COMING HOME TO THE WINDMILL BY THE SEA

CAROLINE YOUNG

This is a work of fiction. Names, characters, business, events and incidents are the products of the author's imagination. Any resemblance to actual persons, living or dead, or actual events is purely coincidental.

Copyright © Caroline Young, 2024

The moral right of the author has been asserted.

All rights reserved. No part of this book may be reproduced or used in any manner without the prior written permission of the copyright owner.

To request permissions, contact the publisher at rights@stormpublishing.co

Ebook ISBN: 978-1-80508-675-8
Paperback ISBN: 978-1-80508-676-5

Cover design: Emma Rogers
Cover images: Shutterstock

Published by Storm Publishing.
For further information, visit:
www.stormpublishing.co

ALSO BY CAROLINE YOUNG

Welcome to Anglesey

The Forgotten Farmhouse by the Sea

Secrets at the Cottage by the Sea

To Geoff, my husband, and my best friend.

If I can stop one heart from breaking,
I shall not live in vain.
Emily Dickinson

PREFACE

Anglesey, July 1999

Beth and Megan sat on the headland above Aberffraw, on the island of Anglesey, in North Wales, where they always watched the sun go down in the summer. Their exams were over. There was no hurry to return home after their long, luxurious day on the beach, as weeks of contented indolence stretched ahead of them.

"I don't think Mam will even notice I'm not there until Dad gets home and asks where his dinner is," Megan said. "She's always so stressed these days."

"My dad never knows whether I'm home or not either," Beth replied. "It'll take him weeks to realise I've gone off to university."

"You can't wait to leave, can you?" Megan said.

"No, I can't, but I'll miss you desperately. In fact, I don't know how I'll survive without you." As she spoke, Beth's face showed the mixture of excitement and trepidation about what lay ahead for her. Could she cope, away from home?

"Ditto, but at least I have Dylan. His parents want him to stay near home, and so I will too. This is a pretty good place to be a poet, and that's the only thing I want to be, so I don't need to go away to do it," Megan said as if trying to convince herself. "I think you're lucky your parents don't mind your leaving, though, especially as they're, well, not all that good at adult life, shall we say."

Beth said nothing, but she knew exactly what her friend meant. Any mention of her eccentric parents unsettled her, and she had spent her whole life longing for ones that fitted in, like everyone else's parents. Part of her felt she should stay and look after them, as their health was already beginning to fail, but she could not sacrifice her dreams as Megan was willing to do. Ziggy, her younger brother by almost three years, would have to take care of Jed and Tabitha. He had little else to do apart from getting into trouble, after all.

"Dylan loves poetry as much as we do. He says he writes poems too, but he won't show me them. You never know, we might put together an anthology of poems based on the island, now that we're officially *together*," Megan said, quickly adding, "But I know you'll love Oxford and all those intellectuals. It's just not for me and Dylan."

Beth nodded, but still said nothing. She was far from convinced by any of this. Was she *lucky* that her parents seem to care so little what she did and where she went? And did Dylan *really* want to write poetry with Megan for the rest of his days? He often looked awkward and embarrassed when Beth saw them together, blushing to the roots of his gorgeous blonde hair... but of course there was another reason for that, a reason Megan knew nothing about, and never could, as it would hurt her so much. Even in *their* friendship, some secrets were better not shared.

Born on Anglesey just over a month apart, the two girls had been best friends since toddlerhood, to the exclusion of anyone else. They knew little of the world beyond the island because they had only ever visited it on school trips to London and Manchester, when their parents could spare the money, which was seldom. Instead, they steeped themselves in great but often reclusive writers who understood the confines of their narrow world. The three Brontë sisters, marooned in their moorland parsonage, were their favourite novelists, and Emily Dickinson their current poet of choice: they read that Dickinson rarely went out, saw no one, usually wore white and wrote deeply soulful poems, only a handful of which were published in her lifetime. And yet these four women's imaginations had spanned the universe.

Beth ran her fingers through her honey-coloured, curly hair and inhaled the tang of salt in the air with affected ease. She was very pretty in a slightly coquettish way, with a cute, snub nose and luscious eyelashes: her appearance usually got her what she wanted, and sometimes, what she didn't. She had already spent many months, and all her meagre pocket money, assembling a wardrobe to take Oxford by storm. Her mother had semi-jokingly told her to "come back with a Lord on your arm." Megan, meanwhile, had spent years feeling in her friend's shadow: her hair was thick but a drab brown, her green eyes piercing but small, and her chin fell away without the refined jawline she so craved. A tiny part of her was quietly glad her beautiful friend was leaving, as she had recently seen Dylan looking at Beth in a way he'd never looked at her.

That night, as they sat in silence and watched the sky light up with pinks and golden ochres, and the sea below them blazed with the sun's daily farewell, they knew that this friendship, the bond they shared, was at the very heart of who they were and always would be. It was a moment of stillness before the changes ahead, a snapshot of a friendship that they were certain was unassailable. Although they would part ways soon – one would stay and one would go – both girls knew that home, for all its limitations, was a place they would always return to... and home chiefly meant each other.

Neither had any idea that it would be many years before they would both sit together in silence and watch the sun set in this place again.

PART 1
HOMECOMING

London, November 2023

ONE

It was pouring, and the big glass walls of Beth Macintosh's pristine London apartment looked as if they were weeping. Fat raindrops trickled in endless succession to the ground, as they had done for days.

"And I thought winters in Wales were wet and miserable," Beth muttered. "At least there was some *variety* in the appalling weather there. Here, it just bloody *rains*."

She slid open the doors of her built-in wardrobe and looked at the long row of clothes of all colours, patterns, styles and sizes (to accommodate those pre-period weeks and post-holiday pounds), but none seemed right for a day as dull as this one. However many clothes she bought, none seemed to match her mood these days. She had two big meetings today, so it was important she looked smart, but she was tired, and the mirror in the bathroom confirmed she looked it. At forty-two, she had reached heights in the company that no woman had ever done before, and her resilience and powers of persuasion were legendary if there were redundancies in the air. In summary, Beth Macintosh was a woman to keep on the right side of, and to admire for her cut-throat zeal, but she was a woman few colleagues *liked*.

She worked as a senior partner in a management consultancy, based in a towering office block in Canary Wharf. Her job was to schmooze clients, make decisions many found difficult and convince anyone who dared to challenge her that she was worth the enormous salary she was paid, plus the even more enormous annual bonus. There were some, a few, that *did* dare, and others who doubted whether That Bloody Welsh Woman, as she was called behind her back, was as indispensable as she thought she was. Some said she had lost her touch. Recently, she had made a few mistakes, and the sharks were beginning to circle. But Beth chose to ignore all of this, a technique for dispelling self-doubt that had always served her well up to now.

Divorced a year earlier, she was now living alone, renting a sparsely furnished penthouse flat in St Catherine's Dock, which she told herself was both amazingly liberating and an emblem of her newfound lack of responsibilities. She had a few very expensive pieces of furniture, all white or cream, a selection of coffee-table books and absolutely no knick-knacks from her married home at all. Her ex-husband, Hugo Macintosh, was a corporate lawyer whom she'd married straight after graduating from Oxford. She'd been certain that she was guaranteeing herself a life of enviable ease, if not endless passion, by doing so. Sadly, one without the other had not been enough for the marriage to survive. She had kept his surname for professional reasons (but in reality because her maiden name was Tonks). Hugo had kept their large house in Hampstead and their only child, a son, had just gone up to Oxford himself.

Lewis had not wanted to apply for Oxbridge. He was only seventeen and the youngest in his year, but the astronomical boarding school fees his parents had shelled out over the years made it a foregone conclusion that he did so. Hugo wanted a return on his investment, as he told his friends, who all said they understood completely. Lewis was the spitting image of his mother with his fine, sharp jawline and thick, blonde hair, which piqued Hugo, as his auburn hair was thinning fast and he had more than a few greys. Lewis had got into Balliol College to read Classics. His brain seemed to master the complex rules of Latin and Ancient Greek with a facility that astounded his teachers. Even so, when the offer came in, he was devastated, telling his mother that his worst nightmare was about to come true. Recalling these words made her shiver. She misted her hair with hairspray and shook her curls to ensure they were suitably tousled, and to avoid dwelling on them for long.

Beth had been worried, but her response was to regale her son with stories of her time at Oxford, the people she had met, the opportunities it had opened up and the things she had realised she could do with her degree, to try to quieten his panic. Teachers had told her that Lewis was "a little *unusual*", but she had put that down to shyness and his being an only child. Some of the stories they told her were a little more worrying: Lewis hiding in a stock cupboard rather than face a maths test, and pacing up and down the inner courtyard muttering to himself when he told his teachers he felt unsure of how to be, but these were hardly life-threatening misjudgements. He had always had his little 'ways', as Beth called them, and they harmed nobody. Surely it was a good thing to be considered unique, as all really bright people were, she'd told herself then, and tried very hard to believe now.

Applying a neat slick of Chanel lipstick, Beth looked at the full-frontal persona she had adopted in adulthood in the mirror. She remembered Lewis's doubts, his despair, but she still hoped with all her heart that Oxford would give him the courage and confidence it had given her. He needed both so badly. She remembered her mother, Tabitha, calling him "a little lost soul" and plying him with biscuits whenever they had come to the island for a very brief visit. He had followed her father, Jed, and brother, Ziggy, (named after Ziggy Stardust) around like a meek little lamb. Lewis had begged them to take him fishing, or surfing, or anywhere, while Beth shouted into the phone at her PA, or organised cleaners and filled the freezer for her parents with military zeal and more than a whiff of martyrdom. She had not brought her son back to Anglesey for years, as it seemed to unsettle him when he had to leave, but she could not deny the fact he seemed far more at ease there. He embraced her family's idiosyncrasies with understanding and forgiveness, as they did his. Yes, Lewis, at present, was an unhappy, lonely boy, and painfully unlike his father, who filled any room with his confidence and charisma, but she was desperately trying to convince herself that he would fit in and blossom at Oxford, and told him so.

"Look, love, where I came from, to go to Uni at all was a miracle, so I grabbed my chance with both hands, and you must too," she enthused when he repeated his reservations to her. "It's a brand-new start, somewhere you can totally reinvent yourself, as I did."

"But I don't want to go, Mum, let alone read Classics. I know I'm good at all that stuff, but I want to make films or write plays – do something *creative*."

Beth shifted in her seat. Hadn't she had dreams like these, once? Hadn't her heart raced as she read a particular line of poetry, a soliloquy in a Shakespeare play or a perfectly written phrase in a novel at Lewis's age? Her son reminded her so much, and so painfully, of Megan, her closest childhood friend, who had always written beautiful poems she'd only ever shared with her. Where was Megan now? Beth wondered. Even after all these years, she still missed her. There was a huge gap in her life where her friend should have been.

Beth had long since learnt to shut down the part of herself that had revelled in literature and loved every moment of her

English degree. She had put all her beloved old paperbacks in a skip when she moved into their Hampstead house, and now there were only a few award-winning hardbacks displayed on a shelf in her flat, all of which she had not read. Affluence, influence and success had been her reward for the sacrifice of this other, more vulnerable part of herself, and they had seemed more than worth all those for many years... but recently, quiet voices had begun to whisper of another way of living, and of being. Was this really where she wanted to spend the rest of her life, doing a job that she knew, in her heart, was utterly superficial, and seeing people she knew were very far from real friends? But she knew that, however wracked with doubt she was, she could not share that with her son.

"I know, and you write *really nicely*, Lewis, but the great stories of ancient history will give you tons of inspiration," she had told him. "And Oxford is the place to make contacts for life, which you don't realise yet how much you'll need. Trust me. You'll love it!"

"OK, I'll try. But if I can't be a screenwriter, I think I might want to be a chef, Mum. I cooked *loads* in school, because the head cook felt sorry for me being on my own, so he sometimes let me help out in the kitchen."

Beth winced. Surely becoming a chef would not be a good fit for her super-sensitive boy? It was such a stressful job. "You're too young to know what you really want, Lewis. Just give Classics a try, please. Dad will be so proud of you."

"That'll be a first, then," came the resigned mumble.

Poor Lewis. He had gone, glumly, to his fate a few weeks earlier, and Beth had not heard much from him since. She hoped his silence meant he was having far too good a time to reply to his mother's resolutely upbeat messages. Whenever she pictured him spending his evenings putting his coloured pencils in rainbow order, or pacing from one end of a room to another, as she had seen him do so often, she dismissed the image straight away. He would have to make compromises to succeed in life, as she had, and Oxford was full of quirky, wonderful people. She and Hugo had given him an excellent start – one that many would envy, she told herself.

Despite all her efforts to feel confident, sure of herself and her decisions in life, the niggling truth was that she simply could not imagine him following the path they had laid out for him. The thought of his dreams, whatever they might be, being crushed as easily as a butterfly under a boot was too painful to dwell on for long.

TWO

Beth had always wanted children in theory, but not so young, and certainly not within a year of marriage. When Lewis was a baby, Hugo had embraced his two hours of fatherhood each evening, his little son roaring with laughter as he put a big blob of bath bubbles on his nose or made funny noises under his armpit. Beth, however, had resented the boredom of taking maternity leave only months after getting her first job and longed for it to end. Yes, she'd *loved* Lewis when he was born via emergency caesarean, but she was happy to hand over his care as soon as she could and return to work. She chose his name as a romantic nod to her heritage, because she pronounced that "Anglesey is wild and untamed, and has a certain Celtic mystery", but that was the extent of her emotional connection to a place she'd left at eighteen and seldom returned to. Hugo had never spent more than a few days on the island, saying he found it parochial and her family difficult. On their wedding day, he had arrived very late the evening before the ceremony and left with Beth early the next morning for their honeymoon in Tobago. His refusal to be involved in the wedding or the preparations that led up to it had hurt her deeply, but she understood his reservations about some of the things Jed and Tabitha had insisted on, such as a pagan blessing after the main ceremony and plenty of joints to share. Once she was officially Mrs Beth Macintosh, she did not look back: for her, the island held nothing but embarrassment, regrets and bad memories. Good riddance to all three.

But this was no longer true. Occasionally, of late, if she had an evening free of engagements, or a weekend inadequately filled, her thoughts returned to her childhood, her family, on Anglesey. She saw the beach below the village, a perfect arc of sand and sea backed by grass-silvered dunes. Sometimes, her dreams were played out against a backdrop of huge, glassy breakers crashing on the sand, and seabirds that speckled the weed-coated rocks looking for food. Images of her father playing songs on the guitar as she and her mother sang along, of her little brother dancing, flickered across her mind, but it was the sense of *freedom,* both physical and mental, that she mourned the most. Ironically, her life had felt so *constrained* since she had left Anglesey, full of things to attain, achieve and acquire, and people to impress, whereas her growing up had been a time of possibilities and hopes, all of which she had shared with Megan. She longed to regain that freedom, and that irreplaceable close bond with another human being, a bond that satisfied so many deep, unspoken needs. But a lapse in teenage judgement had ruined their friendship, and later, an unforgivable single act of moral cowardice as an adult had put paid to any possible reconciliation. When Megan appeared in these memory-laden dreams, Beth awoke in tears.

Her parents still lived in the old grain-grinding windmill, *Melin Arian*/Silver Mill. They had arrived from nowhere and come with nothing, or so they had always told Beth, describing their life on the island as an escape from Hell. When she'd dared to ask what on earth they meant, they'd refused to elaborate. Initially, Tabitha and Jed Tonks had attempted to convert the semi-derelict mill into a home. But she was still a toddler when they accepted defeat after the challenge of making things fit into round rooms proved too much and the bills to do so got too high. The mill, painted white and long since deprived of its sails which were rotting in a shed, squatted sullenly on the edge of the village, its celebratory bright red door promising a warmth that was rarely found within. Throughout Beth's childhood, the family lived in half-finished rooms with unreliable heating, amongst a collection of random charity shop finds, mismatched furniture and skip-rescued items. All of these combined to imbue the mill with the look and smell of a struggling junk shop and Beth could not wait to leave. Once she had, she only went home for short visits, either to put more help in place for her parents or to extricate her younger brother, Ziggy, from his latest misdemeanour. A generous soul, he had failed at everything he had ever attempted, but his parents wholeheartedly adored him. Beth found this both maddening and hurtful, especially when her own successes were not celebrated as much as she felt they deserved. And yet she was still terribly fond of her quirky little brother, and often quipped to her London friends:

"With a name like Ziggy Tonks, I ask you – what chance did he have in life?"

Jed Tonks, Beth's father, was now in the last stages of lung cancer after a lifetime of smoking almost anything he could set alight, and he had replaced the recreational drugs of his youth as a musician on the road with a morphine driver and rafts of co-codamol. Having grown up in Wrexham, down the Welsh coast, he had spent his life just getting by, as he put it, and was regarded by everyone in Aberffraw as a harmless *twmphat*/idiot, if a bloody good guitarist. He had always seemed an unlikely choice for her mother Tabitha, a mournful, well-spoken woman with a past she only ever hinted at, who found solace in wine. But they had stayed together, their long relationship seemingly energised by familiarity and mutual contempt. Now, Tabitha spent her days fervently knitting instead of drinking, increasingly forgetful, and spitting venom and regret at her husband from an old Parker Knoll armchair.

Beth always dreaded running into Dylan Jones during one of her brief visits home. He was now a dentist, a father of four, a local councillor, and a pillar of the community. A big fish in a small pond, as many locals put it. He lived in a huge, seafront Victorian villa in Beaumaris with his wife Manon, a wealthy solicitor's daughter. He was still handsome, not yet grey, and had unfeasibly white teeth, as Beth discovered when she'd found him on Facebook. She'd slammed her laptop shut and with it, closed her mind to her memories of him – of the sweeping black coat he always wore in an effort to look like Oscar Wilde, his prolific blonde curls, and the peach-soft skin of his body, one that she'd felt pressed against hers one moonlit summer night on the cliff, when she had let herself down so very badly. Many, many thousands of sleepless nights had followed that one.

Beth did another check in the mirror. She had to look perfect, to look in control, at all times: that was her Unique Selling Point. Her hair and make-up were immaculate, and her clothes looked as expensive as they had in fact been. She sprayed a quick spritz of her perfume behind both ears and looked in the mirror one final time.

"Pretty good for forty-two, girl."

At 7.45am, the exact time she had to leave her flat to get to the office at 8.15am, her phone rang. Tutting in irritation, she glanced at the screen and saw one word:

Mum.

"Oh, Mum," she muttered. "Lost your knitting needles again?" Buttoning up her calf-length Burberry mac, she slipped her phone into her Mulberry handbag and let it ring out. Surely it would be OK if she called back later? By that time, today's emergency would have been dealt with by the people she paid to deal with such things. It was never anything serious, and she was tired of having to parent her own parents. Besides, she would be late if she took this call, which was not an option. She dismissed a shot of guilt and set off for the office.

When she next looked at her phone just after 10am, there were six words on her screen instead of one:

Dad has died. Please come home.

THREE

It was a dry, bitingly cold November morning, and Megan Williams could see her breath in small clouds. The condensation on the inside of the small windows of her old stone cottage had frozen into an intricate pattern of filigreed shapes. She didn't know whether it was warmer outside than it was inside. The sad expression on Jonah, her elderly chocolate Labrador's face, told her he wasn't entirely convinced either and he hadn't stirred from his basket to find out. None of the ancient radiators in the cottage worked anymore, and Ioan, her younger brother, kept telling her to bleed them. She had no idea how to do so, however, and he hadn't come round to help her because, like her, he was struggling enough just getting through the day.

His wife, Ceri Jones had left him and their two young children in the summer for Darren Farley, a property developer from Chester, and Ioan was still in shock. A local girl, he had married her at eighteen, though many were convinced she had only agreed to it for a big white wedding and attention from jealous school contemporaries. "She's all show, is Ceri" quickly became their father Twm's mantra when discussing his daughter-in-law. Whatever she was, Ceri's betrayal had sucked all hope out of Ioan. Whenever Megan walked over the headland to visit him, she found his kids, Gareth and Envys, running wild, and her brother barely able to speak for fatigue and grief. Her heart ached to see him so.

"Why is it always the best people who get treated the worst?" Megan asked Jonah, who replied only with a long, baleful look. "Goodness knows how he manages to go to work each day and worry about other people as well." And yet she knew why Ioan carried on doing his job as a senior nurse in the emergency department at the hospital in Bangor, because he had told her many times.

"There are always those worse off than I am, *dweud y gwir*/to tell you the truth. I see them, poor souls, every single day."

Megan knew he was right, however hard it sometimes was to believe. Her energy levels were so low on most days, that she envied anyone who was living life even a fraction more than she was.

Laying an old rug over Jonah and wrapping a blanket around herself, she texted her brother a row of hearts. She pictured him scrabbling around to pack the kids' lunchboxes and then doing the school and nursery run, before a half-hour drive to an eight-hour shift in the hospital. He could hardly be making any money by the time he had paid for after-school clubs, childminders and nurseries. Megan looked after the kids for him once a week, but was too tired to help him more with them, so she fretted about how she could put this wrong right. She had no money to spare: selling a few poems to magazines did not make her much money, and she had given up hope of publishing an anthology, the dream she had held so dear when she was younger. "Life has intervened," she told herself, when she thought of her writing career, but it saddened her to admit defeat.

"You are the epitome of a *calon, lân*/pure heart, Ioan," she murmured. "And you deserve better than the hand you've been dealt."

Although it was absolutely freezing in the cottage, with needle-sharp drafts through every door and window, Megan had yet to summon the energy to clean, stoke and light the solid fuel Aga that morning. Energy was a rare commodity these wintry days, and she needed to store as much as she could for the long hours ahead. She would be forty-two in a month's time, on Christmas Eve. It was an event she found impossible to forget, despite the fact that most of her childhood birthdays had been eclipsed by the family's chaotic festive celebrations. Christmas when she was young largely entailed her parents drinking too many Advocaat "snowballs" and her making something for her brothers to eat when they became cranky and restless with hunger. Some years, her father, Twm Williams, had been so incapable by mid-morning on December 24th that he hadn't wished his daughter "*Penblwydd hapus*/happy birthday" at all. Megan had always wondered: a) if birthdays counted if they weren't marked and b) whether she was therefore, by default, actually several years younger.

These days, her family had all but disintegrated. She visited her mother, Nia, in her tiny flat, or during her frequent stays in "the land of milk and honey", as she called the psychiatric unit in Bangor hospital. Her mother's vacant, moon-pale face and bald head were ghastly relics of the lovely person she had once been. Alopecia had taken all Nia's hair, as it was now taking Megan's, tuft by tuft. Her youngest child, Eirlys, a surprise baby born in her early forties, had died of meningitis at three years old, which had rocked her mother to the very core.

"If only the ambulance had arrived sooner," she wailed, for months afterwards. After that, the woman Megan's mother had been never truly returned.

Megan's father had lost his job at a local factory for siphoning petrol out of the vans and into his car, and was convicted of several small-scale burglaries after that. When he was released from jail, Twm Williams had not returned to the island, or to Nia and his children. The family lost their home, Nia was moved into a gloomy council flat, where she sat, staring out of the window at a life that had passed her by. Yes, Nia had lost more than her hair: she had lost all hope.

To Megan, the word "family" now meant Ioan and his kids, and she knew they would want to celebrate her birthday in some way, even though she had told him not to.

"Birthdays are much overrated, in my view," she'd said.

And yet she had loved them once, for one reason alone. Her girlhood friend, Beth Tonks, had always made her birthdays special, baking her multi-layered, luridly coloured, crookedly stacked cakes which had led Megan to nickname her "Wonky-tonks" for a while. Things unravelled between them once school finished and her friend left for Oxford. They had not spoken a word to each other since that last summer, and Megan had not been invited to Beth's grand wedding a few years later (for which, so gossip ran, the groom had only just turned up in time and some of the guests were found sleeping in a field the following morning). She would not have gone, she told herself, even if she had been invited.

Beth had been her soulmate, the yin to her yang, and Megan missed her. How was she now? Did she think about her too? It seemed painfully unlikely: the snippets of gossip she'd heard in the village shop about her friend's successful, glamorous life in London was worlds away from her own, hugely disappointing one, on this small island. And yet, she nurtured the tiniest of hopes that, despite all that had happened between them, her old friend might miss her too.

FOUR

Megan looked at the clock on her kitchen wall. 11.45am. She needed to get moving: it was a Wednesday, the shop in the village would close at 12.30pm.

"Come on, then, Jonah. Let's hit the road. Places to go, people to see..."

She pulled on an oversized, man's overcoat and tugged the black beret she had worn since sixth form onto her head. Looping the lead around Jonah's neck, she coaxed him through the door.

Megan's cottage was not considered part of the village of Aberffraw, as it sat on a piece of land outside the drystone walls that contained most of the houses. Perched alone on an exposed piece of headland, it bore the brunt of the winter storms, its windows regularly misted with salty spray from the waves that crashed against the rocks. Its front garden was often littered with bracts of seaweed tossed over the wall. Megan had lived there, alone, for almost twenty years, and she had no desire to move nearer anyone else. Like her beloved Emily Dickinson, isolation was something she cherished, and she told herself that she preferred to spend her time reading and writing than with gossip and unkindness. But sometimes, in the small hours, she yearned for company and comfort. It was at these times that Dickinson's words were the only things that soothed her:

A wounded deer leaps the highest.

"I hope I will leap high one day, though how, I have no idea."

That morning, as they both walked slowly along the headland towards the village, Megan looked down at the beach. There was always something new to see: a change in the tideline, a different colour on the rocks. Despite the cold, a gaggle of seagulls bobbed in the shallows, hoping for an unwary fish or small crab. The grassy path was crisped with frost and the ivy trailing over the stone wall glistened in the shafts of wintry sunlight. It might not thaw at all today, which would make finding food difficult for the small birds who congregated around her cottage at this time of year. The starlings were hardier, picking through beaches blanketed with seaweed for food, but the garden birds suffered. Megan loved their chattering company.

"I'll put extra food out for them when I get back," she said. "And hope the rats don't find it first."

When Megan reached the village square, it was clear something had happened. Small groups of people stood in doorways or outside the village shop, heads close together, muttering. For once, she was absolutely certain that the focus of their attention was not her, as none of them even glanced her way when she and Jonah walked past. Today, there was obviously a bigger scandal to salivate over, but still she did not linger or make eye contact with anyone. She had learnt not to do so unless she wanted to be stared at. Megan knew her reputation as "that weird girl who went astray", and when she had read Hawthorne's novel *The Scarlet Letter*, she had wept at Hester

Prynne's similarly lonely fate after an unwise love affair. Entering the poorly stocked, overheated little shop, she found that it, too, was all abuzz.

"There one minute, yelling his orders, and gone the next," one woman said to an elderly, very bewhiskered lady. "He had it coming, mind. Never did anything of any use to anyone in his life that I know of."

"Didn't have to. His wife came from money, they say, didn't she? Though I never saw any evidence of it. God knows why she married him and came up here," the older woman replied. "We'd enough of those hairy hippie types in the 1970s."

"He was some kind of pop singer once, wasn't he, like Gary Glitter?" Siân said. "And look how *he* turned out!"

"Well, have you ever heard of anyone coming from Wrexham with a surname like Tonks? *Typyn bach yn od, dw in meddwl*/Bit odd, I think," said a lady from underneath a huge furry hat. "It has to be said that a lot of questions surround the pair of them, all in all," she added mysteriously.

Megan picked up a small loaf, some milk, bacon, eggs and a bag of apples that had seen far better days and took them to the till. The owner, Siân Owen, looked at her grimy coat with thinly veiled distaste, as she always did, before ringing up the few items she wanted without touching any of them. Siân had dyed her hair a rather lurid coppery colour and teased it into ringlets today.

"Keeping well, Megan?" Siân asked, as if doing so caused her great pain.

"*Go lew, diolch*/Not bad, thanks," Megan lied, adding, "How's your aunt doing? Any signs of death yet?" to an explosive "bwahahaha!" from someone lurking behind the chiller. Everyone knew Siân visited her elderly aunt every week in a nursing home in the hope of receiving a hefty inheritance.

Siân put the change on the counter with pursed lips. Leaning forward to reveal far more wrinkly décolletage than

Megan needed to see, she hissed, "Guess who *has* died, though?"

"Surprise me," Megan replied. "Who?"

"Jed Tonks is who. That posh missus of his, Tabitha, was running down the street screeching earlier this morning. Dr Griffiths had to take her home and sedate her." Siân paused for effect. "She's even weirder these days, I heard from the postman. Stands on the doorstep, she does, in her nightie, and tells him she's waiting for a telegram. *Jesu*/Jesus, she'll be in the loony bin by the end of the week, like your mam, you mark my words."

Megan ignored the nasty dig at her mother. This news was a real shock. "*Bechod*/Shame," she muttered to herself. "Tabitha will be lost without Jed, however much she said she hated him." When she looked up, she saw that all eyes were on her. "He was OK, you know, really. Just, well, a bit... *vacant,* a lot of the time, especially recently when he was ill. He was always very kind to me."

Megan glared at Siân, eyeball to eyeball, until she eventually looked away.

"I hear they've summoned their snooty daughter back from London to deal with her for a while and to arrange the funeral. About time she did her bit, I say. Her brother Ziggy's had such a difficult time of it over the years, managing them both on his own. She never comes home for long and doesn't lift a finger when she does. Just pays for others to do what she should be doing."

Megan felt all the blood leave her face in an instant. "Beth's coming home?"

"On her way, Dr Griffiths said," Siân replied with a smug smile. "Back to reality for that Golden Girl."

Megan paid, grabbed her shopping, turned on her heel and left, dragging a very reluctant Jonah after her, deprived of his customary dog biscuit from Siân. If Beth was coming home to help her mother and manage the funeral, she would be home for longer than the usual day or so. They would have to be in the chapel together, as Megan would have to attend the service: they might even have to *speak* to each other. After all these years, how would that be, for both of them? She could hardly imagine a meeting, and yet, when she dared to, part of her yearned for it to happen with all her heart.

FIVE

Megan did not leave her cottage for several days after she'd heard Beth was coming back to Aberffraw. Above all, she dreaded an awkward, semi-polite exchange; she had always stayed well away from the village when Beth was home. Megan also had a deep fear of her friend asking "what are you up to now?" or "how is life going?" because, if she was honest, it wasn't going well and never had been.

But the main reason was that Megan also knew with absolute certainty that, even after all these years, her old friend would be able to tell how lonely, how lost, she was with a single glance. She tried with all the strength she could muster to keep that hidden most of the time, telling herself that she needed nobody's pity, but it was hard. Almost everyone around her had colluded in what happened by not telling her father what he'd done was wrong, so she would not offer absolution by asking for their sympathy now.

Megan sighed. She would have to prepare herself for meeting Beth at the funeral with great care. Then, perhaps, just perhaps, she would not notice her wrinkles, her worn-out clothes and thinning hair and there would be no time for small talk. She did not think she could ever bring herself to trust her again as she had proved such a fickle friend in the past. Neither could she imagine telling Beth what had happened to her after she went away to Oxford. Some things were best kept secret, however much she wanted to share them; it made them less unbearable.

The weather on the day of Jed Tonks' funeral could not have been worse. Torrential rain ricocheted off the roofs and pavements, and the hearse carrying his coffin had to go even more slowly than usual, wipers slashing frantically, Mervyn, the driver's, fat, florid nose almost pressed to the windscreen. The congregation was small considering Jed Tonks had lived in the village for most of his adult life and had brought up his children here. Megan looked around quickly. She knew that Beth had married straight after Oxford and had a son, but there was nobody here who looked like suitable candidates for her wealthy husband or her boy. Her old friend was obviously still too ashamed of the place, and the life she had come from, to invite them today.

A few elderly people sat near the front. They came to every funeral in the village as a) it was expected, and b) because they knew there was a chance of a chat and a free drink afterwards. There was only one man whom nobody recognised, and who spoke to nobody. His leather jacket and straggly greying pony-tail was enough of a deterrent to any conversation with the great and good of Aberffraw, and Megan could almost hear them thinking "another daft old hippy". She decided she would try to speak to him after the service, as one outsider to another.

The vicar asked all there to *cwtch*/snuggle together to make the scene less desolate, but with little success. Jed had had few friends and owed a lot of people money. Megan sat behind a stone pillar so she could see but not be seen. Ioan had offered to come with her for moral support. He had been very close to Beth in the past, but his sister had always known that he had loved her friend, and that she had broken his heart; there was no need to add to his suffering today. Ioan's holiday days were precious and too many of them were already spent ferrying the kids to and from Chester to see their mother.

Just as the twenty-odd wet people in the congregation began to gently steam in the comparative warmth of the chapel, the pall bearers entered to the raucous opening chords of "Brown Sugar" by The Rolling Stones (with an extra percussive layer of "tut tuts" from some quarters). Megan gasped when she saw Beth and Ziggy with a hand under each of Tabitha's thin arms, all but carrying her up the central aisle to the front pew, both their faces rigid with effort. Tabitha's angular face was strangely blank as if she was in some kind of trance. Around her neck was a diamanté necklace that sparkled in each shaft of light, and reminded Megan of Miss Havisham, horribly resplendent in her grief. This ghastly tableau showed everyone present both that their mother would need her children's support for the rest of her life, even though she was only in her sixties, and that they knew it. This was a day Beth had always said she knew would come, and yet fervently hoped to avoid. Megan remembered her bitter words, years earlier:

"My mother may be the woman who gave birth to me, but she has never been a real mam, like yours. Her head and heart have always been somewhere else."

As a few warbly voices started to sing the first hymn, Megan wondered if Beth knew about the heartache that had engulfed her family since she'd left the village. She returned so seldom, never brought her husband or her son home anymore, and she kept her distance from everybody when she did. If she'd heard the bare facts from the local gossips, surely she would know about Nia's illness after the loss of Eirlys, and Twm's conviction and subsequent abandonment of the family? But she could not be sure, because by the time these things took place, Beth, and their friendship, was long gone. Today, as she tried in vain to sing a tune she had known since girlhood, Megan was thankful that it was appropriate to weep at a funeral.

The service was mercifully short and the eulogy, from Ziggy, even shorter. Megan watched her old friend squirm in her seat as her brother stuttered and stammered, a wrinkled sheet of A4 paper visibly shaking in his hand. Wearing a long military greatcoat and army boots, he cut an awkward figure, and Megan wondered why Beth, who probably delivered presentations on a regular basis, had not said a few words instead. Then she remembered how Ziggy had always been the favoured child in the Tonks family, taken on day-long fishing trips by his father and bailed out of endless "misunderstandings". His walking on the roofs of all the cars in the village square sprang to mind, but she smiled at the tameness of this teenage indiscretion that had seemed so shocking at the time.

As people lined up to offer the family their condolences, Megan stood behind Cai Hughes, a builder who had helped Beth's parents try to maintain the windmill as it crumbled around them. He'd been one of Jed's very few friends. Widowed over ten years earlier, Cai was reliable and skilled, ruggedly handsome, even in his early sixties. She saw him dab his eyes and clear his throat in an effort to speak to Beth and Ziggy. Suddenly, she remembered laughter around the kitchen table, both Jed and Cai flushed with home-brew, and Tabitha, young and smiling, jiggling a toddler Ziggy on her knee. She could almost hear Jed playing the guitar with such skill and sensitivity, his eyes closed in bliss. There had been happy times, and they had shared them, these two women who were now meeting again as strangers.

When Cai shuffled forward to shake Ziggy's hand, Megan found herself in front of her old friend, painfully aware that, despite all her efforts, her best winter coat was threadbare and her tatty beret wholly unsuitable headwear for a funeral. Neither spoke for a few seconds, as Megan took in Beth's smooth skin, immaculate blonde curls and smart black trouser suit. Her heart pounded as she waited for the harsh appraisal she had dreaded, the unspoken distaste at what she had become or *not* become, but Beth's brown eyes were not judging her at all. When tears suddenly filled them, she seemed as surprised as Megan. She had clearly had not expected to feel this body-blow of emotion at finally seeing her friend again.

"I'm glad you came, Meg," she said quietly. "I didn't think you would. *Mae'n fendigedig dy weld di*/It's wonderful to see you."

"I'm really sorry about your dad," Megan said stiffly.

She meant this, but she could not smile. That was too much to ask, after all that had happened. At least the moment she had dreaded was almost over and they could soon go home to forget each other once more.

But then Beth wrapped both her soft, manicured hands around one of her friend's, sandpaper-rough in comparison, and squeezed it.

"I will be back more often now, and I hope we'll meet again. Mum will need me, and I, well, it feels... *right* to be at home more," Beth said slowly, choosing every word with great care. "I hadn't ever expected to feel this way and want to come back here more than I have been, Meg, but I do."

A long pause, before Megan felt a familiar surge of anger in her belly. This chic, charming woman had ruined her life, after all. "I'll believe it when I see it," she said.

Beth blinked. Her smile faded and her gaze moved to the next person in the line. Megan shuffled off and tried to find the ponytailed man, but he had vanished without exchanging a word with anyone. As she walked home, rain lashing her legs and the wind threatening to dash her beret onto the rocks, she regretted her bitter, graceless words more than she could say.

SIX

When Beth found out that Megan lived in what they had always dubbed "The Witches' Cottage" as children, and that she chose not to interact with anyone in the village, Beth was so shocked that she vowed to visit her as soon as she could. But the chaos at home grew a little more each day, so she had no suitable time to do so. Her mother was distraught, her knitting abandoned. She spent each day wringing her hands and bewailing the loss of a husband whom she now almost sanctified. Her memories, increasingly sporadic and confused, tortured her, as so many of them seemed to bear very little relation to a reality anyone else could understand.

"He was an astonishing man, your father," she said to Beth again and again. "We went through so much together, things you never knew about, things you can only imagine."

As she spoke, she clutched her daughter's hand as if it was a lifebuoy. Beth, who had no memory of *ever* holding her mother's hand, even as a child, found this deeply unnerving.

"I always told him I had given up everything for him, but he gave up even more to come here for me, where we thought we could be safe from my family."

Beth, her curiosity piqued, started to ask questions:

"Where *did* you grow up, Mum? You've never told me. And what did you give up, and why didn't you feel safe with your family?"

But Tabitha refused to answer, turning her head away like a petulant child.

Getting her to eat anything was almost impossible, and within a fortnight of Jed's death, his widow resembled an emaciated bird sitting in the big, winged armchair. Her cheekbones, always the most prominent feature of her striking face, were now only thinly covered with flesh. Beth felt a huge surge of pity for this once-proud woman, but when she asked her brother, Ziggy, what had gone on in the years since she'd left home, and whether their mother's unpredictable behaviour was anything new, he was typically blunt.

"Mam and Dad were always pretty *off-piste*, Beth. You know that. Mum didn't fit in wherever she came from and she didn't fit in here either, with her posh accent and hyper-formal manners. She's even more forgetful than ever now, but she was always a bit *different*, wasn't she, wearing those kaftans and beads around the village? And Dad, well there was nothing much between his ears, let's be honest. He didn't really give a shit about anything or anyone as long as he had his guitar, his fags and could go fishing at weekends, did he?"

"He cared about you, Ziggy."

Rolling his eyes, he left the room quickly. Beth was wounded at his lack of concern for parents who had done nothing but adore him, whatever he did. She remained bitter that she had never been afforded such leeway or support, and no longer tried to hide it. Why had they not loved her in the same way, when all she had ever done was try to please them? It still rankled more than she liked to admit.

And yet she knew that her brother had stayed here, tolerating their parents' vagaries and the gossip they provoked, looking after them as best he could, when she had chosen to save herself instead. She had had no choice but to leave, to escape; she had been offered an opportunity to change her life forever, but guilt lapped at her conscience, nonetheless.

Food soon became a big problem in the windmill. Beth had never been a good cook, and a despairing Hugo had employed a private chef in Hampstead. She had lived mainly on soups and salads since her divorce, chiefly because they had enabled her to stay slim when others her age were beginning to "spread". One dull morning, as she was resigning herself to concocting something from the meagre provisions in the windmill, her phone buzzed. When she saw it was Duncan Scott, the senior partner from the office, her stomach flipped. He had sent several emails this week, but she had not responded: surely losing a parent warranted at least a *little* time off? If he was calling her, however, he obviously felt differently. She quickly pulled on her coat, and went outside, where she took a deep breath, and picked up.

"Hi, Duncan. How are you?" she said, trying to sound in control while nerves fizzed in her belly.

"All good here. Sorry again about your dad, but we do need to talk, Beth," he replied. She could hear the steely edge in his voice immediately. Gone was the congratulatory tone with which he had greeted her biggest deals, or told her the fulsome praise from delighted clients. Today, Duncan meant business.

"I'll be back in London in a few days, once we've scattered Dad's ashes, so we could talk..."

"Can't wait, I'm afraid." Beth waited, and visualised Duncan tapping his expensive fountain pen on his desk, or perhaps closing his eyes as if waiting for divine inspiration. "Bad news. The board have decided to let you go, Beth. I'm sorry, but your performance stats are not good this quarter, and the agency has to slim down to manage outgoings. I tried to defend you of course, but losing that Clarkson contract didn't go down well..." He paused, waiting for a response that didn't come. "Right, so you'll be given a generous severance payment, and glowing references, it goes without saying, but perhaps you should stay home as long as you need to... er... think about how to move forward."

A longer silence followed. Beth stood quite still and listened to the distant susurration of the waves on the beach. No traffic, no fumes, no deadlines, no pinging phones and beeping inboxes here – just this peace, this unspoilt simplicity. She could picture herself and Megan as girls, roaming these dunes and running, shrieking, into those cold waves. They had never stopped rolling in over the sand and then out again, in all the years she had not been here to hear and see them.

How much time had she wasted chasing the wrong dreams, in the wrong places? She had felt like this for a while, this diluting of her love for London and her frantic, fake life. What was happening right now had always been her absolute dread, and yet she did not feel sad, or scared. She felt relief flood through her, at finally knowing what to do.

"This may sound strange to you, but I'm glad, Duncan. It's time for me to make some changes, and you've just made the first, and the biggest one, for me."

She heard him splutter some incoherent words and allowed herself to enjoy his unease. Duncan was very difficult to rattle, and she had rattled him.

"If someone could pack up the stuff on my desk and courier it to my flat, I'd be grateful. I don't think I'll be back in London for a while. I'm needed here."

"Yes, yes, of course. I'll sort that asap," Duncan replied. "And I'll be in touch about the... er, final paperwork in due course."

"And sort my payoff asap as well, please," she said. What he was doing to her was heartless, even disgraceful, but she hadn't got the energy to fight it now and it was joy that was coursing through her rather than resentment. As she heard him start to muster another bland, consolatory phrase, she decided enough was enough, and hung up with a brief but bizarrely cheery, "Bye for now."

And it felt so very, very good to do so.

Beth waited all that night for the shock, the pain of rejection, to hit her as she lay awake in her childhood bedroom, but it did not. For the first time in her adult life, she had spectacularly failed. *But she was still here.*

As she listened to her mother mumbling in her sleep, Beth realised that she felt more excited about what might lie ahead than she ever had about the promotions, work trips, team-building exercises or exorbitantly priced dinners with clients. All that was peripheral, transient, and she had always known in her heart of hearts that this day would come. Here, this place and these people were real, and their values and way of life long-lasting. She had come from them, and they were a part of her, whether she wanted it to be so or not. She needed to return for a while, to "recalibrate" and, perhaps, to rediscover the person she had once been before she had irrevocably polluted the purest thing in her life – her friendship with Megan. It would not be easy. It would be painful, but it had to be done.

Giving up on sleep around 3am, she turned on the little bedside lamp that had been there throughout her girlhood, which had illuminated page after page of wonderful literature and breathtaking poetry. She had not read a novel let alone a poem for many years, but that night, she reached up to the shelf above her bed which held the books she had loved and treasured most, and had stayed here when she had left. George Eliot's *Middlemarch* was there, its fat orange spine wrinkled and soft with countless rereadings. All the Brontë sisters' novels were next to it, and her heart gave a fillip of glee as she read each title: *Jane Eyre*, *Agnes Grey* and her favourite of all of them, *Wuthering Heights*.

The girl she had been, the person who had learnt whole poems and quoted paragraphs from novels and speeches from plays, had been buried for too long. She had let herself be gulled into a mediocrity she had never intended to settle for. In an instant, she saw that she had also condemned Lewis to forgoing his dreams, and that she had to do something to save him from the same fate as hers. That could not happen. It would destroy him. She would ring her son in the morning to hear what *he* wanted to do with his life, rather than what she and Hugo wanted for him. She could only hope that he would understand her complete *volte face* and heed her warning.

As she huddled under the crackly nylon sheets and threadbare eiderdown of her childhood bed, Beth could picture herself and Megan in this room. They had spent so many hours here, reading and then discussing phrases, words, and how the characters they read about echoed their own feelings and dreams. What great things they had hoped for, what huge passions they had felt! And what a shame that they had dissipated them over a pretentious boy called Dylan Jones who clearly had such massive insecurities of his own that he needed their validation to feel good about himself. She saw it clearly now, but hindsight is a wonderful thing.

This silent but powerful rivalry throughout sixth form was a tinderbox at the heart of their friendship, a blue touchpaper just waiting to be lit. Dylan's suave confidence, his ability to still conversation when he entered a room, his sheer *charisma*, had both girls swooning like some of the women in the novels they devoured. Their longing for his attention was something he was largely unaware of, but few young men can resist flattery, so he welcomed it from both of them, and they fluttered around him like moths around a flame. Eventually, his limitless charm led Beth to betray her friend in a way she could never tell anyone about and make a mistake which had cast a long shadow over both their lives. She shivered in horror at the memory of it.

"But it was all so long ago. Perhaps we could have a second chance at friendship," Beth murmured, taking down her battered copy of *Wuthering Heights* and stroking it lovingly. "Perhaps *I* could have a second chance, Meg."

As she remembered one of that novel's most famous lines, and how they had changed the "he's" to "she's" so that it represented them, goosebumps rippled across her skin:

She is more myself than I am. Whatever our souls are made of, hers and mine are the same.

The truth was there, shining like a gem at the centre of everything. She could only be truly happy if her friend was happy too.

SEVEN

As November inched past and Beth's abrupt change of circumstances began to feel more real, the dankness of a Welsh winter seeped into her body like the touch of chilly fingers. The windmill had never been properly insulated. The ancient central heating produced a lot of noise but precious little warmth. In the kitchen, the old range emitted minimal heat as Jed had turned it down to save money whenever fuel prices rocketed. Beth now turned it up, which meant that the circle of around ten feet in which her mother sat all day staring, unspeaking, into the middle distance was relatively warm, but the rest of the windmill was arctic unless she lit a fire in the living room. Tabitha seemed to accept that these long hours of just sitting was how life was, and she now lived mainly in her muddled memories and troubled dreams. Alarmed, Beth researched this disconcerting behaviour, and was shocked by what she read. They seemed to suggest early-onset Alzheimer's, which filled her with dread. She tried to ignore it, as she had always done with things that were too painful to acknowledge, but it did not work when she was forced to watch as Tabitha grew a little more distant each day.

Each morning, Beth woke up shivering and it took her several minutes to remember where she was and why. At first, the fact that she now had no job, and that the life and the life-style she had so carefully crafted for herself were currently on hold, if not over, felt like a kick in the belly. But as her thoughts settled, she reminded herself that money wouldn't be a problem once she gave notice on her flat and received her severance pay, so she would survive this. A few weeks without any meetings, presentations, tenders and egotistical clients' demands sounded wonderful, but the prospect of months of enforced inactivity bothered her. It was totally counterintuitive for her not to be ferociously busy, always in demand. Desperate to stay occupied, she decided to do some home maintenance. She covered the inside of the windows in the windmill with plastic sheeting to eliminate draughts, scrubbed the limescale crust from the bathroom taps and experimented with making nourishing soups for her mother. These mundane tasks made Beth feel useful, but they did not fill enough of her time to keep her growing rest-lessness at bay. When she had nothing to do, she started nervously humming, often the same tune for a whole day, which even her mother noticed and told her to stop. "Go for a walk!" Tabitha had said suddenly one afternoon. "It will clear your head and give mine some peace. Your father made *far* too much noise with that wretched guitar of his. Go!"

Beth hesitated. Her mother had not said this many words for weeks, but the fact was that she had not been for a walk since the few times she and Hugo had strolled around the college gardens in Oxford before they were married. As a family, they did not go for walks, even though Lewis, as an only child, had begged for the companionship of a dog that they could all take out on the Heath together. Her son had always said he loved animals more than people, but boarding school, and his father's refusal, prevented him from ever having any kind of pet. Even a goldfish he'd won at a fair one summer was swiftly despatched to fend for itself in a pond on Hampstead Heath.

As Beth put on the only coat she had brought with her – a Burberry mac that was neither warm nor waterproof – she suddenly remembered Wil, the scraggy mongrel they had adopted when she was about ten. Jed had found him hungry and wandering on the beach, and brought him home. She had loved Wil as deeply as he had loved her, and he had been a source of consistency, of comfort, in a household often fraught with chaos. A vivid image of her son's disappointed face the last time he had begged them for a dog came into her head. It could have comforted Lewis, too, she now realised. He was still not answering any of her calls or messages, though she was slightly reassured by the fact that he had at least read them. She could not blame him for not responding. They had let him down by being no better at parenting than Jed and Tabitha, just *different* in their unending capacity for failure.

It was drizzling when Beth set off along the narrow cliff path which led to the next bay. She kept her head down and shoulders rigid in the vain hope that this would protect her from the icy wind. The sea to her left looked like molten lead, grey and surging, and the sky was washed of any colour, as a bank of solid white cloud stretched from one side of the sky to the other. It reminded her of dulled monochrome images from the past, blank and oppressive.

"This is a godforsaken spot in the truest sense of the word," Beth muttered as she walked further along the path. "No wonder nobody lives out here."

But when she rounded a corner, she heard the whoop of children's voices and saw the arc of a rugby ball above a straggly hawthorn hedge. Another poignant memory floated into Beth's mind, of Lewis begging one of them to help him practise his passing skills so he would not be teased in school rugby. Hugo had said he was too busy, because he *was* busy, and she had pleaded lack of skill, but she was quite sure Hugo now regretted it as much as she did. They had such a distant relationship with their only son, and they shared the blame for that.

Peering through a porthole-round gap in the hedge, she saw a small, traditional stone-built farmhouse. Its low roof was softly moulded to reveal where the wooden trusses lay beneath, like ribs under thin skin. She had not even known it was there, as the spot was on the outer edge of the village and hidden from view. It looked as if it belonged here, defiant against wind and wave for centuries. She could almost feel its resilience. When one of the children, a rosy-cheeked boy of about six, ran towards the hole in the hedge to get the ball and saw her, she smiled, but he looked a little alarmed. He laid a hand gently on the head of the grey-muzzled brown Labrador that had shuffled over to see what was happening as if seeking reassurance that everyone was safe.

"Hi. I'm just out for a walk, don't be scared," she said. The boy's face stirred a memory, one of another boy, with a similarly kind and open demeanour.

"Sorry, but my dad doesn't like it when people look through that hole," the boy said. "He'll tell you to go away if he sees you."

His island accent was strong and lilting. It reminded Beth so much of the little village school of her girlhood, of happy playtime games with her best friend Megan, that she felt a catch in her throat.

"Sorry," she mumbled. "And I didn't mean to interrupt your game."

A man appeared now, wearing paint-spattered denim dungarees. His strong features were those she had seen mirrored in the little boy. They had the same tight brown curls, and deep blue eyes. Beth started: this was a face she had known well once, her brain told her. Eventually, all the fragments of memory cohered into one person – Ioan Williams, Megan's brother.

"*Helô. Ga'i helpu chi?*" he said, before immediately translating into English when he saw her hesitation. He didn't recognise her. "Hello. Can I help you?"

"*Helô. Esgusodwch fi. Dw'in mynd am dro, ac... Ioan? Beth dw'i, Beth Tonks.*/Hello. Excuse me. I'm going for a walk, and... Ioan? It's Beth – Beth Tonks." Using her maiden name again felt right, here and now, as did trying to speak in Welsh to him for the first time in many years.

The man's expression slowly changed to one of reluctant recognition. He shuffled his feet shyly, just as he had done as a boy, and as an awkward teen.

"Beth. OK. I heard you were back. Didn't know you at first. You look so *different* now. So smart," he said with an air of disapproval. "Sorry to hear about your dad. *Pob cydymdeimlad*/Many condolences."

"*Diolch*/Thanks, Ioan," she replied. "It's... good to see you again."

The man looked down at his work boots. "Yes, thanks," he said eventually.

Beth felt a palpable wave of dislike emanating from him, as cold as the stares from some of the villagers. But coming from him, it was more upsetting because this was Ioan, with whom she had spent so many happy hours when they were young, poring over books in the library, fishing down on the beach, or just chatting. They were always completely at ease with one another. At one point, he had even told her he loved her, but he was a few years younger than her, which was not "cool" at the time, so she had rejected him. She hoped he had been happy since then, but this did not look like a happy man at all.

They had both loved art books in particular. Ioan had lost himself in the hugeness of scale and possibilities great art offered him, a free spirit, his imagination roaming over centuries of beauty. He had spent hours painting the landscape of his home in A-level art class, dreaming of bigger canvasses, bigger lives. Yet here he still was, on Anglesey. He had never left to study art history at university, as he'd always intended to. He had stayed, and married Ceri Jones, she'd overheard in the shop years earlier. It had filled her with grief for the man he could have been. His still-handsome face was slack with tiredness and shadowed with a greying stubble. He looked as if his "free spirit" had gone for good.

"*Sut mae'r Ceri?*/How's Ceri?" she said.

"She's not here anymore," Ioan replied, his shoulders slumped. "Left me."

His deep voice was so full of loss that Beth really wanted to reach through the gap in the hedge and grab his hand. But she didn't. "It's just me and the kids now, as she didn't contest custody. And the dog, of course. She didn't want any of us."

His daughter, a toddler of three or four, joined him at the hedge. Her face had a translucent fragility that reminded Beth of another girl she had once known – Megan's little sister. What had her name been, and how had her life turned out? She wondered but could not ask. Ioan was clearly in no mood for pleasantries.

A pause. "I'm sorry. That must be tough for you," Beth said, calling upon the skills she had learnt in the workplace as a maelstrom of mixed emotions washed over her. She was sorry he was miserable and alone, but a tiny, guilty part of her could not help but note the fact that he was now unattached.

"It is tough, yes, but we're both luckier than Megan, who has nobody," he blurted. "At least I have these two, and you have a rich husband and piles of money, or so I hear from Siân in the shop." He rubbed his face to hide his blushes at such blatant rudeness.

Beth hesitated, stung. What was she supposed to say to that? "Actually, I'm divorced, and have just been made redundant," she said. "And don't believe everything Siân Owen tells you, by the way. She resented me in school and no doubt still does. People seem to hold on to their grudges up here."

Ioan said nothing as her words sank in, but his expression softened a little. "*Ydi me'n wir*/Yes, that's true. But you've got a son, I remember hearing," he went on eventually.

"Yes. Lewis. He's just started at Oxford."

"Wow. Impressive. And I hear you were a big success in your work – whatever it is that you do, or did," Ioan said, his voice deliberately robotic. He was interested, she could tell, but he had no intention of showing it. "Siân's information was inadequate in that area, haha."

"Management consultancy, for my sins. Not sure what I'm going to do next, but yes, I'm lucky financially. Mum needs me now, so I'll be here for a bit."

Ioan grunted. "She always has."

Overhead, a seagull screeched, swooped and then pooed copiously on the little boy's sleeve. When his father and sister laughed, Beth allowed herself a small, guilty smile.

"Good shot, seagull," Ioan said with a smile that transfigured his face.

"*Ych a fi*!/Yuk!" his son replied, his little face scowling in disgust. "Don't laugh at me!"

"Do you remember when a seagull did that in my hair once?" Beth said. "I was crying, so you spat on a tissue and scrubbed it off."

Ioan's smile vanished instantly, and his face clouded over.

"That was a very long time ago. We were different people, in so many ways."

She nodded. "Yes, I guess, but still the same in others."

"*Ella, ella ddim*/Perhaps, perhaps not."

"It feels right for me to be back home now, anyway," Beth said, her crisp tone concealing her hurt.

"You're lucky to have a choice, Beth," he replied. "*Reit*

pawb. Amser cinio. Dos i mewn/Right, everyone. Lunch time. Come inside."

As he strode off, his children scampering behind him, the little girl cast a sneaky look back at the posh woman her father seemed to know but clearly didn't like much.

"*Envys! Dos i mewn rwan*/Envys. Come inside now!"

She was swiftly yanked inside and the door slammed shut.

"Envys. What a beautiful name. If I'd had a daughter, I would have called her that, 'Rainbow'," Beth said softly.

The wind had dropped a little when she started to walk back towards the village. This often meant that rain was coming soon, Beth remembered. With each step, she found herself imagining how different her life would have been if her brief fantasy of marrying Ioan had come true. She might never have fallen under the spell of Dylan Jones if she had simply accepted the fact that Ioan was a few years younger than her and let herself love him, as he'd said he loved her. Would either of them have been any happier now? Would they have left together and made a new life somewhere else, or would she have been content with what he and the island offered, and stayed home? Part of her thought she might have, but now, she would never know.

He was clearly far from happy about her return, which felt like a kick in the guts. Why did these people resent anyone wanting more in life? Especially when a lot of their time was spent complaining about what they didn't have here. For example, during every brief visit home, the businesswoman in Beth had thought that Siân Owen could make so much of the village shop, and the adjoining low-beamed room that had once been a thriving tearoom. Instead, she'd let it decline into a barely profitable, badly run eyesore. But Beth had never said so. On Anglesey, Beth Tonks would always be the disloyal snob who had betrayed her friend and abandoned her family in her selfish quest for success.

"They have no idea what a high price I've paid, and how pointless it all seems now," she murmured.

No, it was not all her fault that Ioan was miserable, or that Megan was unhappy. They had made their own decisions – some good, some bad. But a voice reminded her that she had hurt them both deeply. Emily Brontë's words drifted into her mind:

I have not broken your heart – you have broken it: and in breaking it, you have broken mine.

Heavy rain began to fall, and the darkening sky threatened more. Beth shivered in her flimsy coat. For all the glorious fresh air and sea views, the prospect of listening to her mother's agitated ramblings during the long months ahead, and of watching her brother waste his life, suddenly seemed utterly stupid. Her clothes were soaked. There was no way of drying them in the windmill, and she still had a clean, warm flat in London waiting for her. Her skillset would be perfect for many prestigious roles in the City, despite her recent run of bad luck, she told herself, her pace quickening. Perhaps she should start job-hunting once her mother was a little calmer...

And yet, deep down, she knew she hadn't been happy with her life. What was worse, she had made her son unhappy too, holding up her values as ones to emulate, and expecting him to be a person he could never be. She called him once more, but when the call went to voicemail yet again, she didn't leave a message. She couldn't think what on earth to say to him.

EIGHT

When Megan went to see her brother next, she found him chopping wood in the lean-to behind the house. She knew as soon as he turned around and she saw his face – from the deep angry frown lines in his forehead – that he had seen Beth; she also knew how much he would have dreaded seeing her again.

"You saw her, then?" she said. "I did, too, at the funeral. It was very, well, *weird*, but not as bad as I'd feared, actually. I hope you weren't mean to her."

Ioan winced. "I wasn't mean, but it was awful, *dweud y gwir*/to be honest," he said. "She was peering through our hedge, all dolled-up, chatting to my kids as if nothing had ever happened between us."

Megan sighed. "All that's ancient history, Ioan. If I've got over it, why can't you?"

"But have you, really? Got over it, I mean?" he snapped. "I don't think so."

She shivered. "Whatever. Can we go inside, please? I'm freezing."

Her brother had let nobody except her cross the threshold into his house since Ceri had left. Each time she had been inside, she had been more shocked. Ioan went ahead of her to open the door.

"Gareth's at school, but Envys is playing upstairs," he mumbled. "*Panad?*/Cuppa?"

Megan nodded. The smell in the kitchen hit her immediately: a miasma of full bin, burnt food and wet dog. Jonah immediately went over to greet Whale, the chocolate Labrador snoring in a basket by the range, and his younger brother by ten minutes. Whenever they met, their reunion was always a tender one.

The kitchen was dark, as the windows were filmed with salt spray and dried, mottled condensation. Spiders' webs and bleached cocoons of their eggs lined each windowsill, and the layer of dust on the Welsh dresser was visibly thick. Sheets of paper daubed with bright designs, paintbrushes in jam jars of murky water and pots of poster paint on the table showed that the children enjoyed painting, but there was no room to eat a meal there. Clearly, nothing much had been cleaned or cleared away since the day Ceri had left, almost six months earlier. Ioan's wife had always prided herself on her excessively "*tŷ twt*/tidy house", which her husband had accepted as necessary for her happiness, if bemusing. But this was verging on the squalid. Megan wondered if things had begun to go awry between this couple long before Darren, the property developer, had tempted Ceri away, as they were so ill-matched and such very different people.

"I know it's a mess," Ioan murmured, bringing their teas over to the table. "I just can't bring myself to care."

Megan laid a hand over one of his. "But think about the kids. This is their home. They can't like living like this, especially after..."

"After their mother abandoned them, you mean? Was that my fault too?"

"No, of course not," Megan said, blushing. Her brother was

fragile, and his fuse short these days. She dreaded saying anything that might upset him.

A pause, while they sipped their tea in silence.

Eventually, Ioan said, "She never wanted children, you know – Ceri. Made me wait years before she consented to even try for a baby, as we'd married so young and she said she had 'things she wanted to do'. I have no idea what they were, but I guess she's doing them now. I had dreams, too, once. Dead in the water now, of course."

Megan waited for his sorrow to subside a little, as she had learnt to do.

"I guess we all have different dreams, and this wasn't hers. It's cruel, but life is often cruel. We know that more than most." Her soft, almost musical voice was as soothing as it had been when they were children and she had hugged him whenever there was thunder and lightning. It was a voice like honey, he'd always told her as a little boy. "And you can still paint, Ioan. Even now."

"But this hurts more than anything I've ever felt," Ioan murmured. "Her leaving, I mean."

Megan nodded, and waited again. "I know. And it will, eventually, fade, I promise you, but until then, let me help you as much as I can today."

"*Diolch*/Thanks. Don't do too much, though. I know how tired you get."

He smiled weakly, and she saw a glimpse of the handsome man he still was, before he got up to finish chopping logs. He was still as muscular as he had been in his rugby-playing heyday, but his open, tanned face bore signs of suffering that aged him. She watched his stooped shoulders pick up the axe, and it saddened her to see him so diminished.

Megan started with the pile of greasy saucepans in the sink, before mopping the filthy kitchen floor, which revealed tiles of a completely different colour. As she worked, she could hear her little niece talking to her toys upstairs, her piping little voice clearly audible through the floorboards. She wondered how much she had heard, how scared she had been, during these past dreadful months, as her father had wept and railed about his loss. Such things could scar children irreparably. She would never have a child of her own now, but she could help these two heal by keeping on visiting, however little her brother seemed to want her to.

When she went to clean out the fireplace in the living room, Megan saw that all Ceri's generic prints from Next and M&S had gone. On one wall of the room, Ioan had stuck up what looked like sheets of paper torn from a sketchpad, with vivid watercolour scenes and tiny, cross-hatched drawings of birds and flowers. On another wall were what looked like the pages from an old calendar showing some of the great paintings she remembered from Ioan's library books in the past. It gave her enormous hope to see these things in his home once more. He was still in there, somewhere, her kind, sensitive brother who had so loved art and beauty.

She made them a fresh pot of tea, and Ioan returned with a basketful of seasoned logs from the woodshed and stoked the kitchen range. Within minutes, a wave of heat billowed across the kitchen and both dogs groaned in bliss and stretched out on the rug, their front paws comfortably entwined.

"It wasn't Beth's fault that Eirlys died, or even what happened to me. You know that, don't you? I really want you to let it go, now, as I have tried to do. She'd left for Oxford by then, and probably never even knew about any of it."

"I know that, but I believe it *was* her fault that you suffered as you did. If she hadn't taken Dylan away from you and then jettisoned the pair of you, you might not have had your heart broken." He stopped to gauge if it was safe to continue, and feeling it was. "Mam and Dad should never have sent you away to Uncle Alun's when... when they did. It was archaic, and cruel. Things had progressed beyond the Dark Ages by then, but that didn't bother Dad, of course."

"No, it didn't. But I was too heartbroken to protest, remember," Megan said sadly. "Perhaps it wasn't a good thing, but it was kind, on Mam's part at least. Uncle Alun was her big brother and she knew I would be cared for there," she replied. "Now Mam will never be well again. We've all paid a price for the past, in different ways."

"I'm sorry," Ioan whispered. "I wish I had been able to protect you, keep you safe."

"I should have kept myself safe," Megan replied. "And I should have seen Dylan Jones for what he was – weak and vain. I had too many stars in my eyes to see the truth about him, or anything else, in those days. And we were all so young..."

From upstairs, they heard laughter, as Envys upbraided one of her toys for "getting things dirty". Megan caught Ioan's eye, and knew he, too, had made the connection between his daughter's dislike of mess and his wife's near-obsession with neatness. Megan sipped her tea, and said nothing.

"Are you OK? You are looking *braidd yn gwla*/a bit peaky..." Ioan asked.

Megan drained her cup, stood up and went to the bottom of the stairs. She could not tell him how she had found this winter the hardest of all the many winters she had spent alone. He was still too broken by his own tragedy. "I don't need you to worry about me. I'll do just fine if I take things steady. Now where is that lovely niece of mine?" she said, calling, "Envys! Jonah is here and he and Whale urgently need a cuddle!"

The little girl clumped downstairs and buried her face in warm chocolate Labrador.

"So, will you celebrate your birthday here, and stay over, for Christmas Day?" Ioan said. "I know you usually stay home, but it would be nicer for you, and for the kids, and for me, if you were with us this year."

Megan nodded. "Of course. I would have come every year if Ceri had invited me. You know that, don't you?"

Ioan sighed. "Yes. She wasn't the most... *welcoming* of people, I know."

"Especially to me," Megan said drily. "The terrible whiff of shame, and all that."

Ioan shifted in his chair. "We're not living in times when 'fallen women' are ostracised, though Dad treated you like that, the sod."

Megan sighed. "Dad was a bully, and bullies pick on the weak."

"Mam has never set foot in this house either, I'm ashamed to say," he went on. "Ceri always worried that she would scare the children, with her bald head and her nerves, you know, so I never invited her."

"Perhaps she would have scared them a bit, but she is their *nain*/grandmother," Megan said. "Should you invite her for Christmas too?"

"I have already, but I know she won't come," he replied. "It breaks my heart to think of her sitting there on her own day after day."

"She's ill, and she never means to hurt you, or me."

Ioan shook his head. "I guess I just miss her, the mam she used to be, and I need her now more than ever." He paused. "I don't know how you find it in your heart to forgive people their failings so easily, Meg. I really don't."

She laid her hand over one of his. "Life's too short not to try, but sometimes it's not easy at all, believe me."

PART 2

TO STAY, OR NOT TO STAY

NINE

The imminence of Christmas was all but ignored in *Melin Arian* that year, despite the fact that the village was festooned with decorations and some of the houses positively throbbed with fairy lights. In the past, Jed had made sure that their home was also extravagantly decorated. Once, he had enlisted Beth and Ziggy's help to spool hundreds of metres of lights around the entire mill while hanging precariously from a rickety ladder. He also bought everyone expensive gifts "on tick" or by borrowing money from friends. When, in February, Tabitha realised what he had done, she took to her bed, and a teenage Beth was given the task of sorting out a repayment schedule. This childish excess had been as much a part of their Christmas as turkey and mince pies, and deeply stressful, but this year, nothing felt festive without it and the family mourned Jed's loss.

Tabitha was increasingly lost either in still, silent grief or growing agitation, which added weight to Beth's niggling suspicion that her mother's symptoms could be early-onset Alzheimer's. Ziggy decided it was a good time to go and stay with a mate to help him repair his roof, which Beth resented deeply, as it left her in sole charge of Tabitha.

"You thoughtless git, Ziggy Tonks," she muttered as she tried to soothe her panicking mother once again. "You never did back me up when I needed you to. Same old, same old."

And yet when she allowed these sour thoughts and long-held grudges to enter her head, a small voice reminded her of his many small acts of kindness throughout their turbulent childhood and even since she had left home when he was fifteen. He had sent food parcels of their favourite treats to Oxford, and silly, newsy postcards once a month. He had done so much already for their parents. What lay ahead for him if she returned to London? Caring for their mother as she deteriorated, living on handouts, on his own? That was a prospect nobody would relish. He was still young. Perhaps he had things he wanted to do but couldn't. Beth had never actually *asked* him this since the failure of all his hare-brained schemes when he was younger. Could she really be that callous, that selfish, and leave him to cope with whatever lay ahead alone? The past told her that she could, which shamed her.

The weather was consistently appalling, which did not help lift Beth's thickening gloom. Wild storms racked the island and heavy rain lashed the ground day after day, leaving it so waterlogged that the cattle in the fields struggled to extricate their hooves from the sucking mud. The living room at the windmill was regularly filled with smoke from the fire as fierce gales blew it back down the chimney in puffs of sheer contempt. Beth bought some convector heaters, and everyone breathed a collective sigh of relief when the warmth they produced almost reached to the edge of each round-walled room. But it was not enough. As each monotonous day crawled past, she began to feel more restless, and more unsure that she could stay here for very much longer. She emailed a few marketing agencies in a fit of proactivity, enquiring what opportunities might be available after Christmas. None replied. She had been let go and was in her forties, so she was nowhere near the top of any recruiter's list. What had she expected? she asked herself.

When her phone throbbed at 2am one morning, she was so deeply asleep that she sat bolt upright and stared at the glowing screen, paralysed, for almost a minute before picking up the call. Who on earth could be calling her now? The name flashing at her was "Lewis". When her brain registered his name, it sent a shot of pure adrenaline through her body.

"Mum?" a small voice said.

"Yes... Lewis? Hi, what's wrong?" she persuaded her sleepy mouth to say.

"I'm not feeling too good."

A pause, in which Beth was sure she could hear her son swallowing something and then drinking. Visions of pills and whisky were immediate.

"What are you doing?" she screeched. *"What are you taking?"*

"Two paracetamol. I've got a headache," came the quiet reply.

Beth took a few deep breaths. Her reaction had been exactly the opposite of what it should have been: all those management of people courses she had been on told her that. When she spoke again, she chose her words with more care, but still felt as if she was walking out onto thin ice. Why was her boy ringing now, when he had not rung her for weeks? Had he already tried his father? (She hoped not, as Hugo's new partner, Hilary, would not have welcomed a call at this hour.) Beth took a very deep breath and told herself to wise up, calm down and be present for her son, *whatever* time it was.

"Lewis, love, you scared me, that's all. It is the middle of the night."

"Yes, I know. I'm sorry, but... I can't stay here anymore, Mum. I hate it."

Another slow, calming breath that belied her pounding heart. "I see. Can you tell me why you feel that way?"

"Look, I never wanted to come here, but because I got in, you and Dad told me I had to, but it's not me, and it *never will be*," he said, his voice increasing in volume with each word. "I don't fit in here. Please let me leave."

Guilt coursed through Beth like acid. She had suspected this, but had sent him anyway, like a lamb to the slaughter as Tabitha would probably have said. When she heard a strange, snuffling sound, she realised that Lewis was weeping. She closed her eyes. She had never, ever heard her son cry, even when he was desperately unhappy at boarding school, or when his new tennis racket was smashed over a gate post by the bully who made his life hell there. She had forced her little boy to do something that was causing him acute distress. What kind of mother was she? Shame joined guilt in flooding her body.

"OK, OK, so where do you feel you want to be, Lewis?" she said, trying to sound calmer than she felt. "Do you want to go to Dad, in Hampstead? You know that I'm still up here on Anglesey, with *Nain*/Grandmother, and I'm not sure when I'll be back in London..."

"I want to be there with you, where it's nice and nobody will hassle me and expect me to do *things I will never be able to do*," he hissed. Beth was so distressed as she listened to him sob that her fingers were clutching at her childhood eiderdown as if it was a lifebuoy.

When he could speak again, she heard him pour out his frustration and fear, including the losses of his childhood, the harsh words, the tellings-off, the refusals, the denials of who he was and what he wanted, and they washed over her like a scalding tidal wave. All he had asked was to know that he was loved.

"I know I'm different, that my brain works in a different

way, but why is that a bad thing?" he said. "*Everyone's* different, aren't they?"

"Yes, darling, of course they are," she said, feeling the unfamiliarity of the endearment as soon as she'd said it. "But I need to ask, have you really thought about all this? It's such a huge decision, to leave Oxford..."

"That's exactly what Dad would say. And that's why I haven't rung him."

"I understand, and I know he can be a bit *harsh,* but your dad and I will always be here for you."

A match striking, an inhalation of breath. "Actually, I don't feel either of you have ever really 'been there' for me, Mum." A slow exhalation. "I don't know what I want to make of my life yet, but I do know I need to be myself. I can't even *live* if I have to be the person you seem to want me to be."

Beth was so floored by his words and his tone that she could not muster any reply at all. Unbidden, searing words from *Wuthering Heights* floated across her mind:

I cannot live without my life! I cannot live without my soul!

"I am very sorry you feel we've let you down. You tried to tell me how you felt about going up to Oxford, but I didn't listen. Your teachers tried to tell me how things were for you at school, how you struggled, but I thought it would sort itself out. For me, Oxford was an escape, a reward for all my hard work, you see, and I so wanted it to be that for you, but it seems it's a..."

"Punishment," Lewis cut in, his voice steely. "It feels like a jail sentence."

His words stunned her into silence. Outside her window, Beth glimpsed the ghostly shadow of a short-eared owl making its way from the top of the mill out over the dunes that led to the sea. Somehow, watching its slow progress, and steady, silent wing-beats calmed her, and she remembered how thrilled she and Megan had been to spot one of these birds. How she wished she had brought Lewis here more often, so that he, too, could learn the names of these beautiful birds – blue herons, oystercatchers, lapwings, curlews and snowy egrets. Their songs, their daily rituals of feeding, flying and roosting, had filled her childhood and provided a sense of the natural order of things in her life that could have helped him make sense of his. She said nothing, as she could not bear to take her eyes off the little owl as it made its silent passage across the sky, a tiny, fleeting link to the more considerate person she had once been.

"Mum? Are you still there?"

"Yes, love, sorry. I'm here."

"So, what shall I do? It's the end of term in a few weeks, so I could just tell my tutor I had to leave a bit early, for a... family emergency or something. Then we could talk about what comes next for me, plan it together. As long as I don't have to stay here for *one more day*. I can't do that."

Beth needed to think clearly, but shame was still clogging her thoughts, like mud in the spokes of a wheel. How could she have let this happen to her child? Her job as a parent was to make him happier than she had been as a child, and she had failed miserably. When Lewis spoke again, as she had not replied, she could hear resentment threading through his words once again.

"Most people would have gone to their grandfather's funeral, anyway, to be honest, Mum. I know I didn't see him often, but he and Ziggy took me fishing back in the day, and they listened to me when I told them how I felt."

So Jed, her unpredictable, immature father had been there for her son when she had not. This realisation hit her like a blow to the stomach, a physical pain. And *of course* she should have invited Lewis to say farewell to him at the funeral. Why hadn't she? When had she become the kind of person who did not do so? Whatever the answer to those questions, she needed to step up for her son, fast.

"Right, we can sort this, but I don't know how long I'll be staying up here, Lewis, as it's... not easy, but *Nain*/Grandmother needs my help at the moment and, well, I don't have to rush back for work. I've, er, been made redundant, you see."

Another exhalation, which became a splutter. "Really? Bloody hell, that's a turn-up for the books, Mum!" Lewis said, with a cheeriness Beth found both alarming and reassuring. "Have you told Dad yet? He is not going to be happy *at all*, as he'll have to give you more money."

Beth heard a low chuckle, and then another puff of whatever he was smoking. Her mind was racing, skimming over options at warp speed. Tonight, she had to decide whether he should join her on Anglesey. It seemed a crazy plan, but it was clearly what he wanted, and what, if any, were the realistic alternatives?

But if he came, how would they get on? What kind of food did he like to eat? What did he like to do? What would they talk about? She realised with a sharp jolt that she hardly knew this boy she had given life to. She'd handed him over to nannies and nurseries within months of his birth, and despatched him to boarding school at seven. In the school holidays, Hugo had arranged summer camps and residential trips for Lewis which enabled them both to work or have a relaxing break somewhere exotic themselves. She remembered her bitter words to Megan so many years ago, and they struck a ghastly chord:

"*My mother may be the woman who gave birth to me, but she has never been a real mam, like yours.*"

She had done exactly the same, but differently.

"I really need to talk to you, Mum. About... me, actually, and who, or what I think I am," Lewis said quietly.

Synapses fired and connected in Beth's brain. If he was telling her he was gay, that was fine, but somehow, she doubted it. It didn't feel right. With alarming speed, another scenario began to form in her head. She had always known that Lewis was different to the boisterous boys at his school, couldn't cope well with noise, or things he did not expect. Could it be more than that – was he neurodiverse in some way? She had read some newspaper articles about it recently as it was a growing area of knowledge. How would she feel about that if it was so? How would Hugo react?

Shutting down her whirling thoughts, she decided that whatever it was that he needed to tell her, her very first priority was to reassure him that she loved him, no matter what. And so she did.

"I love you, and it's going to be OK, Lewis. I promise, whatever it is. Really it will." She stopped, and took a deep breath. "Right, this is what we're going to do. Can you get a train up here in the morning?" she said. "Tell your tutor you've been feeling a bit... confused, and need to come home."

"My tutor knows how I feel. He says I should get some counselling, talk things through, perhaps..." he paused, before adding, "get a diagnosis, Mum." Lewis's voice was hoarse and strained as if these words were being pulled from him by force. "And anyway, the trains are on strike tomorrow. I've already checked."

Beth did not hesitate for a second longer. It was time to rescue him.

"Start packing your stuff. I'll be there by breakfast-time, and we'll sort all this out together, I promise. See you soon, love."

As soon as he hung up, Beth texted Ziggy, her fingers trembling on the keypad:

> Sorry, gone to Oxford. Lewis v unhappy. Please look after Mum. Should be back in a day or so. Thanks Zig. B

By the time the church clock in the village struck 3am, she was on the road to Oxford.

TEN

Beth's return to Aberffraw two days later with her son caused a flurry of excitement in the village. Siân Owen spotted the car crossing the square in the early afternoon, as she was struggling to inflate a blow-up snowman to be tethered outside the shop for Christmas. A quick glance told her that the young man in the passenger seat was looking unwell, as his face was drained of all colour. By lunchtime, everyone who cared, and lots who didn't, knew that Lewis Macintosh (who was supposed to be studying at Oxford, and destined, obviously, for the same glittering city-life as his mother) had just arrived in Aberffraw in her car and *did not look at all well.*

"He looked pretty ill to me, in fact. Perhaps he's on the drugs," Siân said, adding as if it was significant, "Blonde curls he had, just like hers."

"He didn't even come to his poor *taid's*/grandfather's funeral, did he?" one particularly vocal critic of Jed Tonks opined. "Says it all, really."

"He hasn't been up here for ages. Jed was not someone Beth would want her precious son to be spending time with, now he's grown up," Siân said, slicing some rather tired-looking ham behind the counter. "Her mother, Tabitha, perhaps, as there was money in her family, whoever they were – or so I heard. Money attracts money like bees to honey, as my old mam used to say."

"Siân, that's really not fair," said a man's voice from behind the shelving. "No, the boy hasn't been here for a while, but he came when he could, and he went fishing with Jed and Ziggy whenever his mother allowed him to during their flying visits. I remember seeing the three of them, like peas in a pod they were, chatting and laughing down on the rocks by the beach."

Ioan Williams stepped out, hands on hips, and Siân's cheeks flamed. "They looked very happy together is all I can say," he went on, "so let that poor family be now. They're grieving, and I know how that feels."

"That's very noble, especially coming from *you*, Ioan," Siân muttered, blushing to the roots of her livid red hair. "You've not been so charitable about the Tonks family in the past."

"I know, but it's Beth I have issues with, for what she did to Megan, not her son," Ioan replied sternly. "The boy looks ill, and she's brought him here when he should be in Oxford, so I say *chwarae teg*/fair enough. That makes her a good mam in my books, so let's all try being kind for once, shall we?"

Siân leant across the counter, eyes bright. "So, what exactly *did* go on between those two girls and Dylan, before Beth left for Uni? There was a lot of talk about him keeping them both dangling, but I've never really..."

"It was, and remains, their business, Siân. *Diolch*/Thanks," Ioan replied, leaving the shop and a stunned silence behind him.

As he walked towards home, where only loneliness awaited him, Ioan's thoughts ricocheted around inside his head. He was as shocked by his reaction in the shop as Siân Owen had been.

Why had he defended Beth so vehemently, when he all but hated the woman both for her rejection of him, and her betrayal of his sister? How he despised this new, hot anger that surged through him so uncontrollably ever since Ceri had left. It was not *him* at all – and yet, unfortunately, it now seemed to be.

The kids were with their mother in Chester overnight, and he could not bear to spend the rest of his day off alone, so he headed towards Megan's cottage. She would be there, with a *panad*/cuppa and a comforting word. She always was and always had been, hadn't she? She had all the time in the world, and no commitments, after all. But even as this thought crossed his mind, he realised with shame that he had very little idea what was going on in his sister's life these days. He had been so overwhelmed with the disaster that was his own. Was he inured to any new troubles she might have because she had had more than her quota of them in the past? he wondered. If so, he cursed himself for his selfishness. Others' suffering did not end just because you've had enough of your own.

And he knew that Megan was still suffering, all these years later, however well she hid it. How did anyone ever recover from such a betrayal, such a cruel loss? He could not even bear to imagine it. The more he brooded on it, the more he felt the licking flames of panic. His sister didn't look well lately and sometimes cancelled picking up the kids on a Wednesday as she was just too tired, which she would only do if she was desperate. She hadn't mentioned her poetry for ages; in fact, he didn't know whether she was still writing at all, but he suspected not. Yes, he had always felt awkward when she quoted the stuff at him, but it mattered so much to her. The last time she had done so, many months ago, he'd laughed out loud when she'd suddenly exclaimed:

"As Cathy tells Nelly in *Wuthering Heights*, 'I wish I were a girl again, half-savage, hardy and free!'"

Looking back on this moment, he shook his head at his

immaturity and vowed to ask her about her writing that very day. The often mysterious but always astonishing words she sometimes quoted to him had always been a light that shone out from the heart of his sister, a bolt of brilliance that belied the dreariness around her. Had that light finally gone out? God, he hoped not.

Walking quickly, he mulled over their last conversation about Beth, and whether he had in fact been "mean" to her when she'd passed his farmhouse, as his sister had suspected. He decided he had. She was grieving and had been nothing but friendly. His rudeness, his lack of grace, embarrassed him. They had been so close once. He could never quite forgive her for betraying his sister's trust, or for rejecting him, however kindly, but he would try harder to hide his conflicted feelings, for Gareth and Envys' sake.

But when he arrived at Megan's cottage, she was not there. Ioan knocked on the door and heard Jonah's half-hearted bark, then he walked around to the back of the cottage and peered in through the kitchen window. The old dog's tail wagged furiously, his ever faithful face alight with love. Ioan reminded himself in that moment how lucky he was to be adored by Jonah, and his own dear Whale at home, and he felt a lump in his throat.

"I'm like Paul on the road to Damascus today, with all these bloody revelations!" he said, wiping his hand roughly across his eyes.

When he dialled Megan's mobile number, it went straight to voicemail, but as she would probably never listen to a message, there was no point in him leaving one. He knew where she kept a spare key, but to snoop around her home without her knowledge or consent did not feel right. Waiting for her to return might make her feel he was keeping tabs on her movements, which she would hate. There was no choice but to leave.

But he turned to return home with a heavy heart. It was

only noon, but already the day felt as if it had reached its peak and any feeble warmth was beginning to ebb. Gusts of wind whipped flurries of dry leaves along the path in front of him, and the waves were tipped with white. Suddenly, a shaft of wintry sun lit up a large, round patch of water far out on the horizon, a spectacle Ioan had always dubbed "God, saying hello" when he was a child. As the light intensified, almost blinding in its brightness, the impression of something divine, a message from somewhere above this earth, grew even stronger. This astounding natural spectacle echoed the celestial sunbeams he had loved in the classical paintings he'd often pored over with Beth in the school library during wet lunch breaks. They'd always been astounded at the heavenly splendour great artists like Michaelangelo and Caravaggio were able to capture on canvas. Those, Ioan had loved, but it was the artists who managed to transfix a blissful moment of the everyday that he loved even more – painters like Vermeer and Rembrandt, though they were of a different age and time. When, as a teenager on a school trip to a local gallery, he had first glimpsed the North Welsh artist Kyffin Williams' vibrant paintings of hill farmers, sheep dogs and low-roofed cottages next to churning seas, he had gasped aloud. This was *his* world, peopled by those he recognised, and made beautiful. How he had longed to do the same, but it would never happen now. That had been one of the many heartbreaks he had endured over the years.

Ceri, his wife, had neither understood nor shared this passion. She'd discouraged him from doing an Art History evening class as his shifts at the hospital already took their toll on family life and studying paintings was not worth his time in her view. Beth had always understood, though, and celebrated his interest with respect. They had talked about which techniques they felt were most effective, and how the bold strokes of Van Gogh or Picasso compared to the far more delicate touch of

Monet or Seurat. He smiled at these happy memories, perfect moments in time – a time long gone, but not forgotten. And Beth had been there, at the heart of them. He would always love her for that.

But was she "still the same in many ways", as she had implied when they had spoken? And how could they ever be close again? He had no answer to those questions as he walked back to an empty house, but he knew with absolute certainty that her return to the island would change his life forever, though he did not yet know how.

ELEVEN

Although he had wanted to come to Anglesey, Beth was unsure how Lewis would settle into *Melin Arian,* for a number of reasons. Firstly, it was far more basic than he was used to and entertainment for young people was pretty limited. Secondly, he had never been here in winter, when the main preoccupation of every day was trying to keep warm. His rooms in her London flat and in Hugo's Hampstead house were spacious, warm and clean. At boarding school and at Oxford, his accommodation was comfortable, heated, with a hot shower, a desk and somewhere to put his clothes. In Anglesey, he was given the tiny circular bedroom at the very top of the windmill that had a lumpy old double bed in the centre, leaving only enough space for a chair either side. When, by 10am on his first morning, he still had not appeared, Beth began to worry. Was he OK up there? How could he sleep so long up in that freezing little cell when she woke at 6am every morning with an ice-cold nose?

When he appeared in the kitchen doorway just before 11am, his warm-blonde hair sticking up around his head like a dandelion clock and a broad smile on his face, she had such a vivid flashback of him as a toddler on one of their rare family days out that contentment spread through her body like a sip of good wine. Finally, they would be able to spend some time together.

"Good *evening*, old bean!" Ziggy said, pointing at the clock with a huge grin on his face. He had come back to the mill because, as he told Beth, his favourite nephew was in town. She knew that he meant well, but his influence was not always a good one and Lewis was in a pretty fragile state.

She need not have worried. Lewis grinned at his uncle's teasing, as he always had, and gave him a fake salute.

"Reporting for duty, Tonks," he said. "Let the craziness commence!"

Then he spotted his grandmother huddled in her chair in the corner. "Hey, *Nain*/Grandmother. Are you warm enough there, *miles from the only heate*r?" he said, with a mock-glare at his uncle.

Ziggy was sitting almost on top of the convector heater. He blushed and scraped his chair back a little. "*Sori, Mam*/Sorry, Mum."

"Oh don't call me that stupid Welsh word!" Tabitha exclaimed. "I am pretending I'm not here. I don't aim to be for much longer, you know."

Ziggy sighed. "You're going nowhere anytime soon, Mum."

"But I need to go back to where I came from. Back to my home, back to the beginning," she replied. Then she stared at her son for a moment or two, and said, "Please pass my knitting."

"Goodness knows what you're on about, Mum, but really glad today is a chatty day," Ziggy muttered.

Beth quietly ushered Lewis to the table, whispering, "I did warn you it's a madhouse here, love."

"Should suit me fine, then," he replied, crossing his eyes deliberately.

"Fancy some fishing while you're here?" Ziggy said, once

Tabitha was calmed by getting a ball of wool ready to make a jumper for the "poor lost lad". "I've got all Dad's old rods and stuff..."

"Yeah. That would be great," Lewis replied. "When are you free, as I am, as of today, as free as the proverbial bird?"

Ziggy shifted in his seat. "Well, most of the time, to be honest, boy. Just doing favours for people and so not working much at the moment."

Beth muttered, "Surprise, surprise."

Ziggy flinched. "We can't all be like you, Beth, and claw our way to the top. It hasn't done you much good, from where I'm sitting."

"I can do without your opinion on what I do or don't do, thanks, Ziggy," Beth said. She had hurt him, but he had hurt her right back. This was a very familiar pattern.

The room fizzed with tension. The only sound was the clack-clack of Tabitha's knitting needles.

"I think it's quite lonely at the top, and I think it's good that Mum will have a break, as she's just been made redundant by her boss with no warning. You haven't told them, have you, Mum?" Lewis said, completely oblivious to the huge wave of shock this news generated in the room and nonchalantly buttering himself a slice of toast.

All eyes swivelled towards Beth.

"No, no, I hadn't said anything yet," she said, flustered. "I'm sure I'll get another job before long, but it seemed like a good thing, er, at the moment, given current circumstances, er, to have some time here." Beth heard the tremor in her voice and was shocked to find herself shaking. She was glad she was able to be home to help her mother cope with the loss of Jed, but, yes, she had effectively been jettisoned from her career, after years of stupidly devoted service. It really, really hurt, now that she actually allowed herself to think about it.

Ziggy shook his head. "I'm really sorry to hear that, Beth.

It's total shit, in fact. They must be a bunch of *twmphats*/idiots to let you go, but it's an occupational hazard of having an occupation, I guess." He looked at Lewis for approval of his, oh-so-sophisticated, joke. Lewis grinned on cue.

"And I say you can stay here as long as you like, both of you. If we all take things one day at a time, *and everyone chills out a bit,*" he looked at Beth, and winked, "it'll be happy days all round. Mam'll love it, won't you? The old fam back together. Oops, *Mum.*"

"*Diolch, Zig*/Thanks, Zig," Beth replied, glad the tension had dissipated, as her brother never held grudges for long. "If we're going to be cooped up here, it looks like it's us who are going back to the beginning, just like you wanted, Mum. But let's do things better, this time, shall we, idiot brother?"

Ziggy looked at her askance. "OK, let's, idiot sister."

Tabitha's anxious face was transfigured with a beatific smile as she heard her children's banter. "My darlings, together again. And 'the little lost soul' too," she added, turning to Lewis. "What a beautiful boy he is. He reminds me of someone... look at all that gorgeous *hair...*"

"Me, Mum?" Beth said, forcing a laugh. It was wonderful to be actually having a conversation with her mother, but this comment unnerved her. "Everyone says he looks exactly like me."

"I see you in him, Beth, but there's something else, someone else, now his face is changing from a boy's into a man's..." Picking up her knitting again, she shook her head as if to dismiss the thought.

"Well, I don't see any of Hugo's genes in you, so you got lucky there," Ziggy said, slapping his nephew on the back so hard that he almost spat his mouthful of toast across the table.

"No, the boy doesn't look like his father, but Hugo Macintosh is from very good stock, I'll have you know," Tabitha said. "We knew his people. That's why they wouldn't come to your wedding."

Everyone stared at her, open-mouthed.

"Your family knew Hugo's family, Mum?" Beth asked, incredulous.

"Take no notice," Ziggy hissed. "She says daft stuff sometimes. Thinks she's one of the Mitford sisters some days. Aspirations of grandeur, and all that." He winked at Lewis as if to say, "I'm on a roll today."

Beth smiled, but as Tabitha had never, ever spoken much about her childhood, or where her family were, could there possibly be some truth in her ramblings? Beth's parents had been such an unusual couple that nothing would surprise her, about either of them. There must be a story there, hidden beneath the silt of their years together.

She ran over what she knew about her ex-husband and his family in her mind. They owned a small country estate in Berkshire, kept racehorses and had well-to-do ancestors stretching back several centuries, according to Hugo's parents, Thomas and Petronella. They had not come to Anglesey for their son's wedding, citing a last-minute diary clash, for which Beth had never forgiven them. She suspected they had been forewarned of her parents' more *informal* plans for the day. But this slight paled into insignificance during the years that followed, during which Beth was left in no doubt that she would never be deemed good enough for Hugo. Their response to the divorce had been both telling and hurtful. When Hugo told her that his parents had never really seen her as daughter-in-law material, Beth had wept bitterly.

It seemed incredibly unlikely that Tabitha's family *had* known Hugo's people, as she put it, and yet she had sounded both convinced and convincing. Did her mother's history, whatever it held, lie behind her parents-in-laws' relentless unkindness to her? It would explain a lot, if so. And did anyone else in her family show symptoms of Alzheimer's in their sixties, as her mother was doing?

Beth could only hope that, as Tabitha's muddled recollections ebbed and flowed, some snippets of the truth would seep through the widening fissures in her memory and flesh in more details of her shadowy past. For now, all she could do was watch and wait.

TWELVE

As November became December, life at *Melin Arian* fell into a predictable, dull rhythm: everyone missed the chaos that Jed had whipped up around him in some ways, but his absence was most keenly felt by Tabitha. She could sometimes be found weeping soundlessly in their bedroom, tears rolling down her cheeks, or stroking her husband's acoustic guitar with a vacant expression on her face. Her children enveloped her in a loving cocoon that she could not see but they hoped she knew was there. Beth contacted the GP to arrange a cognitive assessment of her mother and to discuss how to manage whatever lay ahead for them all if her suspicions were confirmed. It was one of the most difficult phone conversations of her life. Tabitha was still distant, but no longer coldly and deliberately so, as she roamed the long, darkened tracts of her memory. In truth, mother and daughter had never been closer, and Beth knew that to lose her now would be utterly heartbreaking.

As each short, dark day merged into one, she set herself a different task for each one of them. It was the only way she knew how to manage her anxiety about what was to come. She deep-cleaned the kitchen, beat the living room rugs outside and wiped the inside of the little windows with a mixture of vinegar and water so that any precious slivers of sunlight could penetrate the rooms. Having had a cleaner ever since her marriage to Hugo, she was amazed at how satisfying these simple tasks were – far more than any "brainstorming session" or "client face-to-face opportunity".

Lewis settled into life at the windmill immediately as if his former life had been deleted the moment he arrived. If he had made any friends at Oxford, none got in touch with him. It seemed as if he had always belonged on the island and he told Beth he felt safe, and had returned to his true home, which she found a little odd but vaguely comforting. He still paced to and fro up in his room, as they could hear him, but he seemed calm rather than agitated when he came down afterwards, so nobody ever referred to it. When Beth did some research, she discovered that this behaviour was called "stimming" and was a way of relieving stress for some neurodivergent people. All she cared about was that Lewis was happy, and he was. Within a week, he had taken over all cooking duties in the windmill, was offering to walk dogs for elderly villagers if it was raining, read the newspaper aloud to a blind neighbour and did some shopping for people who struggled in the icy weather. Ziggy began to call him "*Sant*/Saint Lewis", a nickname he both hated and adored.

He was outside for hours each day, whatever the weather, armed with his mother's battered old *Collins Gem Book of Birds*, and returned with rosy cheeks and tales of all the different birds he had seen. He recorded the mournful cries of curlews on his phone and listed the gulls' cliffside nesting sites so he could revisit them in the spring when they would be busy with chicks. He also told his mother he was writing his first play up in his chilly attic room (or "The Garret" as Ziggy called it), but he wouldn't let anyone read it. Beth didn't mind because she'd read on a parenting website it was good for a teenage boy to be expressing his feelings openly and she had never seen him so relaxed.

"When I walk and feel the force of the wind against my body and the spray on my face when the waves break, I feel properly alive, Mum," he told her very earnestly one day. "I've never really felt that before."

"I know what you mean, love," she replied. "I feel it too."

"And when I make something nice for us all to eat, I feel good about that as well. Better than I ever felt about anything, actually."

"Well, I'm very grateful when you cook, so carry on the good work," Beth replied, keeping her slight reservations about some of the spicy dishes he cooked for Tabitha quiet, as her mother ate them all with gusto.

With each passing day, she felt more sure of her decision to extricate her son from the life she and Hugo had lined up, at least for a while, and bring him here. She felt that both of them were coming to terms with the person he was, and that they could only do that when the pressure to conform was sloughed away. She had not yet told her ex-husband much about Lewis's state of mind, or how long he might stay on the island. Hugo had to be managed, and that would take time and tact. She would talk the future through with Lewis's Oxford tutors in January. Taking at least a year out was possible, and her only concern now was to take care of him and let him heal after years of rejection and disappointment. Hugo would understand that, eventually, she was sure. The way forward would become clear, over time, when Lewis felt ready to talk to her about it.

One thing nagged at Beth's peace of mind, however. Her son was spending a great deal of time with Ziggy, whom he had always worshipped, as he was fun, funny and much more available than his busy father had ever been. Within days of arriving on the island, Lewis was following Ziggy around devotedly as he had as a little boy, and even started copying his eclectic, charity-shop-based dress sense.

Was Ziggy going to involve Lewis in one of his ill-thought-out schemes? she fretted. More failure was the last thing Lewis needed right now. She had not forgotten the so-called noodle van that she and Hugo had lent her brother money to set up, which ended when a storm blew the van into the river as he hadn't locked the shutters properly. Another scheme, funded by their parents, had entailed Ziggy walking along the beach offering freshly split coconut halves to sunbathers. That ended when there was rarely enough sun to bathe in and he had a glut of unsold, very expensive, coconuts. But despite her doubts, Beth could see that her son adored Ziggy and that her brother adored him right back. When Lewis started nagging her daily to let them go fishing in the old rowing boat the family moored near the beach, he seasoned it with lashings of emotional blackmail.

"Uncle Ziggy promised to take me years ago, but you said 'no', of course. You and Dad always said 'no', but I'm an adult now, so can you *chill out* please?" he said, adopting the phrase his uncle used at least ten times every day.

Cornered, Beth parried with, "Why don't you keep fishing on the shore for a while, where it's safe? You loved that, remember, when you went with Ziggy and *Taid*/Grandfather years ago?"

"They were some of the happiest times of my life, of which there were very few," Lewis said, sending another shot of guilt through his mother. "But can I go out when Uncle Ziggy says the weather's good enough? I can cook whatever fish we catch and *Nain*/Grandmother needs all the vitamins and protein she can get, remember, for her *brain health*."

Fortunately for Beth, the weather in December was predictably unpredictable, so Ziggy and Lewis had to stay on the rocks on the beach for a while longer. They caught precious little, but Lewis was totally absorbed and enjoyed it immensely, as he could "finally be myself", he told his mother. For all his perceived shortcomings, she watched Ziggy treat Lewis with kindness, respect and understanding, and she saw their relationship deepen with tentative pleasure. She decided that it was time to let her son make his own way: trying to rein him in anymore would probably push him further away, *whatever* Hugo said.

Which was plenty, once she told him of recent events in more detail, as she knew she had to. He was aghast at "The Oxford Commando Raid" as he'd dubbed Beth bringing Lewis home from university after an overnight drive. He was also far from convinced that his son's friendship with Ziggy ("which is all he bloody texts me about") was altogether a good thing. As the mobile reception was poor in the windmill, Beth had to walk along the headland to take her ex-husband's calls at a set time each week. It was an obligation she would gladly have dropped as they were such very different people now, and it was always tricky, but Hugo loved his son, and cared what happened to him, so she kept him informed.

"But, Beth, there's nothing for him there," Hugo said sadly, in one particularly fraught call. "He must stick out like a sore thumb in that backwater. He's a bit of an oddball, isn't he, much as we both love him?"

Beth stuttered a "I don't know... I think..." but he had hit a nerve. Should she voice her concerns about Lewis's behaviour now, or wait until she felt completely sure? Hugo made up her mind for her, by what he said next.

"And surely he's not going to forgo a place at Oxford to be a *cook,* a *dog walker* or go fishing with your reprobate brother? He needs sound guidance, and perhaps some professional support to sort himself out..."

"I know, but not yet, and I really don't see him going back to Oxford any time soon, Hugo," she said firmly. "He was so miserable when I brought him here. I was seriously worried, but he's happy now, you should see him..."

"Bloody hell, I know it sounds trivial, but I've spent thousands of pounds on that boy's education, Beth," Hugo muttered. "Surely you understand my concern that he might waste it?"

"It was my money, too, remember, but none of the choices he made were his. They were *ours*," she said. "All I want is for him to be who he wants to be, not what we feel he should be to please us. He's finding his own way now."

"That's a luxury I was never afforded, but I take your point," Hugo replied with a deep sigh. "Well, just make sure your brother doesn't influence him too much in this quest for 'his own way'. He's not really an ideal role model, is he?"

Beth felt a surge of defensive fury and her carefully controlled tone wavered. "Hugo, you have met my brother three times in our entire marriage, so don't judge someone you barely know. He's kind and patient with Lewis, which is more than you ever were, so cut him some slack please. I'll ring you after Christmas."

She hung up and marched along the coastal path towards home full of righteous indignation.

It was the black beret Beth recognised first. The hunched shape shuffling along the headland path swaddled in a long overcoat and pulling a shopping trolley behind her stirred no recognition, but that beret... it had to be Megan.

The wind was strengthening. Beth watched from a distance as her old friend struggled to keep the shopping trolley under control with one hand every time a strong gust blew it sideways, and almost off the cliff edge. The other hand was keeping that beret on her head as if her life depended on it. As one of the few remaining emblems of the person she had once been, Beth decided that perhaps it did. She walked towards her.

"Meg, let me help you," she shouted into the wind. "It's wild and getting wilder out here."

Megan lifted her head, but the rim of her beret was pulled so far down that Beth could only glimpse a sliver of her achingly familiar face. She looked very, very tired.

"Let me at least take the trolley, will you?" she said. This risked sounding patronising, but Beth knew this was no time for pride. Weather like this could become dangerous very fast indeed.

Wobbling like a drunkard as each gust buffeted her, Megan tried to steady herself but could not. As her thin arms flailed and the beret flew off, Beth's arm slipped through hers and she rooted it to the ground with a stamp of her left foot.

"That beret is a priceless artefact," Beth said, stooping to pick it up. "It's a part of you. Always has been."

"*Diolch*/Thanks, Beth," Megan murmured, tugging it back onto her head quickly. "I didn't know the weather would turn so quickly. How daft of me."

Beth smiled. "We all make mistakes."

A pause, where unspoken words hung.

"We do indeed. But whatever the weather, I have to get to Ioan's with these Christmas gifts for his kids. It's his only day off this week, and he ordered them to be delivered to my house. Ioan needs to hide them before they get home from school," Megan went on. "The things I do for that brother of mine."

"I know that feeling!" Beth replied, laughing.

Megan stopped and turned to look at her. Beth knew exactly what was coming next: poetry.

"Beth, do you remember that Emily Dickinson quote we used to say to each other when our families were driving us particularly mad? I do:

"Look back on time with kindly eyes, He doubtless did his best."

"Yes. You're right. That's all any of us can do, our best,"

Beth murmured. "And Ziggy is so good with Lewis, my son, and with Mum."

"Kindness is a much-underrated quality," Megan said. "That, and forgiveness."

Beth looked into her friend's eyes. Did she forgive her, finally, for her weakness in tempting Dylan Jones away from her to satisfy her own ego, and eventually prising them apart with a betrayal she could never forget? The upshot of this weakness in her own life, and the cloud it had cast over her happiness, she could hide forever, but the consequences for her friend could not be hidden: she was alone, unhappy, and her poetry remained unpublished. It was an awful lot to forgive.

THIRTEEN

Whale, Ioan's Labrador, was at the gate when they reached the farmhouse, barking rather unconvincingly at a branch on the lawn, blown down from an apple tree in the garden. A glowering sky threatened rain, and both women knew what that could mean on the island in December: they had better be quick dropping off the gifts and get home even more quickly. Still arm in arm, they staggered up to the front door and knocked. When there was no answer, Megan opened it and went inside. Beth loitered tentatively in the doorway; would Ioan want her to come into his home? He had been so hostile when they had spoken before.

"*Whale, dos i mewn*/come inside," Megan said. "I've got her brother, Jonah. They're from a long line of Anglesey Labs, and so loving."

"They're both gorgeous. Do you remember Wil, that stray my dad found? I loved him so much – still love dogs, in fact. What you see is what you get with a dog, which is a rare thing in people."

"Well, there's a new litter of pups now, looking for homes, Ioan told me, but I hope he's not tempted to get one. He's got more than enough on his plate." Megan sat down at the table with a grunt of relief. "He needs *human* friends, not more canine ones, that brother of mine."

Beth, still in the doorway, felt the hairs on her arms stand up. A Labrador puppy, ready for a new home, and local too? She knew someone who had waited his whole life for a loving friend like that...

"Don't look so scared, Beth. Come in. Ioan won't eat you," Megan said.

"Are you sure?" she replied. "He looked as if he wanted to, the last time we met!" Warily, she closed the door behind her.

The kitchen looked slightly less chaotic than it had before Megan's efforts to clear up a few weeks earlier, but it was clear that Ioan was still struggling to manage his busy household. The bin was overflowing, the sink full of dishes and a load of damp washing was steaming in the wicker basket by the range.

"His wife left him, he told me," Beth whispered. "So sad."

"So bloody selfish, you mean. She was a real cow, but he loved her for some unknown reason. Never realised how lucky she was, but karma will come for *Ceri bach*/little Ceri, you mark my words." Megan cackled, wagging a finger.

Both women laughed, stopped, and then covered their mouths with a hand in one, synchronised, movement. This was how it had always been in the past, Beth remembered happily: two bodies, one mind. A loud crash from somewhere upstairs, followed by the slam of a door, made them both jump.

"The wind's really picking up now," Megan said, frowning. "Ioan! Are you here?" she called out.

A muffled thud, some swearing, and her brother appeared in the other doorway, rubbing his eyes like a recalcitrant school-boy. He'd obviously been asleep in the living room and just fallen off the sofa.

"Meg, hi... oh, and Beth, hi." He tousled his hair roughly as if doing so might wake him up faster. "I've got *déjà vu*, seeing you two standing there together."

He did not move closer, and the atmosphere in the room was suddenly unnervingly tense as if a field of static electricity was humming in the air between them, waiting to crackle and zap if the wrong words were said.

"Right, host of the year. How about a *panad*/cuppa?" Megan said, quickly brushing a scree of crumbs off the table. "It's really rough outside and getting rougher by the minute. Beth saved me from certain death on the way, so we won't stay long."

Ioan nodded curtly at Beth, who was still standing in the other doorway, as if to thank her. Then he went to fill the kettle.

"Well, the wind's put some colour in your cheeks, Meg, which is good to see. You haven't looked well lately."

"I'm fine, or I will be if you make me a bloody hot drink!" Megan said. "And invite Beth *in*, perhaps?"

"Sorry, yes, come in and sit down, Beth – if you can find a chair with nothing unsavoury on it! The spillage quota is high around here."

By the time the kettle had boiled and Ioan had put a teapot and mugs on the table, the sky had darkened from dark grey to a bluey-black, and the kitchen was plunged into a thick, viscous gloom. Within seconds, they heard the first "plip plip plip" of raindrops on the windowpanes and soon afterwards, treacly torrents of water were streaming down the glass and a thundering noise filled the room as rain cannoned off the roof slates. Ioan watched, open-mouthed, as the corrugated iron roof of his woodshed flew past the kitchen window like a shot in a surrealist film. They all heard it crash to the ground on the front path, and winced. New sheds were expensive.

"You'd better stay here until it eases off – both of you," he murmured. "Nobody's going out in that. They'll keep the kids safely at school too."

"Thank goodness. I've got the Christmas things for them, the ones you ordered," Megan said, pulling the shopping trolley towards her. "Here you go."

The two women watched as Ioan pulled each garish box or package out, his face glowing with boyish delight. There was a remote-controlled car and a Polaroid camera for Gareth, a *Frozen* doll and a pink feather boa for Envys. He also pulled out a small set of toy carpentry tools for her, and a set of toy pans for his son. "In case I'm accused of gender bias," he muttered. They all laughed.

"I can't give them their mother back, but I can give them these," he said, his face clouding with a sudden sadness. He sighed as he put all the toys away. "I asked Mam again about coming for Christmas Day, but I don't think she understood me. It could be a quiet one, Megan. You don't have to join us if..."

"Quiet is my favourite vibe, and the kids will love those gifts," she cut in. "I'm not exactly drowning in invitations, you know."

"I know that, *cariad*/love. And yes, they'll love these until they see what Lady Ceri and Lord Darren have given them," Ioan said bitterly, going upstairs to hide the gifts.

As Megan poured tea, Beth remembered Christmas gift-giving in her family, when Hugo had insisted on their giving Lewis a "ring-fenced amount of cash" and something "small but useful", like rugby socks and a Tory politician's autobiography. These were the kind of gifts he had been given by his parents, she knew, but she regretted not being a *little* more extravagant. Seeing this young father's joyful anticipation of his children's happiness at their gifts was in such stark contrast to her memories of Lewis as a boy. Oh, what she would give to see Gareth and Envys' faces on Christmas morning, when they opened *these* gifts! How could she ever hope to make it up to her son, when the days of train sets and Action Man were gone forever? And what could she possibly offer him now that could be any kind of consolation for all those times she and Hugo had said "no"?

While Ioan was upstairs, Megan moved to the sofa, and closed her eyes, clearly exhausted by her battle with the weather. Beth looked around her and sipped her tea at the table quietly so as not to disturb her. As Ioan had said, she didn't look well. And why on earth had she not taken that wretched old beret off, now they were inside?

This dingy room was clearly in need of more care and attention than Ioan had time to give it, but it was cosy, nonetheless. She saw the faint outlines of two or three pictures, obviously recently taken down, and much smaller art prints stuck up inside the frame of dirt they'd left on the wall. Van Gogh, Cézanne, Gauguin and Monet's vivid colours glowed in the soupy gloom, injecting a spark of life and colour that nothing else could do on that wintry day.

On the biggest wall in the kitchen was another, less vibrant print – beautifully mounted and framed with seasoned pine – showing a tumbledown traditional Anglesey cottage with a softly undulating roof and small windows like eyes that looked out over the sea. When Ioan came back into the room, she had to pull her gaze away to look at him.

"You like that one?" Ioan said.

"Yes, I do. Kyffin Williams, of course," she murmured. "I should have known you would love his work as well."

"I do indeed. So, you do too?"

Beth smiled and nodded, and felt a fillip in her belly, something akin to what she had felt whenever she had glimpsed him powering down the rugby field to score a try, or coming out of the sea after a swim, all those years ago. He'd retained his rugged good looks, despite everything that had happened to him.

"I've only ever seen his paintings in books, but I think he

captures the bleakness of this place better than any other artist ever has, or ever could," she replied.

Ioan nodded. "It's so difficult to capture the *wildness* of it, yes, but he does it somehow. You can almost hear the waves and feel the wind on your face when you look at these, I think." A pause, which Beth did not feel the need to fill. "I met him once, you know, when I was out on the cliffs trying to do some painting myself. He walked past me in his big old coat with his dogs skittering beside him, and told me to "*dalia ati*/keep going" – with the painting, I mean. Even said I had got a sense of the wideness of the sky. I'll take that."

"And so you should," Beth said, feeling a surge of pleasure. This was how it had been between them in the past, when they shared things that others might well have thought rather soppy, when they were both teens trying to find a language they could share. How could the few years between them have mattered so very much to her then, when they mattered so very little now? The sadness of all they had lost was almost over-whelming.

"Actually, have you been to *Oriel Môn*/The Anglesey Gallery, in Llangefni, to see Kyffin's paintings? We could go, *os dach chi isio*/if you like." A deep blush suffused his cheeks and disappeared again in an instant.

Beth saw Megan, who was still lying on the sofa, open a sly eye, but she said nothing.

"Sure. That would be great," Beth replied, hoping her own blushes were hidden by the gloomy light in the room.

"OK, let's exchange numbers, and sort it sometime."

She handed him her phone, but his use of the more formal form "chi" had stung her a little. And was he was just being polite, with his "sometime"? Perhaps he still wanted to keep her at a distance – and who could blame him?

"I'm pretty busy with my mother and Lewis, to be honest," she said. "On that note, I really need to get back soon. It sounds as if the rain's easing off, but what about Megan? She looks so tired."

"I'll drive her home in a bit. But do you think she's OK, Beth?" Ioan asked, in a hissed whisper across the table. "She won't tell me when I ask, but I'm worried about her."

Beth hesitated. Did she have the right to express an opinion, when she had been no part of these siblings' lives for so many years? She felt not.

"I don't know the answer to that," she said. "But I do think she's lonely and I think she's sad, and she needs something to look forward to." But as soon as the words were out of her mouth, she realised that Ioan probably blamed her for his sister's circumstances. It was her that had stolen Megan's only love, after all, in tempting him away from her and triggering their final split. There was a silence, a gathering of thoughts, but when Ioan eventually spoke, he did not react in that way at all, and she felt her discomfiture vanish.

"Aren't we all, inside, lonely and sad?" he replied instead, shaking his head. "What a total mess we've made of things, the three of us. Let the past stay in the past."

"Yes, it is a mess, but you and I have our kids, as you told me the other day."

"I'd like to meet your Lewis one day. People in the village shop say he's a nice lad, that place being the source of all intel around here!"

"He is. He's a wonderful lad, and I think you'd get on well." After she had spoken, Beth realised that the warm feeling now spreading through her was pride. It was a wonderful feeling.

It was on the tip of her tongue to suggest that all three of them go to the gallery, as Lewis would also love Kyffin Williams' paintings, but she did not. Somehow, she wanted to keep that as a possibility for herself alone. Before she left, she had one more question to ask Ioan.

"Do you happen to have the number for the people who

breed Labradors, and have a litter to find homes for at the moment? Megan mentioned them."

When Ioan smiled at her then, his face lit up and two small dimples appeared in his cheeks, as they always had, Beth remembered.

"I do indeed. Pass me your phone again and I'll give you it."

"I must be mad, even considering getting a dog when I have no idea what the future holds, for me or for Lewis," she said.

"Which of us has any idea of that? Not me, that's for sure. Take a risk, Beth – say 'yes' not 'no'. It might change your life. Dogs can do that."

He was right: she had said "no" to so much and had led a life dictated by values she knew she no longer held. Yes, she would get Lewis a dog at last, and fill his life with the unconditional love Wil had given her as a child, when the world was often a confusing, lonely place. As she walked back to the windmill in the wind and rain, she felt lighter of heart than she had done in a very long time.

FOURTEEN

Beth always looked back on the storm that had reunited her with Megan and Ioan as a gift, a fortuitous twist of fate. The next bout of bad weather to hit the island she remembered for different reasons, however, though both affected her life in ways she could never have anticipated.

The morning she finally consented to let Ziggy and Lewis go out in the boat was a dull, chilly one, but it was dry and there was barely any breeze. A bank of cloud was hunkering on the horizon, but that was usually the case on these bleak December days. It was a week before Christmas, and even the weather seemed to convey a feeling of hushed anticipation as if it didn't want to do anything too dramatic in case it spoilt things. Beth had no reason not to trust Ziggy when he told her that they a) would not go too far out, b) would stay near the rocks at the mouth of the bay, c) that she would be able to see them from the shore , and d) that she just needed to *chill out*. She knew that he was right on the last count, and she was trying very hard to do so.

"I've had the old outboard motor serviced, so we have power

if we need it," he told her, carefully decanting wriggling lugworms into a plastic bait-box.

"Well, that's reassuring," she replied. "Dad always refused to use it, didn't he, wanting to rely on the pure power of wind and wave, I seem to recall?"

"Yup, silly old hippy," he replied. "I like to hear the plash of the old oars in the water too. That's the way island fishermen always used to fish close to shore. But I also remember having to go out and rescue Dad at least once a month because he'd mistimed the tides. Ioan always leaves his rib moored over there, above the tideline, so he can save us from a watery end if necessary."

He left the room before Beth's open mouth could produce any sound.

Lewis was beyond excited at the prospect of a trip out on the water with Ziggy. He had been up late the previous night, checking their rods and flies, and zealously googling what they might catch. How could she even consider curtailing his pleasure at such a wholesome outdoor pastime when she had never seen him so happy? It was unthinkable. She told him that she would sit in her car in the car park with her binoculars and a flask of tea, mitigating her overprotectiveness by saying she was proud to see a family memory come alive again. This was partly true, but in reality, she was both reluctant to let him out of her sight and painfully aware of how long she had wanted to do exactly that. What a waste of so many hours, days, months and years they could have spent together, enjoying each other's company. She was more than thankful for this second chance, but she knew she had to afford him the freedom to make his own choices and decisions now, however hard this was for her. He had to be at ease with himself, whoever he was.

. . .

The tide was low when uncle and nephew scrunched across the shingle down to the water's edge, carrying Jed's old boat above their heads like a huge tortoise shell. When Ziggy came back for the outboard motor, he gave Beth an unconvincing thumbs-up as he passed the car. The wind was picking up a little, and his face said he knew it. She added another sugar lump to her tea.

But the next hour or so passed in a semi-blissful haze. Beth fixed her gaze on the little boat on the near horizon and watched as Lewis and Ziggy cast and reeled in their lines in beautifully choreographed repetitive movements. As the car windows steamed up and she felt her body relax in the warmth, she dozed off, leaving the window open a crack so she could hear any imminent emergency. When a strong gust of wind ruffled her hair, she sleepily opened her eyes as her brain registered that the sky seemed to have changed colour since she'd closed them. It was now a dark, leaden grey and the sea was craggy as huge waves heaved up and down and battered the rocks with spectacular arcs of spray. She could not see the boat at all, as the horizon was now all but obscured in a thick sea fret. With a lurch of panic, she pushed the car door open and squinted into her binoculars, and out to sea. In seconds, the Dior scarf she was wearing was whipped off her neck and vanished into the distance, twisting and cavorting like a dervish. Then the rain started, incredibly heavy from the off, obliterating everything within seconds in a wall of impenetrable water.

"Lewis! Ziggy!" Beth screeched, hearing her own words fly back in her face.

Staggering down to the shore, she was just able to make out the vague shape of the little boat rising to the top of each wave before plunging down again and then disappearing in the deep trough. There was no possibility of them rowing ashore in this. Would Ziggy be able to start the outboard motor in rain this heavy? Scenes from apocalyptic disaster movies flashed across her mind, but Ziggy was no Bruce Willis.

Looking back, it astonished her that she was able to do what she did next. She always credited her gruelling experiences in the boardroom for the steely calm she displayed. She called Ioan, praying there would be enough signal, and that he would not be at work or too busy with the children to be able to help. She had no idea when the schools broke up for Christmas. When he picked up and she heard his deep voice through the howling wind, it was so hard to keep all her seething feelings at bay that she sobbed and spluttered into the phone incoherently.

"Beth? What's up? Are you all right?"

"No! Lewis and Ziggy are out in Dad's boat!" she blurted. "I can't see them anymore, but they set off from Traeth Mawr. They have an outboard motor, but I don't think they'll... Ziggy said to contact you, if..."

"*Paid a phoeni*/Don't worry. I'll be there as soon as I can," Ioan replied.

And he was. Only five minutes later, Beth saw his Land Rover skid to a halt above the beach and watched him sprint down to the shore and into his boat, his outboard motor cradled in his arms. She ran towards him, but he was already pushing the rib's trailer over the shingle and out into the churning waves. With a ghastly realisation, she wondered if she had asked him to risk his own life in saving the others'.

"Where were they, roughly, when you last saw them?" he shouted back at her as he lowered the outboard propeller into the water.

Beth pointed towards where she had been watching Lewis and Ziggy fish before she'd fallen asleep. "By that outcrop of black rocks on the far right of the bay. Please take care!"

Ioan nodded and yanked the starter cord. His outboard immediately roared into life, and he vanished into the blanket of grey rain leaving a thin trail of diesel fumes and a wide, white furrow in the water. In seconds, he, too, disappeared into the gloom.

The next five minutes were amongst the longest of Beth's life. She could hear nothing, and see nothing, but her imagination was in overdrive. Why on earth had she allowed her sensitive, city-bred son to go out in a battered old rowing boat in winter with her lackadaisical brother? Was this some cruel fate, that Lewis should be taken from her now, just as she had realised how much she loved him? And Ziggy, too, was in terrible danger! How would her mother cope with losing him as well as her husband? A sudden surge of love for her unusual, vulnerable mother spread through her body unbidden: she could not bear to watch her suffer any more pain or loss. And Ioan had two small children... no, she could not imagine anymore.

She was nearing hysteria when she heard the faint buzzing of the motor returning to the shore, growing stronger second by second. She bent double in relief but only when she saw the fuzzy outline of three heads in the rib did the tears come. She raced down to the water's edge.

Lewis and Ziggy were soaked to the skin, their hair plastered to their heads, but they were both smiling. Ioan, at the back of the boat, head down, was not. None of the men said a word until they were all onshore, and the rib securely fixed to its mooring. As they climbed out, the rain stopped as suddenly as it had started, and the wind dropped. Beth was lost for words: she was relieved, but she was shocked, and angry too. Thankfully, Ioan spoke first.

"Well, I could do without that on a regular basis," he said, sweeping his hand through his dripping hair. "Next time, check the forecast, Ziggy, OK?"

Ziggy winced. "I did, honestly, but it said 'showery'."

"Hmm, but things change quickly at this time of year, don't they? The word 'shower' can mean many things up here, as you know full well."

"Yes, and I'm sorry, both of you," Ziggy said sheepishly.

"Mum, your dad's boat sank and we lost all the rods. We had to swim to the rocks, but we weren't that far out. Sorry if you were a bit worried," Lewis said.

Beth could only nod, astounded at his nonchalance.

"*Duw*/God, Ioan's right. The weather up here can get far worse than that. Don't you remember, Beth, when we got cut off by the tide at Llanddwyn?" Ziggy said, when Ioan was out of earshot.

Beth spluttered indignantly. "Ziggy, I don't care. I have aged *ten years* in the last hour. If you ever take Lewis out on a boat again, I'm coming with you."

Ziggy smiled. "One for all, and all for one, just like when we were kids, eh?"

"And that got us into many a sticky situation, I seem to recall, like when I followed you up that tree and onto Mrs Griffiths' garage roof and broke my bloody arm," she said, folding her arms in mock sternness.

Ioan came towards them, and when he smiled directly at Beth, she felt a wave of peace spread throughout her body. Minutes earlier, she had been terrified for her son's life, but this modest, kind man had made everything right with the world again with that smile.

Years later, she would look back on this chaotic afternoon as one of the most important of her life, and as one that took it in a direction she could never have foreseen. It also took her one step nearer to feeling she had come home.

FIFTEEN

Megan's birthday, on Christmas Eve, began badly, as it so often had in the past. The moment she opened her eyes, she felt a deep sense of foreboding as if what lay ahead of her for the rest of the day was emblematic of her future: an endurance rather than a celebration. She had promised to go to Ioan's after lunch and spend today and Christmas Day with him and his children, but she was so tired, and her heart was heavy at the thought of it. Her brother's home would certainly not be offering the perfect "Happy Christmas" that was on all the cards, and in all the songs and TV adverts at that time of year. The absence of Ceri would loom large, which would probably see Megan having to console her brother if he drank too much, and entertain Gareth and Envys for much of the day. She simply could not be bothered with any of it, but she knew she had no real choice but to go.

She heaved herself out of bed into the cold that lurked beyond the relative warmth of her old flannelette sheets, threadbare Witney blankets and hot water bottles. Her breath formed into small clouds, and there was a thin film of ice on the inside of the window as if sealing her inside. Built with blocks of pitted dark grey stone hewn from a local quarry, her cottage had always emanated more gloom than comfort.

"No wonder we called this place 'The Witches' Cottage' when we were kids," she muttered to her still-sleeping dog. "It would take some serious sorcery to make this place feel good."

Despite herself, she went to the front door first of all, to see if any birthday cards had been delivered. The postman very rarely came to the cottage, and when he did, brought only council tax bills and junk mail, but today, perhaps, might there be something nicer? she dared to hope. The doormat was bare. She opened the door, just in case there was something on the mat outside, but nothing greeted her except a carpet of frosty grass and the frozen crusts of bread she had thrown out for the birds the previous evening.

Her mother Nia couldn't remember what she'd had for breakfast, but Megan had hoped that Ioan might have reminded her of her birthday and organised at least the sending of a card. The fact that he had not hurt her more than it should have done, and she ate her porridge alone at the table as hot tears rolled down her cheeks. This was not the life she had planned at all.

Once, she'd hoped for so much, before she'd mistaken lust for love. Before then, her life had looked full of promise and her head had buzzed with thoughts and words and ideas. Now, she was middle-aged, worn out, creatively frustrated and obviously pretty unloved, given the lack of post today. How had the Megan Williams she had once been allowed this to happen?

A sharp knock produced a paroxysm of barking from Jonah, who heard only the loudest noises in his old age. Megan pulled her tatty dressing gown around her and scrunched her old beret onto her head to hide her bald patches before opening the door to be greeted with Beth, clutching a large plastic food container to her chest. In contrast to her immaculate appearance at her father's funeral, Megan noted that, today, her friend was not wearing any make-up and the huge overcoat she was wearing had clearly been borrowed from Ziggy. Behind her, a posse of hopeful, hungry gulls dipped and hovered.

"*Penblwydd hapus i ti*/Happy birthday to you!" she said. "I made you a cake."

"Well, if it's not bloody Wonkytonks!" she exclaimed, sounding happier than she had intended to because she was, truly, happy to see Beth today. So she had remembered the date of her birthday, after all these years. "*Dos i mewn*/Come in," adding a muttered, "and excuse the mess."

"I don't care about any mess. It's bloody freezing out here. We might even have a white Christmas at this rate," Beth replied, coming inside and stamping her wellies to try and warm her feet up. "I can only remember our having snow once or twice when we were kids, but it was brilliant when we did."

"Ziggy used your mam's tea-tray as a sledge and went down old Ieuan Parry's field so fast he nearly went off the cliff," Megan said, laughing.

"Sounds very like him. He's just as daft now, I'm afraid, and I think Lewis is learning the dark arts from him."

"Yes. Ioan told me about their hairy fishing trip."

They both laughed, and then stopped laughing as one.

"Right, let me show you my latest culinary creation before it collapses."

Beth took the lid of the plastic container and gingerly manoeuvred a large, pink, icing-slathered block out of it and onto the table. It had a miniature plastic "Happy birthday" banner stuck in it and sloped very severely to the right.

"You've surpassed yourself," Megan said. "It looks, well, amazing! *Diolch, Beth*/Thanks, Beth."

"Let's have some cake and a *panad*/cuppa for breakfast, eh? What's not to like about that?" Beth replied with a shiver.

"Sorry, I know it's cold in here. The radiators don't work,

but let me stoke the range, and warm us up a bit. I'll get some clothes on too."

"Don't get dressed for me, Meg," Beth said. "I really don't mind what you wear, or don't wear." She glanced at Megan's beret, however, and it was understood that she was gently asking why her friend was wearing it indoors.

"Alopecia. Big bald patches," Megan said, taking the beret off and pointing at her head. "Mam got it too, when things got bad. No idea why it's decided to start for me now, but it doesn't really matter. Who cares if I have hair or not?"

"It does matter, and I'm sorry about it, and I hadn't even noticed before today. I don't mind if you've got bald patches, honestly. And I'm sorry about your mam too. I heard she's... struggled an awful lot over the years I've been away."

A pause while Megan wondered how much Beth knew, and Beth, in turn, waited for her friend to fill in the gaps in her sparse knowledge. She did not.

"That seems to be what life is, an unending struggle," Megan replied. "Remember when we used to say:

"She felt herself supremer—

A raised, ethereal thing."

"Yes, '*And life would be all spring*'," Beth said. "I guess Emily Dickinson felt as invincible as we did at that age."

"She had her fair share of hard times, but at least she kept all her hair," Megan said, grinning.

Jonah shuffled across the kitchen and stuck his nose into Beth's crotch, his tail wagging. Both women laughed again, relieved at the lightening of mood.

"Sorry about that! He's pretty daft now, but I think it's safe to say he likes you!" Megan said. "Sit down and he'll probably leave you alone. We don't have many visitors in this squalid little pit I call home."

Beth met her gaze for the first time. "I'm glad to be here, in your home, Meg."

When Megan returned, dressed, and without her hat, the conversation that followed was oddly stilted, peppered with silences in which both women remembered how close they had once been. To Beth, they seemed like two lionesses, circling, observing, gauging each other, unsure whether to risk tackling trickier truths. Their shared teenage fixation with Dylan Jones was the obvious "elephant in the room", but did they discuss it now with seriousness, or dismiss it as adolescent silliness? But both knew it had been much more than that; it had become a rivalry that had severed the bond between them with a finality neither would have believed possible and its shadow still darkened their friendship like a swirl of ink in water. As conversation dwindled, both knew that they were making progress, but they were still not entirely comfortable in each other's company.

Outside, a cold, unpromising day was gradually becoming a better and brighter one. The ground steamed as wintry sunshine thawed the frost and revealed scrubby grass, drifts of black leaves and the slick slate pathway leading to the cottage. Beth was unsure how long Megan wanted her to stay, but she did not want to leave, however awkward being there felt at times. There was nowhere else she wanted to be that morning. When Jonah made it clear he needed a walk by filling the air with ghastly smells, she was happy, because walking might make talking easier. It did, but not in the way she'd hoped for, or expected.

SIXTEEN

The December sky was an incredibly vivid blue as they took the cliff path heading away from the village. The sea was calm, a sheet of rippled glass, with a gentle swell replacing the thunderous waves of a few days earlier. The rhythmic pulse of the water as it met the shore below them and then crept away again, leaving a lacy veil of soft froth on the sand, was so soothing that the two friends soon matched their pace to its slow, easy movement. They chatted sporadically, mainly about how they were both dreading Christmas tomorrow and how early they thought they could escape to bed and leave everyone to squabble over the TV remote control, but there was an expectancy in the air between them. Both women were wondering who would dare take this chit-chat into less comfortable territory. Megan cracked first.

"So, tell me about that ex-husband of yours, Hugo Macintosh? Ioan told me you're divorced. I haven't heard much good about him, *dweud y gwir*/to tell the truth. Did you love him?" she asked.

Beth was accustomed to direct questions in her work, but this one took her by surprise. "Well, I thought I did," she managed eventually. "He seemed to offer me the full package – good looks, a good job, a good future. Lots of ticks in lots of boxes. And he was funny, sometimes, and kind, sometimes. I guess we just grew apart, wanted different things. He's happy now, with an uptight solicitor called Hilary, but I still miss him."

"So in the end, he offered only disappointment, am I right?" Megan said bluntly. "Men tend to do that, I find." Her face was hard, her lips pressed tight shut.

As these words sank in, Beth silently acknowledged that, yes, men did often disappoint, but it was her own decisions that had disappointed her more.

"He was what I wanted and who I thought I wanted to be, when I married him, but people change," she murmured.

"Oh, they sure do," Megan replied pointedly. "We invest our hopes in these men, don't we? At least you have your son. What's his name again? If you told me, I've forgotten, sorry. I tend to do that with details."

"Lewis. His name is Lewis," Beth replied, blushing at her friend's brusque tone.

She had expected bitterness still to seethe beneath their rekindled relationship, like red hot lava glimpsed through cracks in the earth, but it was painful as her friend jabbed at her long-hidden guilt. Her schoolgirl betrayal had had such a devastating impact on Megan and blown the trust between them into a million pieces. How could she ever hope for forgiveness for what had happened later, which was even worse? She could not.

Without warning, Megan stopped dead on the path and looked out to sea, where a fishing boat was chugging steadily across the silver line of the horizon.

"I thought we could both find our dreams, Beth, but I think it's fair to say that you found yours at the expense of mine," she said. "You had everything, but you took the one thing I wanted, just because you could."

Heart pounding, her breathing fast and shallow, Beth could barely speak. "But I didn't mean to hurt you, Meg. I was young, and silly... and he wasn't worth it."

"I know. You were selfish and he was stupid, but what you did... made things impossible for me."

Beth stared at her. "But how, Meg? I don't understand. I told him to leave me alone in the end. He didn't really want either of us – he just used and abused us both."

"Yes, he did," Megan whispered. "But what you had done had repercussions that lasted a lifetime for me."

"But how?" Beth pressed. "Tell me, please. I flirted with him, which was stupid, but there must be more to it for you still to hold that against me, Meg."

"There is," Meg murmured.

Beth braced herself, sensing that her friend was about to tell her something that was very important indeed. And dreading it.

Megan looked away. "I had a baby. After you'd gone away to Oxford. I had Dylan's baby, a boy, and my parents made me give him away because Dylan refused to marry me. He said he liked you more, even though you rejected him, toyed with him, and then dumped him. He was just a dalliance, a challenge for your ego, but to me, he was everything. He left, you left, and I was on my own."

As Beth stared at her friend it seemed that her face, so familiar, so loved, dissolved into a million tiny pieces, pixellated by this shattering news. There was no platitude she could offer in response to this. She had spent years wracked with guilt for tempting Dylan away from her dearest friend, but now it seemed that she had actually caused her friend's life to implode, and then simply left to live her own. This realisation was unbearable.

"I had no idea you were pregnant," she said. "I really, honestly, didn't, Meg."

"I know. You'd gone, and Dylan went too, despatched by his

parents to dental college in Cardiff to grow up a bit and forget all about me," Megan said. Each word was causing her such pain that Beth could see it etched on her face. "I was sent to my mam's relatives on their farm in the mountains until my baby was born. Dad insisted they arrange for him to be brought up by people he knew, but I was never allowed to ask who, or where."

Wringing her hands, Megan paused as if to summon the strength to go on.

"Oh, it would never happen now of course, but back then, there were grey areas, cracks in the system that wily people like my dad knew how to exploit. Nobody would question it up in the hills, where you could go weeks without seeing another soul." Her gaze met Beth's for the first time, as she said, her voice a whisper, "I still dream about him you know, and see his perfect little face. I never even knew his name."

"And you never went home again, back to your mum and dad's?"

"My parents were old-fashioned. They wouldn't let me back in the house, and I didn't want to be anywhere near them. I moved to my horrible cottage to lick my wounds, I suppose. Nobody ever wanted to live there, so the rent was peanuts," Megan said with a sad smile. "Only Ioan has ever come to see me there all these years. I think Mam realised how cruel it had been, especially when she lost Eirlys, and she just couldn't cope with all that grief."

Beth started. "Eirlys, that was your little sister's name, I remember now. She *died*? Oh my God. How?"

"Meningitis. Dad delayed calling an ambulance as he was sure it was 'just a cold', and it arrived too late. Mum crumbled, hence the alopecia, the breakdowns, all of it. She's never recovered. Felt God was punishing her."

Neither woman spoke at all for several minutes. Above them, the sky was now ominously black, a change neither of them had noticed. Jonah whimpered when the first raindrops came seconds later. Megan bent down to stroke his head tenderly.

"Sssh, Jonah. He hates getting wet, you see. What a weird Labrador, eh?" Megan said, but she did not succeed in dispelling the sadness in the air.

"I'm so very sorry about Eirlys, and about your mam, about everything. And I can't begin to imagine how that would feel, to know you have a child out there that you've never met," Beth said.

"You weren't to know what Dylan and I were planning, what he was promising me. He was weak, as most men are. You were always the pretty one, remember? I was the weirdo."

"We were *both* beautiful, Meg, in different ways," Beth exclaimed. "I won't hear you say things like that, nasty things your father used to say to you that are best forgotten."

"Ah, we were both so young, weren't we? Dreaming of a Mr Rochester or a Mr Darcy coming to scoop us up. Do you know, I reckon Dylan hated poetry, really, but just said he liked it to get into my knickers?"

Beth nodded, shutting out a vivid image of tangled limbs on a darkened clifftop, her fingers running through thick, blonde curls. "I always thought he was such a *poseur,* but I still couldn't resist him for some reason." Later, she had learnt what a total and utter fake he was, but now was not the time to confess it.

"I would so love to see my son, even if it's just once, or at least to know he's well and happy," Megan said.

"Have you ever tried to trace him? He might still live in the area..."

"Ioan feels I should try to find him, and he was the only one who told Mam and Dad that they were wrong in what they did. They never forgave him either."

Beth waited, deciding how much she could ask, before whispering, "Would you think about trying to find your son now, Meg?"

A long pause followed, fraught with longing. Jonah nuzzled Megan's hand, sensing her distress, but she pushed him away gently.

"No. What good would it do, to anyone? None at all. It's ancient history now, and our lives parted a week or so after he was born. I'm resigned to it. I have to be."

But when Beth looked at her friend's face, she was not so sure. She looked bereft of hope, and everyone needed hope, because the future was utterly bleak without it. They stood on the headland as the blanket of misty rain slowly crept overhead and made their view grow fainter, softer, as in a pointilliste painting. The only sound was the soft purr of the boat's engine far out to sea, and the reedy peeps of some nimble-footed redshanks scouring the shallows for food. It was time to go back to their separate homes.

But in that moment, Beth was certain of another part of her purpose in coming back to the island. As well as growing to love her family and getting to know her son, she would search for her friend's lost child and reunite them.

PART 3

OLD LIFE, NEW LIFE

SEVENTEEN

January is always bleak on Anglesey. A resolute greyness seems to quash any flickers of colour or life, like a huge steely blanket laid over the flat landscape. There are no leaves on many of the trees, no heartening crocuses yet to cheer the soul and very little light or sunshine. As a girl, Beth had always hated this time in *Melin Arian,* chiefly because living in the dark, circular mill made her think of life inside a pepper mill, like Mrs Pepperpot, a character in some of her favourite girlhood stories. And yet this year, this January, felt different in the windmill, because it was a time of growing happiness.

Beth had given Lewis a male black Labrador pup on Christmas Day, and none of them could ever have imagined how much difference a little dog could make in a household. Lewis called him Zebedee, or "Zeb" for short, and adored him from the moment he lifted him out of the cardboard box he'd arrived in, both of them trembling with excitement. Despite the poos and puddles, everyone else soon loved him too, and within a week, nobody could imagine life without a fluffy, furry, licky Zeb in it. Wherever Beth went, he lolloped after her. When he was tired after hours of chewing, zooming, sniffing and exploring, Tabitha asked for him to be lifted up onto her chair where he snuggled next to her leg as she stroked him with a rapturous smile and a gentleness Beth had never seen before. Ziggy made various things for him to play with. Most of them involved wooden spoons and tennis balls, and the little dog slept on Lewis's bed from day one, giving him the love that only dogs can do.

"He *understands* me," he said, whenever Zeb sat at his feet waiting until he felt ready to play with him, or licking his hand gently whenever he seemed anxious. "Nobody else ever has."

As the start of a new university term approached, Beth got in contact with his Oxford college before they emailed her yet again asking what Lewis's plans were. She explained how her son felt about returning to continue his studies (panic-stricken) and obtained permission for him to defer for a year in the first instance and then consider what to do after that. In her heart, she knew he would probably never resume his degree, but this agreement softened the disappointment for Hugo. Lewis was delighted to be able to stay on Anglesey for the foreseeable future, but in case he spent all of every day flitting from old passion to new project, Beth insisted that he use his time well and help her and Ziggy with the care of her mother. Tabitha needed more managing by the day and it would take all their efforts to keep her safe.

"All absolutely fine with me," Lewis had said, when she told him. "I love taking care of *Nain*/Grandmother, honestly. I know she's a bit *weird*, at times, but so am I, so we get on perfectly. She will have one hundred per cent of my attention at all times."

Tabitha's appetite had improved since Lewis had become the house chef, but her behaviour had worsened. A heart-breaking assessment and diagnosis of early-onset Alzheimer's was helpful, in that it told everyone in the family what to expect and how to try and manage it, but there was no cure.

The progression of the disease was unpredictable, and often rapid.

Without any particular reason, Tabitha started wearing the beautiful old necklace Beth remembered from childhood over her nightdress, gazing at herself in the mirror as she turned to see it glitter reassuringly in the lamplight before she went to sleep at night. More and more frequently, she left the windmill at odd hours, wandering around the village looking for her "home". If they gently returned her to *Melin Arian*, she was angry rather than relieved, and set off again as soon as she was able to sneak away. The family began to dread a phone call from the police, telling them that she'd been run over, or from the coastguard telling them that she had fallen into the sea and drowned.

Beth deliberately did not go and see either Megan or Ioan for a week after Christmas. She was happy to leave them in peace and focus on her own family. It would probably have been an emotional, exhausting time for both of them, she suspected. She, too, had things to sort out once the new year began, as she needed to go back to London, empty her flat, and "shut down" her previous life. It was a task she was dreading, but one that could not be shirked.

Leaving Ziggy and Lewis in charge at the windmill with a long list of cleaning tasks, useful phone numbers and tips on how to keep Tabitha's wanderings to a minimum, Beth caught an early train to Euston. She had emailed Duncan, her ex-boss, to tell him that she would be in town and felt they should meet briefly and to nudge him into sorting out her severance payment.

Pulling into Euston, past mile after mile of outer London's graffiti'd hoardings, anodyne warehouses and sickly, blackened saplings by the train tracks, Beth realised that in the six or so weeks she had been out of the city, she had already become accustomed to a different environment – to bitingly cold air, quiet, slow days and velvet-dark nights. Here, where tannoys blasted across the station concourse, traffic lights blinked and billboards blared at her, she felt so disconcerted at first that she had to sit on a bench outside Euston and take some long, slow, deep breaths. She got a cab to her flat rather than the Tube, as the thought of the endless shuffling of humanity at each stop and the vile, yeasty smell of the carriages was repellent.

When Beth put the key in the door to her flat, she closed her eyes for a few seconds before turning it. Inside, would be all the relics of the person she had been only a few weeks earlier, who already felt so alien to the woman she was today. She had booked a storage unit in Walthamstow and arranged a removal company to pack up and take her stuff there next week. Whatever lay inside this urban box was the past, and she wanted nothing more to do with it.

The flat was warm despite her long absence, as the heating for the building was centrally controlled, but its silence reminded her more of an office than a home after the noisy, chaos of the mill. It had absolutely no character whatsoever, but was purely "a functional and sustainable contemporary living space", as the letting agent's glossy prospectus had put it.

"And who wants to live in one of those, for Christ's sake?" Beth muttered.

Two taped cardboard boxes from the office sat on the granite worktop. Her assistant had obviously brought them over. Opening one of them, she found some stationery items, a cactus, a lumbar support cushion and a framed picture of Lewis at a prize-giving event at his school, taken several years ago.

"Not much to show for all that striving, is it, love – for either of us?"

Her exit strategy was short and sharp. Within a couple of hours, she had cleared every cupboard, the fridge, the freezer and put the, very few, clothes that would be useful on Anglesey into a suitcase. The rest, she left for the removers to take out of her sight, and hopefully, her mind: she had no need for any of it now and would deal with donating them to charity further down the line.

Her phone pinged: a two-line email from Duncan confirming that her surprisingly generous severance payment would be in her account by the end of the working day but that he could not meet her today, after all. He hoped "to cross swords with you again"; wished her well "going forward", and trusted she would "never lose her can-do spirit".

"There's no danger of that, Duncan," she muttered. "In fact, I can do anything I like, going forward, and none of it will ever involve YOU!"

EIGHTEEN

Beth felt obliged to say goodbye to the four women she had got to know in the city and tell them of her plan to return to Anglesey, but she was nervous as she walked towards Soho to meet them.

They were a disparate group. The youngest, Isabel, was in her early thirties. Beth had mentored her at work and dried her tears in times of crisis, a kind of surrogate-motherhood she had found easier than the real thing. Gemma, her contemporary, was an artist she'd sweated and grunted next to at a hot yoga class, and who had very kindly offered her a bed for the night. Flora, a single, retired English teacher, was in her early sixties, and had been at a stalwart of the Hampstead book group she'd attended (sporadically, as their book choices were always "anything by Iris Murdoch or Ian McEwan"). Finally, there was Sabrina, a glamorous, private-school educated PA who'd married her, older, boss and had a baby at the same time as Beth. They'd met her at weekly Aquababy classes and had bounced and splashed their babies and tried to look as if they were enjoying themselves, blurting their true feelings in the changing rooms afterwards. Beth had tearfully confessed to not having truly bonded with Lewis, for reasons she could not quite pinpoint, and Sabrina had said she hadn't wanted a baby at all, but her husband refused to use contraception, so here he was.

Almost twenty years later, Beth accepted that her feelings had been very real, but looking back, they made her incredibly sad. Surely those surreal, unreal early days as a young mother should have been savoured, however tired and frustrated she had felt? How many hours had she wasted pining for whatever she thought she was missing, and envying other twenty-two-year-olds their babyless lives? They were so short, in retrospect, those days of baby and toddlerhood, and they would never, ever come again for her. She wished with all her heart that she had seen them for the fleeting gift they had been.

Beth Macintosh was never, ever late, but today, she was going to be, as she had underestimated the distance. All four women were sitting at the table when she arrived, and she sensed the uneasy vibe between them even as she gave her coat to the maître d'.

"Hi, Beth!" Isabel cried, rushing over to "mwah mwah" her. "I miss you sooooooo much in the office. It's not the same at *all*."

The others smiled and leant forward in their chairs expectantly as Beth took her seat at the head of the table. She was their only common link, the reason they were here, their pack-leader: to be safe, they needed to stay close to her.

"Thought you'd want to sit there, at the top," Gemma said with a melodramatic wink. "Top dog, and all that."

Beth smiled but felt a niggle of unease as she realised how little she actually knew this woman. She had never seen Gemma in outside-the-yoga studio *clothes*. This evening, she was wearing a very colourful African-print tunic. Her matching fabric head-dress reminded Beth of a rather lurid Mr Whippy ice cream. If Gemma, born and bred in Lewisham, hadn't been aware of cultural misappropriation when she'd got dressed this evening, everyone else in the restaurant would be. This was not a good start.

Flora, in total contrast, was wearing a sensible navy and white striped dress and a large, gold St Christopher necklace. Her now-greying hair was in the same severe bob, clipped back on both sides, as it had been all the years Beth had known her. She found this strangely comforting, as it reminded her of a character in a Wallace and Gromit film.

"I am so jealous of you, moving to live by the sea," Flora said. "Think of it – no more stifling summers or loud, over-blown people. London's *full* of them these days, I find."

"You live in Hampstead, don't you, Flora?" Gemma snapped. "Full of arty-farty people, I find. I live in Catford."

Flora retreated behind the menu.

"I live near Hampstead too, actually," Sabrina said quickly. "Quite near where Beth used to live when she... before she... I mean, back when..."

Beth rescued her. "Before I got my release papers?" she said.

But Sabrina's face did not register this weak joke, and she attempted to gloss over any awkwardness by babbling about her children, their schools, their gap years, their university courses. Sabrina had never returned to her PR job after her first child, and now had three more. The deep hollows under her eyes and stressed demeanour betrayed how exhausting her life had been. There had also been plenty of gossip about her unfaithful husband too. For Sabrina, there'd been no let-up in the breeding cycle and Beth could only imagine how soul-destroying that might feel if she had been a reluctant participant.

Isabel soon looked bored with kid and baby talk, as Beth had heard her put it. "Shall we order, Beth? Any suggestions?" she said, adding, "There are some real vintage gems on this menu! I mean, who eats salmon en croute and prawn cocktail these days?" She laughed insincerely. "Their profits will plummet now you're not bringing clients here on company expenses!"

Beth "hahaha'd" in response, but when she saw Isabel smirk, she was suddenly struck by how *immature*, this woman was, and how gauche – traits she had pushed aside in work, where Isabel needed and flattered her.

The evening did not improve with the addition of food, or even wine. The harder Beth tried to find common ground between these women, the more difficult conversation became. Isabel made generic responses to everything anyone said, her eyes glazed with boredom. Gemma left early after starters as there were no sensibly priced vegan main courses on the menu. In one way, this was good, as it gave Beth the opportunity to go to a hotel tonight, but in another, it was unsettling. They had spent so many hours alongside each other, grimacing, mirroring each other's poses and giggling at the inevitable urge to fart in the classes. Had all her adult friendships in this city been this hollow, this *insincere?* she wondered. She feared they had, as none of them seemed to be standing up to any scrutiny this evening.

Isabel left next, saying that she never ate pudding and was watching her weight. When she didn't even offer to pay for her meal, Beth knew that her hunch that she had just been putting in an appearance had been correct. She wished her luck in the full and shameful knowledge that she had behaved exactly the same on her own way up the slippery pole.

Once only Sabrina and Flora remained, the atmosphere became far more relaxed. It transpired that Sabrina had been to the girls' school Flora had taught at, so they had a lot of common acquaintances. Flora, always shy, came out of her shell as she talked about her long career, and her pride in it. Beth let them chat, genuinely happy that the nicest women had probably had the nicest evening. Sabrina left at around 10pm, following an angry text from her husband, and her offer to pay for her meal was gently refused.

"Come and visit me on Anglesey," Beth said. "We'll walk and talk. You'd love it."

"I will, and I would."

When the bill arrived, Beth opened the age-softened leather glasses-case she had grabbed from her mother's bag when hers could not be found in the detritus in *Melin Arian* early that morning. Reading glasses were a new addition to her life that she still found difficult to remember to take everywhere with her. They spelt *age*, and she resented having to wear them.

"This is on me, Flora," she said. "To thank you, for coming."

Flora made suitably formal, grateful noises, and patted her hair nervously. Beth knew that she must have felt much older than the others that evening, and that, for this shy woman, it had been a huge effort to come at all. Grateful for her decades-long loyalty, Beth vowed to value it more.

Suddenly, absent-mindedly watching Beth clean her glasses, Flora exclaimed:

"Tabitha Acaster? Oh goodness me! Is that the name in that case? I went to school with a girl called that. It must be the same person – it's a very old family name. She was a little older than me, and very beautiful, I remember. Came from a very well-to-do family with a house in Mayfair and a country seat in Sussex or Surrey... we all wanted to get invited there, but never did. They had amazing parties, she told us, with jazz bands and dancing and champagne fountains. All very 'Great Gatsby'." Flora paused, and a shadow crossed her face. "To be honest, though, Tabitha never seemed very happy. Very *un*happy, in fact, poor girl. Where on earth did you get her glasses case? In a charity shop? I did hear her family fell on hard times after we all left school... lots of scandal, death and tragedy, apparently."

Beth felt all the hairs on her arms stand on end. It was as if a rough sketch that had always been present in her memory suddenly had a dash of colour, a smidgen of detail, added to it. She had seen her mother's maiden name, Tabitha Acaster, inside the glasses case years ago, but she had always refused to talk about her family. But even if this was her golden opportunity to find out *why*, Beth could not lie to Flora to do so.

"To be honest with you, Tabitha is my mother, but she never, ever talks about her past," she said. "And she's called Tabitha Tonks now."

Flora spluttered water across the table. "Of course! I remember now! She ran off with a musician, didn't she? What with that, and her brother's unfortunate death, I think it went downhill for the Acasters after that. So very sad."

Beth felt as if she was moving underwater as she slowly and deliberately paid the bill, stood up and let the waiter help her on with her coat. Flora was looking slightly nervous now.

"Look, I didn't mean to talk about your mother in a... gossipy way. It's just such an astonishing coincidence," she said. "Do send her my best wishes. She'll remember me if you say what my nickname was at school: 'Borer Flora'."

Beth smiled. "That's a nasty nickname. I hope Mum never used it."

"She didn't," Flora replied. "She was always very kind, to everyone."

"Would you mind if I got in touch again, Flora, to find out more about Mum's history? We've known nothing, my brother and I, about where she came from, and she keeps asking us to 'take her back' there. She's been diagnosed with early-onset Alzheimer's, and it might help us understand what she wants us to do."

"Of course, and I am sorry to hear she's... unwell. She was a most extraordinary young woman, let me tell you."

"She's an extraordinary old one," Beth said.

As the two women parted and vanished into the anonymity

of a London street, neither knew how significant their meeting would prove to be.

NINETEEN

Beth returned to a bitterly cold Aberffraw to find the village in a state of panic. Siân Owen's wealthy spinster aunt had finally died the previous night, and she was already busily telling everyone that she planned to shut the shop for the foreseeable once her expected huge inheritance was confirmed. Cai Hughes, clipboard in hand, had called an emergency meeting of locals that afternoon. Many were anxious, as there was nowhere else to buy a newspaper, pint of milk or loaf of bread unless they drove five miles to Brynsciencyn or waited for the rare bus to Rhosneigr. Ziggy and Lewis were keen to be involved, and urged Beth to join them. She agreed, but only for Cai's sake.

Cai Hughes had shown more kindness to her parents than anyone over the years and his unfailing good nature was something to marvel at. He was the long-standing bingo caller in the village hall; he often gave people lifts to the hospital in Bangor rather than let them rely on the sporadic bus service, and he always led the biannual beach litter pick, whatever the weather. He had once started a Lepidoperists Club in the village, as the dunes behind the beach were famed for the butterflies that lived there, but his enthusiasm for butterflies was sadly not matched by anyone else. Beth knew that if there was a "pillar of the community" award in the village, Cai Hughes would deservedly have won it. When they arrived at the meeting, he was already in full flow, his permanently rosy cheeks ablaze with indignation.

"Siân, you can't close the shop! The pub's only hanging on by the skin of its teeth, relying on the tourists in the summer to get by. We've got the *Neuadd Goffa*/community hall, and it does some good things, but without the shop, the village will have a real gap at its heart. Not everyone wants to do all their shopping in big supermarkets, or order an online delivery – a *lot* of us don't, in fact. There are too many delivery vans speeding around on our little roads as it is. We have to save this place somehow."

Siân folded her arms, and said, "Look, I know it's a blow, but I've got cruises to go on and pools to lounge beside, and Elwyn and I have waited years for a proper break. I'm not working here day in, day out, if I don't need to, sorry. Life's too bloody short."

The low murmur around her expressed complete understanding.

"It's not the end of the world, *pawb*/everyone. Someone else will just have to run the shop, at least for a while. It's hardly rocket science, and there's enough of you to choose from," Siân said. "Perhaps you could do shifts, or job-share. Isn't that all the rage now?"

There was a different buzz now, as everyone in the shop shuffled about, raised eyebrows and exchanged brief, alarmed, comments. The majority of the villagers at the meeting were elderly, having retired from the working world.

"We wouldn't have a clue how to run a shop, Siân. Most of us are old and worked on the land. We're not business people," one grizzled old man said.

"This is a job for the young ones," another elderly man muttered.

Lewis, now very popular in the village for all his good deeds, pushed to the front of the gathering, and Beth watched a couple of older people beam, and slap his back in greeting. She also saw Ziggy nudge his way to the middle of the room as if keeping his options open. What on earth had they got planned?

Beth stayed back, unsure how she would be treated if she volunteered. These people remembered her only for the fact that she had abandoned her family, and never been back for longer than a few days until her father's recent death. A few would know about her and Megan's teenage tussles over Dylan Jones, and fewer still, given her friend's swift exile, would have guessed what the consequences of that infatuation had been for Megan, but many would still have put two and two together and made six. This was probably more of a poisoned chalice than an opportunity, and it certainly was not what she had envisaged for her new life. Nope, she did not need to do this.

Pulling her hood up, she shuffled back still further until she felt herself bump into someone equally reluctant to be the centre of attention – Ioan.

"Why are you hiding in the dry goods?" she hissed at him. "Nobody's press-ganging you, are they? I'm just waiting for them to twist my arm."

Ioan shook his head. "They'll be nagging me to manage this place and I'll be saying 'OK' before I even have time to tell them what a totally daft idea that would be," he said. "Managing a ward is enough for me, but I'm a prime candidate in their eyes, and I'm under sixty-five, unlike most of them here."

Beth grinned. "Me too, and Ziggy told me how important this place is to everyone. I can see why people are upset about the prospect of it closing, but it needs someone who *cares* about it to survive in this economic climate."

A pause, in which Beth sensed a gear change in the conversation. "Remember how we always used to spend our pocket money in here," Ioan said eventually. "And how Megan used to keep Siân's dad, Mr Owen, chatting, so that he might pop a few extras in the bag for free?"

Beth nodded. "I do. What about that time I found some money on the ground and cleared out his entire stock of 'Lolly Dippers'?" she said.

"I had all the lollies, and you had all the pink fizzy powder."

"And I can still see my pink vomit fizzing in the bottom of the loo," Beth laughed, overcome by a sudden rush of memories.

"So, this old shop *is* important to you, then, isn't it?" he said softly. "It means as much to my kids as it did to us, and they still spend their pocket money in here and try to get freebies from Siân – which is no mean feat, let me tell you."

Beth sighed. "Why didn't we appreciate what we had, when we had it? It was those little sparks of joy that make life worth living, like finding that money totally unexpectedly."

A white-haired woman turned around and smiled at them. "That's the biggest lesson life teaches us, *dw'in meddwl*/I think. Look for magic in the everyday: you can usually find a sprinkling of it somewhere."

To her left, another, almost identical-looking, elderly woman was now nodding furiously. *"Mae'n wir iawn*/It's very true," she said. "Nesta always gets to the knub of things."

"We get there together, Mai," Nesta replied firmly.

"You look *wedi blino'n lân*/utterly exhausted, Ioan," Mai said.

"I am. I could do with a bit of that magic right now," Ioan said, shaking his head sadly. "The hospital is so busy, and it gets worse with every shift. What with that and the kids, I don't know how long I can keep going."

Beth felt an urge to hug him but knew better than to try.

The meeting was getting even rowdier when she suddenly heard Ziggy's voice rise above the babble.

"Beth! Where are you? Beth, get over here, you're needed!"

"Uh-oh. You've been rumbled," Ioan whispered. "Look, I know it's a far cry from your big city role, Beth, but I think you'd make a cracking job of sorting this place out. You really would."

Beth shook her head. "I may be unemployed at present, but I'm not that desperate for something to do, and money's not a problem."

"Lucky you, but I still think you need to occupy that ever-active brain of yours," he replied, with a dimpling smile that made Beth long for more of them. "Go for it, Beth. And think how much people here would appreciate it."

She winced. "So, I should do it as my penance for leaving, you mean?"

"No," Ioan said, slightly less convincingly. "Perhaps more as a way of reconnecting with where you came from. There's the big room next door that used to serve afternoon teas if you're up for a real challenge."

"I remember it. I was a waitress there one summer. You could feel the damp seeping into the serviettes on wet days."

"But it has a lot of potential," Ioan replied. "The right kind of café could be a great addition to the village with a bit of imagination and forethought."

Just as Beth was mustering another dismissive response, she felt a sharp tug as Ziggy pulled her to the front.

"This is my very clever sister, Beth. She's finally done with making her fortune in London, divorced her dubious husband and come home to look after Mam and keep me in check. Her son Lewis you probably know already – he's a star and is already making a real difference in good old 'Berffro/Aberffraw." Muffled applause, at which Lewis blushed scarlet. "Anyway, Beth's had oodles of management experience and has plenty of free time right now, so I propose we ask her to take our beloved shop under her wing when Siân and Elwyn go walkabouts, if she's willing that is." He paused. "*Are* you willing, Beth?"

Horrified at this public outing of her personal circumstances, Beth stood in the middle of the scrum of people, many of whom she vaguely recognised from childhood, and all of whom were now staring at her with a wide selection of expressions on their faces. In her discomfiture, only the ones that could be perceived as disapproving came into focus.

"I... er... I don't think I'm the ideal fit for such an... *important* role," she began, reaching for the familiarity of management-speak to hide her discomfiture.

"Mum, you're the perfect person for it." Lewis had appeared at her side. "You could make it a real success and make a lot of the people in this village very happy by doing so. It's time to... *woman-up.*"

Ziggy laughed, and nodded his furious approval. "Too right, old bean."

More murmuring, positive and warm. Beth hesitated, until Siân Owen slowly unfolded her arms. A silence fell: everyone knew that she was about to speak, and woe betide anyone who didn't listen.

"Beth Tonks, you may not have *been* here for years, but you are *from* here, and I can see that here matters to you," she said. "It won't be forever, don't worry, but I would rest easy if I could go and have some fun knowing somebody as bossy and clever as you is looking after my shop. That's the way I see it, anyway."

A roar of approval rang out.

Beth looked around, and as she felt her panic slowly begin to ebb, she saw only smiling faces, nodding their encouragement. She ran through her options with a rapidity bred of years of experience. Perhaps she *could* help them by getting things organised, streamlined, and then hand over to someone else so that she could leave, or do other things? It would certainly stop her worrying about Tabitha's illness and Lewis's future all the time, and to actually say "no" would be pretty churlish (and Siân Owen would probably disembowel her).

"Everyone will pitch in, sis," Ziggy said. "Even me, if you'll let me. Honestly."

"And me, Mum," Lewis added, looping his arm through hers, which made her glow with happiness as it was so rare for him to do so.

"And everyone's so glad you're back now, to look after your mam," one of the white-haired sisters said. "You're doing the right thing."

"Better late than never," came from one corner, but was greeted with a chorus of "tut-tuts."

"This might be *your* little bit of magic, keeping this place as the beating heart of our village," the other sister said with a smile. Beth blushed, wrong-footed because she could not tell which was Nesta and which was Mai, to thank her.

"They're a force of nature, the Parry twins, let me tell you," Cai Hughes said to her quietly. "Both taught in local schools, and neither married, but don't worry about offending them. Even their father often couldn't tell them apart."

People were now coming forward to voice their opinions directly to Beth.

"I can't imagine not getting my paper and packet of ready-rubbed here each morning, before I start work," a stocky young man said.

"So few shops still stock sweets in jars, or strings of liquorice," added a woman wearing a white puffer coat so big that she resembled the Michelin Man.

"And where else would we get a can of corned beef when we need one on a Saturday afternoon?" cackled another, older man, with a beard that almost reached his navel. "Can't beat a bit of corned beef hash to keep the chill out."

"It might be ten years old, that bloody can, but Siân would

definitely have one!" shouted another voice, which produced a gale of laughter.

"It's always been here, a part of my childhood, and I would like it to stay a part of every child's life in this village," said a soft woman's voice from the back of the room. Beth turned: this voice was very familiar, but surely Megan would not have braved this big crowd to come today?

A man spoke now. "I think that's why it matters so much. Familiarity, routine, tradition and the bonds we all share, that we want to carry on in the future, for the next generation."

Beth was sure this was Ioan but could not see him in the mêlée.

"So? Will you take it on, Beth?" Cai asked, his twinkly eyes kind but earnest.

The silence that awaited her response was almost deafening.

"I suppose it's too much to ask to be allowed to think about it overnight?" she said.

"Yes," was the well-meaning but firm response from the room.

Everybody held their breath.

"All right, I'll give it a go," she said, which was greeted by a collective exhalation and a smattering of applause. "But I'm going to need all the help and advice I can get, OK? I have never run a shop in my life!"

As everyone closed in to shake her hand, or tell her they would help her, Beth glimpsed Ioan, grinning from ear to ear.

TWENTY

The rest of January crawled, as only January can. Each morning, waking to an icy darkness before anyone else was stirring in the windmill, Beth's first thoughts were about the task ahead. Her brain teemed with ideas about what to stock, where to get it from, and how to improve the way the shop was run so that people could buy ingredients to cook meals for their families rather than just snacks or a pint of milk. To have something that could really serve this community appealed to her. In the small hours, she even allowed her imagination to roam over the possibility of reopening the tea shop that had once been next door. It felt good to think about how her skills could make others' lives better, rather than how to make more money for people who already had more than enough of it.

Instead of huddling in a chilly bed in a chillier bedroom, Beth decided to get up and out every morning. In London, she'd never, ever got up this early, or gone out for walks. She'd enjoyed weekend lie-ins and the occasional luxury of a working from bed day, but on the island, the moment she awoke, she needed to be outside and moving. This was a feeling she remembered from childhood, when she had always been the first up, and expected to stoke the range, let their dog Wil out and wash the dishes so they could have some breakfast before she and Ziggy went to school without even seeing their hungover parents.

Tugging on every pair of socks and every sweater she could find (almost all of them either Ziggy's or Lewis's), she set out just as the sky was showing the very first signs of light. On dry days, slivers of delicate ochre came first, often followed by a rippling sequence of pink, orange and gold as the sun gradually rose above the horizon and cast a blazing pathway across the sea until it touched the shore in front of her. It was breathtaking, and to be given this unique gift each morning felt like a blessing indeed. She took Lewis's Labrador pup Zebedee with her, as he was as desperate to get out as she was, and she impressed herself with her skill in applying the few puppy-training tips she had found online. He was obedient and responsive, and loving him was not difficult: he reciprocated in bucketloads.

"Perhaps I'm not such a dead loss as a parent, after all?" she muttered whenever he willingly sat, stayed or came back when she called him.

One morning, after three dark, mainly wet weeks, a faint light was filtering into Beth's bedroom when she opened her eyes. For the first time that year, she could hear a blackbird trilling and a distant pair of robins calling and answering each other, as well as the usual cacophony of hardy gulls. She grabbed a slice of buttery toast and set out with a lighter heart, deciding to risk the rougher path that led towards Megan's cottage, as she could now actually see her feet on the ground.

She rounded the headland and looked over to the rocky-edged bays beyond before quickly glancing back towards the village. In that very moment, the orange street lights that delineated its little, winding streets all went off as one as if someone, somewhere, had pressed a switch. There were a few lights on in bedrooms and bathrooms, and the sound of a delighted dog barking at its morning release drifted towards her on the breeze. It was such a small place, a place that encompassed so few people in comparison to Hampstead, or St Catherine's Dock, where she had last lived, and yet Beth could almost *feel* a sense of belonging emanating from that little huddle of homes like the warm, spectral glow on a Christmas card.

"I could never have guessed that I would come back here, and want to stay here, Zeb," she murmured. "But I do. I really do."

She walked on, eating her toast, circled by several gulls. The sun was now up, a glowing orb above the watery horizon, and when she turned to face it, and closed her eyes, there was the faintest hint of warmth in it too. The sudden realisation that she would still be here in the summer, the time she and Megan had always loved most, because they could splash in the waves and sit and chat in the dunes together, as they always had, brought tears to her eyes.

"Thank you, Duncan, you absolute total pain in the arse, for setting me free. Who needs board meetings and sales drives when you can have *this*?" And she clapped her hands together in childlike glee.

She spotted a figure down on the shingly shore below Megan's cottage. It was a woman, Beth was sure, and she had a gentle, slow gait that was strangely familiar. A large dog ambled alongside her, stopping to sniff at regular intervals and then catching up with a spurt of energy. Beth watched, unseen, as the woman peeled off her coat to reveal what looked like a long-sleeved black T-shirt and leggings. She was also wearing chunky black gloves, and black booties.

"Oh my God, she's going to go in the water!" Beth exclaimed in horror. "It's *January*, for goodness' sake!"

Just before the woman walked towards the water, Beth watched her pull a flat, black hat off her head and shake her straggly hair free of it. Even from this distance, the round, pink patches of skin on her scalp were visible and she knew it was Megan. Was this her dear friend's morning ritual, and had it been thus all the years when she had not been here to witness it? Wild swimming had become popular down South too, but she had laughed at women going shopping in their expensive designer swim-robes. Now that she knew Megan that swam in these cold seas and then returned to her freezing cottage to face another day alone, it almost broke her heart.

She watched as Megan walked into the waves, throwing her arms into the air to let the froth slap on her belly. She made no sound and did not break her stride as the cold water hit her thighs, her pubic bone and then her waist. Next, she splashed water up onto her arms and shoulders, glanced back at Jonah to check he was not following her in, and plunged under the next wave. Beth gasped, astonished, and waited for her friend to bob up again. To intrude on this moment felt wrong, but for a split second, she considered the ghastly possibility that Megan did not intend to emerge from the sea. She dismissed this thought before she ran down to try and save her. It was an almost sacred experience, she could tell, and she would not disturb its peace. This was something positive for Megan, something that made her feel *alive*, not a wish for death. Her life had so little happiness in it, that perhaps the sea reminded her of how that felt.

Megan did not stay in the water for longer than a few minutes. Staggering back onto the shore, she peeled off the wet layer, revealing her underwear and vivid red skin. She tugged on her coat and beret and walked briskly back up to her cottage, the dog following slowly behind her. Only when the cottage door closed behind them did Beth turn to walk home.

Just as her friend needed to be reminded of her desire to survive by plunging into icy waters, Beth, too, yearned for a richer, deeper life, with richer, deeper friendships. She also needed to feel the thrill of the cold water on her body, to reconnect her with the almost-elemental young woman she had once been. She vowed that sea swimming with Megan would be another part of that new life, along with all the others that were gradually falling into place. The gap that still yawned at the heart of both their lives was obvious, and it was one that only each other could fill.

TWENTY-ONE

In the first week of February, as a scree of snowdrops appeared around the village gardens and the small, green knubs of daffodil shoots peeped above the grass, Siân Owen called another meeting in the shop. She went to *Melin Arian* just before it, to chat to Beth so that she knew what to expect and what was going to happen when they got to meet everybody. Beth struggled not to stare at the vivid blue highlights that now threaded through Siân's hair.

"I don't want you to keep things the same as I have, and my father did," Siân said. "I know it could be much better, much more, that little shop, but I've got a bit jaded with it all, and I actually think it's made me into a bit of a bitch."

Beth wrestled with how to respond to such frankness. She had heard how nasty Siân could be, and how much she loved salacious gossip. "Well, I'm sure you..."

"No, it's true, and I admit it. I have become a prize bitch and I don't want to be one anymore. *Digon!*/Enough!" Siân said firmly. "I haven't got the *hwyl*/energy to do what needs doing in the shop, let alone think about the big room next door. You have, so you have free rein. We'll discuss what happens when I come back, *if* I come back, haha."

"Well, I don't know what my long-term plans are, but I won't let things go to rack and ruin, I promise. It'll be a steep learning curve, and I can't say I'm not nervous."

"*Paid a phoeni o gwbwl*/Don't worry at all. You aren't on your own. You have everyone behind you, people with skills and talents you probably don't even know about yet. And there's such gratitude for your taking this on, there really is. People here appreciate loyalty, and you've shown it," she said, adding "Finally" and a hefty wink.

"I only hope it will stay at the heart of the community it's always been," Beth said. "Supermarkets have their place, but a village shop is a local treasure."

"*Ydy wir*/Certainly. And, let's face it, the only place you are guaranteed to get all the best *sgwrs*/chat, of course," Siân replied. "I'll really miss that, *dweud y gwir*/to tell the truth!"

Beth laughed. "The best *gossip*, do you mean? I thought you said your bitchy days were over!"

"Oh, they are, really," Siân said, "but surely everyone, everywhere, loves a bit of goss? Perhaps, even you...?"

Beth smiled. "*Definitely* even me."

"Then you'll fit in just fine, *cariad*/love," Siân said, buttoning up her cardigan as if preparing for battle.

The shop was packed for the meeting at which Siân formally announced that she was "handing over to new management" at the end of February. Beth, Ziggy and Lewis stood at the front, next to her, and Cai, Nesta and Mai formed a supportive huddle on the left. Beth was delighted to glimpse both Ioan and Megan near the chiller and was now sure that it *had* been her friend's voice at the last meeting. She decided to find a way to involve her in this venture, as she clearly still held this place dear, and had so much to offer, but above all, because people needed to forget Megan's past as willingly as they seemed to have done hers. The fact that she had felt able to come to these meetings, and seen that nobody had even noticed, let alone judged her, gave her real hope that this could happen.

When Siân folded her arms ominously, a hush fell. She knew that some locals still doubted she really would go (as she had declared she was doing so fairly regularly for years). To dismiss any residual doubts, she spoke very plainly indeed.

"So, it's happened, *pobl*/people. Aunty Elen's inheritance has come through – hallelujah – and so Elwyn and I will be off to stay in my second cousin's house in Madeira for a couple of months, and then cruising the Med. After that, who knows? Elwyn can't wait. It's all he can talk about."

A few sniggers; few people had ever heard Elwyn Owen, a retired electrician, utter more than three words in succession.

"He'd better take some earplugs with him if he's got to listen to you all day for months!" Tomos Owen, a pig farmer, said to a wave of titters.

Siân scowled. "Hidden depths he has, my Elwyn. Don't underestimate the power of a silent Welshman, Tomos," she said. When a billowing of laughter followed, she held one finger up for silence: everyone immediately obeyed.

"*Reit 'ta*/Right then. Beth and I have had a long chat, and I want to tell you now that any changes she makes here, she does with my blessing, and if I hear that anyone is making her life difficult, *in any way whatsoever*, there'll be hell to pay when I return. *Ydi pawb yn dalld?*/Does everyone understand?"

Nods, grunts and a few mumbles confirmed that they did.

"What about a farewell party in the pub?" Cai called out. "First round on me!"

The roar of approval guaranteed the party would be very well-attended.

"OK then, thanks, Cai. *Gwych*/Excellent. The second round's on me," Siân said, beaming.

"And the third, on me," Beth added.

The noise that followed this almost shattered the shop windows.

When Lewis returned from walking Zeb through the village on the evening of the party, he said the air of excitement was almost palpable, seeping out of cracks in windowpanes and draughty cottage doors. It felt as if this celebration distilled how much everyone cared about their remote little community, in which few important things had changed for decades. Tourists came and went, and houses were bought, upgraded and then rented at eye-watering prices during the summer season, but some things remained constant. Fishing boats still skimmed over the waves, followed by a noisy congregation of gulls; the beach was a place of paradise for countless dogs, and neighbours exchanged gardening tips, local news or details of their latest ailment over fences or squat, stone walls.

In the days since Siân's announcement, many people had come forward to volunteer in the shop. Beth, slightly over-whelmed, decided to close it for a fortnight so that she could plan properly and do a deep clean: Nesta and Mai, despite their age, had promised to help. She planned to check and update stock too, and Cai Hughes was so keen to assist that he bought a MacBook especially. Lewis agreed to set up a *"Siop bach*/little shop" social media page so everyone could keep in touch. Ioan drew up a rota, so that Beth would still be able to spend time with Lewis and Tabitha, and Megan gladly offered to produce some handwritten signs and labels in the beautiful, calligraphic handwriting she had had since girlhood. Spirits were high, and the village hummed with the rare anticipation of something new happening.

For the party, Beth wore a dress she had not worn since coming back to the island: its frilled neckline and gauzy fabric hadn't seemed appropriate before, but tonight felt like the true beginning of her new life, and she was going to celebrate it. When she walked into the pub packed with people she had grown up amongst, all of whom greeted her warmly, Beth felt the pricking of tears, and heard several admiring "awwws" at her outfit. Lewis and Ziggy high-fived people left and right, Siân and Elwyn nodded approvingly, and Ioan gave a thumbs-up and gestured that he and Megan had saved her a seat at their table. Megan was wearing a soft blue jersey dress and looked happier and healthier than Beth had seen her for weeks. She had put her hair up in a bun which both hid the ravages of alopecia and highlighted her cheekbones.

"You look lovely, Meg," she whispered as she sat down behind a row of about ten glasses of white wine people had already bought her. "And I am going to struggle to drink this lot, so help yourself!"

"You scrub up well, Beth," Ioan said with a bashful smile. *"Ti'n edrych yn hyfryd iawn*/You look very beautiful."

"Diolch/Thanks," she replied, blushing scarlet, noting that he had used the familiar "ti" form this time. From a man of few words, these few words were gold-dust.

Dai Evans, the publican, had laid on a magnificent buffet, and the level of chat and laughter ballooned as everyone ate and drank more. Beth, ever alert to her friend's mood and movements, noticed that Megan was watching Lewis as he moved from person to person, charming everyone with his complete openness. Was she wondering what her own son might look like now, and how it would feel if he was here? Her loss was unimaginable, even after all these years. She had a son whom she had never been allowed to know.

"Are you all right?" Beth asked her gently. "I really didn't know if you'd come, as it's very noisy and busy. I'm so glad you did."

"This is the first party I've been to in over twenty years, Beth. I was not going to miss it, however difficult it was to get myself out of the door!"

"Well, I appreciate it. Oh, and I want to join you swimming in the sea once the layer of ice has melted," she said, grinning. "Bet you didn't expect *that!*"

"Well, we used to swim as kids, even when it was freezing and pouring with rain," Megan said, giving her a side-eye. "But you were always the wimpy one."

"Agreed," Ioan said, his cheeks flushed with beer and contentment. "We could hear your screams from here when the water was a bit chilly."

Happy and relaxed, Beth realised, for the first time, how far she had come, in so many ways, since she'd come home. Would she rather be listening to Hugo drone on about the pressures of work in Hampstead, trying to stay in favour with a totally insincere Duncan or eating another tasteless ready meal in her immaculate dockside flat right now? she asked herself. No, she most certainly would not. She would much, much rather be here, eating cocktail sausages and drinking warm white wine. She reached for Megan's hand, and squeezed it.

"I'm really glad to be home. There's lots to do, but I think we can do it, together."

"Of *course* we can! There'll be bumps in the road, but this feels momentous, for all of us. I haven't had energy like this for, well, for years." She paused, and her animated expression stilled.

Beth looked at her. "I feel a quote coming on..."

"You know me too well! Here it comes! Emily Dickinson sums up the way I've felt for years, Beth:

When I hoped, I feared.

But now, I don't fear anymore. And I dare to have hope. *Diolch*/Thank you, my friend."

"*Croeso*/You're welcome."

TWENTY-TWO

Siân and Elwyn left on March 1st, St David's Day, after ceremonially putting the "Closed" sign on the shop door at 6pm on the last day of February. They drove away in their old minivan with "Siop Aberffraw" painted on the side, seen off by a gaggle of customers waving Welsh flags, daffodils and the odd, limp leek. Elwyn had removed the three beer cans tied to the back bumper, muttering grumpily about "not going on bloody honeymoon."

Beth's phone was pinging all day, with texts, messages and emails from suppliers she had contacted. She had only two weeks to bring all her plans to fruition before reopening. The biggest change she wanted to implement was to make the shop focus more on selling local, home-grown products, and celebrating the huge variety of the island's food. This would not please the wholesalers, but if small shops were to survive, they had to offer something special as well as personal service, the newly formed committee felt. Setting up a supply chain that kept prices reasonable (despite competition from the supermarkets) but maintained quality and sustainability, would be a huge challenge, but Beth was determined to try.

March arrived with a week of spectacularly bright-skied days and the landscape was magically transformed. On the grass verges, thousands of tiny celandines opened within minutes of feeling the sunshine on their waxy yellow petals, splaying wide to welcome the return of warmth and light. Daffodils blazed in most hedgerows, and primroses punctuated most of the green swards around the island with gorgeous spots of colour. A bitter wind still reminded anyone rash enough to venture out without a coat that they had made a mistake, however. In fields all over the island, the sight of tiny white lambs jumping and tumbling over each other for the sheer joy of being alive raised everyone's spirits and the grass glowed when the sun hit its lush greenness, nurtured by many, many rainy days over the winter. Spring on the island was a time of hope and expectation.

But in *Melin Arian*, the changes that came were less welcome. Tabitha fell in her bedroom while trying to throw feathers from her pillow out of the window for the birds to make their nests with. She was rushed to hospital in Bangor in an ambulance and spent two nights on a busy women's ward, confused and distressed, while her bruises healed and her mood stabilised. Ioan, who had met her from the ambulance, told Beth how shocked he had been at how much she had changed since Jed's death.

"She looked like a shell of the woman she used to be," he told Beth. "I remember her as so colourful, so *different* to everyone else in the village. And she was babbling absolute nonsense, about 'feathers', especially 'white feathers' for some reason. I'm so sorry. It's such a cruel illness, and she's not even old. Please let me know if I can help."

When Tabitha came home from hospital, Beth was torn between anxiety about getting the shop ready, relief that her mother had not broken any bones and a growing sense of dread about what lay ahead. Would Tabitha withdraw from reality more and more until she eventually disappeared into the past, or worse, into a world of muddled memories and regrets from which none of them could rescue her? None of them knew how this illness might have affected others in her family either, which might have helped them. Her mother's more frequent, increasingly plaintive pleas to be "taken home to the Park" were also deeply distressing, as neither she nor Ziggy had any idea what she meant.

"I know someone who went to school with Mum, Flora Carmichael. She told me a bit about her when I last went to London to pack up," Beth told her brother one evening as they sat in the kitchen drawing up a new draft stocklist on her laptop. "She said that Mum came from a wealthy family, and was very kind, but was very unhappy as a child."

"Mum's *always* been unhappy, Beth, but she hid it well, under wacky clothes and a very loud voice," Ziggy replied. "Remember when we used to find her crying as if the world had ended, but she would never tell us *why*?"

"Yes, I do. And what about that necklace she insisted on wearing to Dad's funeral, and puts on over her nightie these days? I remember finding it in an old brown envelope in her room when I was about six or seven. '*To Tabby, from Luci,*' was written on it. I never understood its significance, of course, and she wouldn't answer my questions then, and she can't now, but perhaps it was a clue about her past?"

"Sounds likely. And what if those are *real* diamonds? That would mean she must have been rich. I think Dad knew more than he let on about what she'd left behind, and why they came here," Ziggy went on, clearly intrigued. "They both described it as an escape, didn't they? But from what?"

"'Hell' was all she ever said to me, but whatever it was, I think she deserves to feel at peace with it now," Beth said. "Let's try to find out more."

Their initial internet search on "The Acaster Family"

revealed only a brief summary of the family's history and long heritage, plus an obituary of a "George Acaster", who'd died in 1968. There was also a murky photograph of a well-groomed family of mother, father and three, obvious, siblings – two girls, and an older boy. The father was wearing a sharp morning suit, his hair slicked back, and he was smoking a cigar. The mother looked very fragile, as if wary of the camera. The boy in his mini-sized suit and tie, looked defiantly at the camera and the older girl smiled confidently with her hand on the younger girl's shoulder whilst she, in contrast, scowled miserably, her shoulders slumped. The writing in the small, mock-heraldic plaque at the top of the photo pronounced *"George, Martha, Henry, Lucinda and Tabitha Acaster at Featherstone Park, 1952".* Ziggy zoomed in on the three children immediately.

"I guess that sulky-looking girl is Mum," he said. "Typical! But my God. Doesn't the boy look like Lewis?" he said.

Beth hesitated. "Yes, I see what you mean. He did look rather like that when he was about ten or twelve. Not that I saw much of him then, let alone met any of Mum's family," she added sadly.

"Mum keeps saying that Lewis reminds her of someone. Perhaps it's her brother, Henry?" Ziggy said. "Let's see if we can find a photo of him when he was a bit older. He would have been the main Acaster heir, so there are probably lots. Daughters didn't count in families like this, even in the sixties."

Beth recalled Flora mentioning her brother's death but said nothing to Ziggy yet. Perhaps, even back then, the media could get their facts wrong...

His fingers flew over the keyboard as he sought more information, but she was uneasy. She was curious to know more about her mother's hidden history, but this felt more than a little like prying. Tabitha's childhood had not been a happy one, as this photo made very clear, and the fact that she never spoke about it did not bode well. Whatever her mother had left behind had caused her enormous pain, however much she said she wanted to revisit it now. But Beth had another cause for unease too. The photo of Henry Acaster did, vaguely, remind her of Lewis, but it reminded her of someone else as well.

"Here he is again, at Brasenose College, in Oxford!" Ziggy exclaimed. "Henry Acaster. What an arrogant-looking arse he looks, Mum's brother or not."

Beth looked at the college photograph of six young men dressed in dinner jackets, wing-collars and white bow ties. All of them were looking directly into the camera, cigarettes artfully held to one side: they were near-clones of their time, and their class, but Henry stood apart, and had a slightly different air about him, almost an aura. With a mane of blonde curls that spilled down over his collar, and full lips, Beth struggled to remember who he reminded her of: when she did, she almost cried out. This cocksure, *beautiful* young man looked so very like the Dylan Jones of all those years ago, whose charismatic irresistibility had led her to betray her friend, and herself. It *wasn't* him, of course, but he exuded that same vanity, and probably had the same almost-magnetic effect on others. No wonder she and Megan had fallen for him so completely as naïve, sheltered teenager girls steeped in historical romances and noble heroes. They had had no defences at all against a young man like *that*.

For a few, agonising seconds, she could hear Dylan panting in her ear, kissing her neck. She winced at the memory of her half-hearted attempts to stop what was happening, years after she had left home, the night before she was due to marry Hugo. Desire had overtaken them completely. The photograph of this young man brought it all back with shocking vividness. Breathing in short, shallow breaths, she was glad that Ziggy was focused on the screen, and not on her.

"I think we need to try and find out what led Tabitha Acaster to end up with Dad," he said. "We don't know how they met, why they came up here, or anything about her family's reaction except that she never saw them again, which is a big clue, I suppose. I reckon there are some very serious skeletons in some very valuable cupboards in all this business. We can't ask Mum anything really, so it's up to us." He clicked on link after link, tutting when most proved to be worthless.

Beth sat back, relieved that her brother had moved on from the photo, but as he scrolled through page after pointless page, she became impatient. If they were going to do this, they should do it properly, and with respect.

"Should I message Flora, Mum's school friend, and find out if she can help? At least we're talking to a real person who knew Mum. We won't say anything to her until we know more, and then we can decide what, if anything, to tell her."

Suddenly, Ziggy sat bolt upright. "Hey, look at this! It's an article from the *Sussex Downs Gazette*, from December 1960."

Beth looked at the screen and felt as if all the air had been knocked out of her lungs. The headline ran:

Featherstone Park heir found dead; youngest daughter missing.

She skim-read the article, her heart pounding in her chest. She could hear Ziggy breathing faster than usual too. So, it was true. Here was the brother's death Flora had referred to so ominously. Were they finally about to uncover the mystery that had always surrounded their mother? If so, a large part of her didn't want to.

Henry Acaster, 23, heir to the Featherstone estate, was found dead in the grounds of their substantial property outside Shoreham-on-Sea. Cause of death is pending a coroner's report. The younger daughter, Tabitha Acaster, 21, last seen by eyewitnesses with her brother and another, unknown man, is missing. Police

are continuing their enquiries. Any information, please ring
Shoreham 01388 458221 without delay.

"Bloody hell," Ziggy said, sitting back in his chair and
scratching his head. "What do you reckon happened?"

Beth shook her head. "No idea. It could have been so many
things. It all sounds a bit cloak and dagger to me. Not sure I
want to know the details."

But Ziggy, instead of listening, was still googling. He
quickly found another article, dated a few years later. This one
was not afforded many column inches at all, and the headline
type was very small. He read it aloud:

"Featherstone Park, seat of the Acaster family for over 450
years, has been sold at auction to fund death duties owed
following the demise of George Acaster in a car accident on
October 31st of this year. Lucinda Acaster, the surviving heir,
will live in a cottage on the estate pro bono, the purchasers state.
The whereabouts of Tabitha Acaster, the youngest daughter,
remain unknown."

Ziggy stopped reading. "No, they don't!" he objected. "I
know where she is! She's upstairs in bed in a draughty old windmill on Anglesey!" he cried. "Crikey, so Mum really *is* posh. I
thought she was kidding all these years, telling me to take my
elbows off the table because she'd have been rapped with a ruler
if she'd had manners like mine!"

"But why did she run away and never go back?" Beth said.
"I bet her family didn't think much of Dad, if they ever got to
meet him."

"You're right there. A long-haired rock guitarist would not
have been their husband of choice for her, I bet."

"Well, at least poor old Lucinda got a cottage, even if all the
rest of the money went to the taxman," Ziggy said. "Behind the
stables, I bet, which are probably all now converted into holiday
cottages with hot tubs and big plasma TVs."

"It might be a long shot, but we could take her back one last time, if only to help her lay some ghosts," Beth said. "I think we owe her that."

"I'm not convinced. It might wake them up and freak her out even more," Ziggy said. "Things can't have ended well, as she ran away..."

Beth sighed. "I know that, Zig, and it will be a risk, but I know how it feels to long to get back to where you called home, before things went wrong."

Ziggy looked at her, a flash of annoyance in his eyes. "Remind me what went so wrong for you, Beth? You married a millionaire, rose to the top of your chosen tree, have plenty of cash and a son who loves you. No offence, but I can't really see what was so tough about your life after you left here, to be honest."

Beth said nothing. How could she even begin to tell her brother how anxious she had been throughout her pregnancy? How she had regrets that had soured most of what he saw as her charmed life. There was no point at all.

"I just mean, you know, all those years when I was trying to be someone I wasn't, Ziggy. Yes, I'm very lucky, I know I am," she said.

But Ziggy was still brooding. "When you look at how things turned out for Megan, who's stuck here, and for me, trying to manage our parents for most of my twenties and thirties, yeah, I think we can safely say you are."

"OK, yes. Point taken."

A gust of wind made the windows rattle and the draughty front door creaked ominously. Beth was glad of the distraction.

"Let's talk about what to do about Mum another time. I'll get in touch with Flora soon, but I really need some sleep now," she said wearily.

"You're right. Sleep first, rejoining the landed gentry next," he said, his face cheery once more. "There might even be some money in it, wink, wink."

"Well, if there is, you can have first dibs as I am already absolutely rolling in the stuff, according to you," she said, in as offhand a way as she could manage.

"Touché. Sorry," Ziggy replied. "And sorry about being a bit... *mean*. I'm happier than I can say that you came back to help me with it all."

"I'm glad too, and am grateful for all you've done for Mum, and did for Dad," Beth replied. "I should have told you that years ago."

"You've told me now, and that's good enough for me," Ziggy said. "But if we're going to be heirs to a fortune, bagsy the chestful of gold coins!"

TWENTY-THREE

The time leading up to the grand reopening of the village shop was so busy that Tabitha's past seemed less relevant as the demands of the present were pressing in on Beth from all sides. What little sleep she had was full of nightmares about overdue orders, angry customers and invoices that demanded her attention *right that minute*. She was exhausted, before things had even begun.

However tired and gritty-eyed she felt, her days still began with a walk along the cliffs with Zeb. It was a routine that nourished her and prepared her for whatever lay ahead better than any pre-work hot yoga class or mindfulness session had ever done. The weather was much milder by the middle of March, the trees on the island were gradually greening and the air was busy with insects and birdsong. After her walk, she had very little time to herself, as days were packed with meetings with potential suppliers, or with Cai Hughes, always eager to help in any way she needed him to. Her team of helpers was both growing and willing and Beth knew that without them, she had no hope of reaching opening day either fully prepared or in one piece. She had to make sure that Nesta and Mai didn't overdo it, though. Every morning, they arrived, pinnies on and rubber gloves in hand, ready to set to work bleaching, scrubbing and polishing... and chatting, non-stop. Beth valued their sincerity and common sense enormously: at home, Ziggy's manic energy and Lewis's constant stream of ideas were sometimes difficult to deal with. For now, she decided not to get in touch with Flora and risk opening a can of worms she had no energy to deal with. Tabitha's secrets would have to wait a little longer.

And yet, she knew it couldn't wait for too long. Every day, her mother forgot more and remembered less, shouted things that made no sense, and seemed more withdrawn from life in the windmill. The door to her memories was inexorably closing and could never be reopened once it had closed. Beth had always resented her mother for being painfully unlike all the other mams in the village, but seeing her so vulnerable, and realising that she, too, had suffered in the past, made her want to offer her whatever comfort she could before it was too late. She spent time brushing her mother's hair, painting her nails and talking to her about things she remembered. When she described a rare family day trip to Chester to see the races, Tabitha's face shone with happiness and she was able to recall the names of all the winners. Beth sensed that she had grown up amongst thoroughbred horses, as Hugo had. That was the world she had left behind.

Churning these conflicting thoughts one morning, days before opening day, an unexpected conversation in the shop shocked her to the core. She was filling the new wicker baskets she had bought with locally made scallop-shaped Aberffraw biscuits. They would go alongside a display of the Welsh cheeses in the chiller, and she hoped her customers would be willing to pay a little more for both. Her period had started that morning – that unwanted, monthly reminder that her body was just-about still capable of bearing a child, but that any opportunity for her doing so was currently zero. She would probably never meet a man she could love up here: she had blown all her chances of that twenty years ago when she had rejected Ioan and batted her eyelashes at Dylan Jones instead.

"At least I have Lewis," she murmured. "Now, more than ever, I thank goodness for the baby I thought I didn't want."

The Parry twins were cleaning the glass counter-fronts for the umpteenth time, as each shaft of sunlight revealed a new smear, which then saw them rubbing and polishing all the more vigorously. Beth was wrestling with an online ordering system that seemed to have been designed to confuse even Bill Gates, and had thus totally bamboozled Cai Hughes. At just after 11am, all three women turned to each other and smiled wearily.

"*Amser coffee*/Coffee time," Nesta said.

"*Mae'n amser eistedd i lawr, yn wir*/Time to sit down, for sure," Mai replied.

"So, do you think you'll ever marry again, Beth?" Nesta said as they sat down on upturned boxes to drink their coffee. "Shame not to, at your age."

Beth laughed, and blushed. She had not quite got used to the twins' lack of filter, much as she liked it at times. "I have no idea! I think once was enough for me, really. But what about you two? Neither of you ever married even once, though, let alone twice."

Mai nodded. "We had our reasons."

Her curiosity aroused, Beth asked tentatively, "Can I ask what they were? You would have been a real catch for any man, both of you."

"Well, I *was* caught, since you ask," Nesta said, putting her mug down. "Caught by a wonderful man too – but he died of pneumonia before we could marry."

"And I decided not to let Nesta grow old alone, so I didn't

marry either," Mai said. "It probably sounds a bit strange to you, but it was best for us."

"That's so, well, *selfless* is the word, Mai," Beth said, trying to disguise her shock.

"But don't think we're saints, either of us. Far from it. My fiancé's death was my fault," Nesta said softly. "I insisted we walk home from chapel on a bitterly cold night as I'd heard there might be shooting stars. He caught a chill, and he died." Her voice was almost a whisper now. "But I still go out at night in search of shooting stars, and make Mai come with me. Isn't that stupid?"

For a long minute, the only sound was the gentle humming of the freezers, and the three women sipped their coffee without speaking. Beth could not think of an appropriate response, and she had a big lump in her throat.

"No, it's not stupid," she said eventually. "It's you remembering and perhaps asking for forgiveness for a genuine mistake. Part of me coming home is about that too. I made some mistakes, some bad ones…"

As one, Nesta and Mai put their index fingers on their lips to shush her.

"We don't need to talk about them," Mai said. "We are human, designed and destined to fail, as our father used to say. You're lucky, because you have the chance to put things right, as Nesta never had, because Dai was dead."

Beth hesitated. Something very strange was happening here, something she had not expected. *These women knew something big about her* – she could see it in their faces, but what did they know, and how did they know it? The terrible question she knew she needed to ask came out of her mouth before she had time to edit it.

"You know about… me and Dylan Jones, the night before my wedding, don't you?" she said. "Were you both out *that* night, looking for shooting stars?"

The twins' mouths said nothing, but their eyes said everything.

Beth hid her face in her hands. "Oh, what must you think of me? And did you know that Megan had Dylan's baby, just after I'd left for Oxford? I didn't know, I swear. She told me only recently."

"Hush, Beth," Nesta said, laying a hand over hers. "Yes, we knew about Megan, and we felt sorry for her when her parents sent her away, too, but it was kept very quiet."

"Megan was sent away to relatives, and Dylan Jones to Cardiff, quick as a flash. His parents haven't spoken to him since."

"But we still felt sorry for you, because I know you'd... *fallen under his spell*, in the past and that it had destroyed your friendship with Megan. Everyone knew how full of himself Dylan was – and still is, so the gossips say."

Beth shook her head. "I was such a terrible judge of character in those days."

"You were young, that's all, but I know how guilt and regret feel, how they eat away at you." A pause. "How did you feel on your wedding day, for instance?"

Tears began to roll slowly down Beth's cheeks: she had felt mortified, sullied, all that dreadful day. She hadn't spoken to anyone about this, ever, as it was her greatest shame of all. "I've regretted what happened that night ever since, and I am trying so hard to make things right with Megan now, but I don't know if I ever can. She lost so much, because of me." She stood up and turned away to hide her very real distress.

"But you have a second chance," Mai murmured. "At friendship, and perhaps even at love."

"As I did not," Nesta said.

"I'm not sure what you mean," Beth said, but in her heart, she was very sure. The twins had noticed how she and Ioan looked at each other, were with each other. They were very exceptional women, just as Cai had told her.

"We think that you lost something important that starlit night, before your wedding," Nesta said. "You lost faith in *yourself*."

"But luckily for you, *cariad*/love, everyone here has plenty of it!" Mai said.

"*O Diolch*/Oh thank you, but please, please don't tell anyone, about that night, I mean," Beth said, drying her tears. "You are the only people in the world, apart from Dylan and I, of course, who know... and I just couldn't bear it if..."

Without speaking, both twins stood up and wrapped their arms around her, and she knew that her awful secret was safe.

TWENTY-FOUR

The final evening before the reopening was frantic, with everyone who had agreed to help pitching in to ensure it all went smoothly. After a final flail, at 10.15pm, everything was set up and the weary team went home.

The great day itself was gloriously sunny, but with a chill wind common in spring on the island. Ziggy had strung colourful bunting between all the buildings in the square, and the little flags fluttered hopefully above the proceedings, giving definite party vibes. There was a small queue of people outside the shop by 9am, shuffling glumly from foot to foot to keep warm, but when Beth pulled up the shutters to reveal the stunning window display, she saw their faces light up. Fresh local vegetables took centre stage, with cabbages, broccoli and the last of the season's stems of sprouts, all arranged into soft, green mounds. Free-range eggs from a farm near Llanfaelog nestled in tiny baskets, and fresh loaves, delivered an hour earlier from a local independent bakery, took their place on gingham-lined wicker trays. A dozen currant buns completed the array, each one topped with a glistening sugar glaze and a cherry. Beth had chosen sunny yellow drill aprons for her staff, which they wore, standing in a line to greet their customers, with enormous pride. Megan had filled glass jars with primroses and dotted them along the inner edge of the window: everything seemed to proclaim hopefulness, and new beginnings. Cai, the twins, Ziggy and Megan were on the rota today, as the committee felt they deserved the honour of being in the thick of things on opening day.

Hung across the entire display was a banner with "*Croeso yn ôl i siop ni*/Welcome back to our shop" stitched onto it in bright, patchwork letters.

Inside, the shelves were no longer crammed with dusty packets of tapioca and cans of processed peas. Each section was arranged for ease of access, with healthy family meals very much in mind. Small bunches of hedgerow daffodils were arranged in bright jugs and scattered around the shop, and their fragrance mingled with the delicious smell of the rich coffee from the small independent bean-roastery in the village of Nantlle, up in the mountains. Megan had produced a small library of handwritten, bilingual recipe cards for customers to borrow, all using products that the shop now stocked. Lewis told his mother that he was very enthusiastic about selling filled sandwiches and baps, and organising cookery workshops sometime in the future. Beth nodded and smiled but made no promises. His brain's capacity for schemes and passions still baffled her.

Many of the recipes were for the simple but tasty traditional dishes Megan remembered from childhood, such as *stwnch* (a comforting mix of buttery mashed vegetables such as potatoes, swede and broad beans) and *cawl* (a traditional thick soup guaranteed to warm a winter's day). The *bara brith*/currant loaf recipe was the most popular of all.

"I remember eating slices of that at summer fairs, when your mam made it," one woman said. "The best I've ever tasted, spread thick with butter."

"I'll tell her you said so," Megan said, wishing that she could. These days, any talk of the past upset Nia, so it would never happen.

Things began to settle down after lunchtime, and Ziggy seemed so at ease with taking charge that Beth made herself and Megan a *panad*/cuppa, and they took them out to the weed-lined courtyard garden at the back of the shop. Sheltered from the wind, this space led to the large room that had once been a thriving tea shop.

"I remember serving thousands of 'Welsh cream teas' in that clammy room," Beth said. "I earned every penny of my measly wage!"

Megan smiled. "You've come a long way since then, Beth Tonks. And no doubt you've got a lot more planned that you haven't shared with us yet."

A pause, a shared smile. "Perhaps, but I can't do it on my own. I thought I could, in the past, do everything alone, but now I know how much we all need each other – how much I need *you* – to make this work."

"The shop you mean?"

"No. My new life, up here. It doesn't make any sense, without you," Beth said. "We deserve this second chance, don't you think?"

"Yes, we do, especially after all the shit that's happened – to both of us, I mean," Megan said, a shadow crossing her face.

For the first time, Beth wondered if Megan had guessed how lonely she had sometimes felt in her marriage to Hugo, as they'd drifted further and further apart. She felt sure she had.

"And there's so much we could do together now, Meg. With Ziggy and Lewis, of course, and even Ioan, if he's got time, and is willing, that is..."

"I think he's more than willing," Megan said. "He'd do anything, for either of us – you know that. And like us, he needs someone to colour in the future for him. It's just an outline at the moment, isn't it?"

Beth felt a fluttering in her belly. Could she be a part of that future? she wondered. She did not dare even imagine such happiness could be hers.

As they sat in companionable quiet, drinking their tea, she could not help but hope that the future would also see her friend finally meeting her lost son. That was the part of her image of the perfect years ahead that seemed to be missing, and it made her sad. She decided to ask Ioan if he had any clues as to the boy's whereabouts the next time they met, but they would have to be careful. Just as with investigating Tabitha's past, reopening old wounds in an effort to heal them could go very wrong. Above them, a plane hummed, leaving a pristine vapour trail in the blue sky on its way across the Atlantic. The two friends listened to the chatter in the shop, the regular "ping" of the vintage till Ziggy had found and the sigh of the wind in the trees, and neither felt the need to say a word.

Yes, it would be risky, Beth told herself, but she remembered some words of Emily Dickinson's, because they seemed so appropriate now:

Is bliss, then, such abyss,
I must not put my foot amiss
For fear I spoil my shoe?

Surely, uniting a mother and her child was worth taking a risk for?

PART 4

HOPES AND DREAMS

TWENTY-FIVE

For the first few weeks of April, Beth felt happier than she had done for many years. The island was coming alive a little more each day after the long winter months, as trees and hedgerows exploded with colour, and even the ever-bracing sea looked more inviting when it reflected a clear, blue sky. She was tired, as the shop was very busy, and keeping track of what sold well and what didn't proved more complex than she'd expected, but it was exhilarating when customers congratulated her on what she was doing, or put in large, weekly orders instead of going to the supermarket for their shopping. Beth decided that it was the right time to start wild swimming with Megan, because that, she was sure, would sharpen her wits and clear her head. She was finding the relentless small decisions she had to make, and questions she had to answer, hard to cope with. At times, she felt like the target at a firing range.

"I worked with huge corporations, so why am I finding deciding which farmer to order our Anglesey new potatoes from so difficult?" she asked Ziggy, after one particularly trying morning.

"I think you're doing too much, and trying to be too nice to everyone," he replied. "Delegate, and go for the jugular to get us the best deal, Beth. The farmers will respect that, and 'profit makes perfect', doesn't it?"

Beth laughed. "Hmm, I'm not so sure about that, having been very profit-focused in my previous life."

Ziggy winked. "I was only kidding. Profit is nice, but it's not everything."

"Thank goodness for that. I thought you'd undergone a personality transplant, and that I'd soon be pining for the old, lazy, good-for-nothing Ziggy!"

He gave her a big bear hug, and she returned it. In recent weeks, the easy, mutual trust that she and her brother now shared had brought her enormous joy. He still wore crazily mismatched charity shop-bought clothes and had a very brief phase of growing a handlebar moustache, but his sheer good nature meant nobody judged him and she felt ashamed that she had done so in the past. He approached things in a different way to the slippery, semi-truthful methods she had had to use in the business world, and she admired him for it. She no longer saw him as a sponging waster, and wondered if, in fact, he ever had been. He was straightforward, honest, loyal and dependable. He was exactly what he seemed, with no "side" or pretensions, and that was both great and very, very rare.

Lewis had also transformed since his arrival. He persuaded Beth to lend him money to buy a vintage tricycle and renovated it with a precision and skill that amazed her. Whatever the weather, villagers soon knew that if they rang Beth and placed an order, Lewis would deliver it with a cheery smile and the "ding ding" of his bell. Many elderly customers invited him in and plied him with tea and cake as an excuse to engage him in endless *sgwrs*/chat. When Beth noticed that he was putting on weight, she was delighted, but Hugo felt the need to comment on this when his son Facetimed him, as his parents had probably done to him whenever he returned home from boarding school.

"Hmmm, it looks like someone's got their feet firmly under the table," Hugo said. "It always was pretty carb-heavy, the diet up there, I recall."

"Actually, the diet up here, and everything up here, is amazing, Dad. I caught fresh mackerel for our dinner last night, and we had free-range poached eggs for breakfast from Gethin Jones, a farmer. He's my friend," Lewis replied.

Hugo, embarrassed, mumbled, "Good stuff. I'm glad, really I am. I just meant that you're looking well, son: it's just, you know, you look *different*."

"That's because I'm *happy*, Dad. See you." And he hung up.

It was all that Beth could do to stop herself from rushing in and hugging him for standing up for himself so well. He *did* seem happy, and she saw much to admire in her son, but she still could not entirely dismiss her unease at some of his "ways", as he too now openly called them. People could be unkind, and fitting in was so vital in life, she knew, and she worried that he would not.

She reminded herself time and time again that Lewis had always been a little different, and that she had always known it. Since boyhood, he had developed great passions for things that had taken over his life, occupied his thoughts 24/7, and then vanished like a popped bubble when he moved on to the next one. A particular film had obsessed him as a toddler, and he had played certain games for hour upon hour. Here on the island, for instance, there was now no more talk of screenwriting, or birdwatching: those things had vanished from his world. He was still an enthusiastic cook at *Melin Arian*, but he seemed unaware when flavours jarred, or when a dish was too spicy and rarely followed a recipe for guidance. When Beth talked to Ziggy about this, he told her that her son's behaviour was "endearing", and that he had always been "one of a kind", but this did not entirely allay her worries. She began to research neurological diversity, in all its many forms, in more detail than she had ever dared to do before and a template began to form into which Lewis fitted, and which made sense of so many of the things he did and said. When he came to her one day, and told her, very matter-of-factly, that he, too, had been doing some digging, and thought he was very probably somewhere on the autistic spectrum, she was momentarily taken aback to hear him say the words, but within seconds, she threw her arms around him with relief. To have him realise this himself took a huge weight off her shoulders.

"I'm happy you've told me, love. You are your own person, Lewis, and you will forge your own path," she told him.

"I am, and I like who I am, but I might run some things past you sometimes, if I'm not sure about them, if that's OK," he replied.

"Of course it is! And you will tell me if things bother you, or you want me to do things differently, won't you?"

"Yes. For starters, can you please stop hugging me now?" he replied, with a wriggle and a smile.

TWENTY-SIX

Beth fully expected her first sea swim with Megan to be mainly an exercise in endurance, but she had committed to it, so she had to do it. The sky was a ragged patchwork of dull, grey clouds, and a brisk wind sent flecks of foam scudding over the surface of the water. The two friends met at Megan's cottage, which seemed to have metamorphosed into a much more pleasant place to be since the last time Beth had visited. The windows had finally been cleaned to admit some sunshine, and the rooms smelt of freshness and spring. Having some purpose and hope was obviously doing Megan good, and it was patently clear that she had been deeply depressed for a long time.

Megan was wearing only a threadbare black swimsuit to swim. Beth had brought along a wetsuit Ziggy had briefly surfed in as a teenager, but when she finally wrestled herself into it, it hung off her body in huge floppy folds.

"Aren't you going to wear anything else?" Beth asked, looking at her friend incredulously. "I know you do this all year round, but it's still only April, Meg!"

"You get used to it. And if you cover yourself up too much,

the water can't bring you to life again," Megan replied. "That thing will just get in the way."

Beth winced. "Refinement through suffering, eh? That sounds a bit 'Victorian novelist' for me. I'm going to wear boots, gloves, a hat – as much as I possibly can without risking sinking, in fact."

Jonah followed the women down to the shore, where he flumped down on the sand as if proud to maintain his reputation as a lifelong, water-hating Labrador. Megan immediately set off towards the water's edge.

"You said you'd do this, so you better had, or I will never forgive you," she muttered as she walked past a shivering Beth. "Just sayin'."

Within a minute, having splashed her face and arms with water when she was waist-deep, she had disappeared beneath the glassy surface of the sea. The only evidence of her presence was a trail of bubbles behind her feet as she glided soundlessly beneath it. Beth was still getting dressed for the event.

"Shit, she's like a bloody mermaid," Beth said, galumphing down to the water in the oversized wetsuit with a rictus grin on her face. She suppressed a shriek as the chilly water seeped into her wetsuit shoes, but could not do so when, lumbering further in, she tripped on a rock and fell, face first, into the sea. Arms flailing, mouth gasping for air, she felt the icy water penetrating through every seam, into every baggy inch of the wetsuit. Soon, its weight became so much that standing up was difficult, and almost scary.

"Take it all off," Megan called from further out. "You won't regret it."

Beth hesitated, shivering violently. Could she actually do this? As kids, they would have done so without thinking, but now, with the caution of adulthood in the way, it seemed insane, like shucking off both common sense and reason. But no bottling was allowed today.

Quickly, so that she could not change her mind, she peeled off the wetsuit, the gloves, the hat and kicked off her sodden neoprene shoes. Then she took a deep breath and ran at the water with a wild yell. She did not stop until she felt a wave breaking over her head and came up seconds later to see a coronet of gulls circling curiously above her, her body tingling as if touched by lightning. There was nobody else in the world she would rather have been with than her dearest, oldest friend, and the realisation that life had come full circle and she was home, where she knew she belonged, filled her with incredible joy.

When she let out a strange cry of primeval exaltation, she heard Megan's laugh drift across the water, just as it had in childhood when they had swum here in all seasons, and all weathers, and felt that the world was theirs to conquer.

TWENTY-SEVEN

The week after their swim, Beth deliberately rota'd her first full day off working in the shop so that it coincided with Ioan's. She needed to try and find out what he knew about Megan's baby. She texted him on her morning walk a few days beforehand.

> Hi, how about that trip to Oriel Môn/Anglesey Gallery on Wednesday? I need to get out of the shop and there's a new exhibition on there. B x

He did not reply for several hours, but just as Beth was wishing she hadn't texted him at all, he did:

> Gr8. I could do with a cultural shot in the arm. Pick you up at 9.30am. I

Her first reaction was hurt that he had not added a "X" as she had. Her second was a spike of terror that they were now going to spend a whole day together. How would that work out? Would they have anything to say to each other? she wondered. Suppressing her fantasies of them rekindling some kind of romantic relationship, she decided to try and keep things light and focus on chatting about Kyffin Williams' paintings. Only if things were going really well, would she risk asking him a little about Megan's baby, and where he might be now. This was a risky strategy, and she had no idea how he might react, but she was conscious that this could be her only opportunity to find out.

Ioan was punctual, tooting his horn outside the windmill at 9.29am precisely. Beth kissed the top of her mother's head, told her very clearly that Lewis was around all day to take care of her, and headed for the door. When she opened it, the sky was so blue and the spring sunlight so bright after the darkness inside *Melin Arian* that she squinted and covered her eyes with her hand for a few seconds.

"My good looks dazzled you, eh?" Ioan said. "Happens all the time."

Beth laughed. "Yeah, yeah. In your dreams."

When his old Land Rover roared off, backfiring copiously, and she heard the soothing voice of Joni Mitchell on the stereo, her nerves began to melt away. The fact that she had rejected his clumsy, teenage love all those years ago (which had left him vulnerable to the charms of Ceri Jones) was territory best avoided. The last thing this man needed was a mixed-up, pre-menopausal middle-aged woman right now. They were friends again, going to spend the day discussing beautiful art and that was more than she had ever hoped for. Anything more was simply impossible.

The twenty-minute drive to Llangefni from Aberffraw took them through some of the smallest, most meandering little roads that criss-crossed the island. Ioan's route took them past stone-built farmhouses with daffodils at their gates and muddy yards that retained both their traditional character, and their closeness to the land. Beth could see that here, away from the tourist hotspots on the island, life had probably not changed much for generations. Cows chewed the cud resignedly, sheep grazed without ceasing and their lambs, slightly larger and less cute now, gambolled around them. When they drove past a large white placard promoting *"Easy care sheep – the breed of the future"* on one farm fence, they both laughed out loud.

"I need some easy-care kids," Ioan said. "My two are driving me bananas."

Beth, glad that they were sitting alongside each other, as it always made talking about sensitive subjects easier, replied, "I guess it's hard, without their mother, however good a job you're doing of being both parents."

"It's tough, yes, but the worst thing is that they don't understand why she went. All they see is that their PE kit is never washed in time and their packed lunches are rubbish," Ioan said. "We managed to keep our differences hidden, Ceri and I, and there were no big showdowns with Darren, her new partner, which was all well and good, but it means that her leaving us makes no sense to the kids at all. They just don't understand it."

Beth sighed. "That's not easy, and I'm sorry. I can't say Hugo and I did the same. Lewis knew exactly how much we both wanted out by the end."

Ioan slowed right down and met Beth's gaze directly.

"Ceri wants a quickie divorce, Beth. Do you think it's best I just agree, without a fight?" he asked earnestly. "She isn't contesting custody, says she'll have the kids to stay for some weekends so they can stay in school here, and doesn't even need any money from me which means I don't have to sell the house, but it seems such a *downbeat* way to end a marriage and dissolve a family."

Beth saw both the tears glittering in his eyes and his gulping effort to quell them. Talking about this was acutely painful for him; she was honoured that he trusted her enough to do so.

"I don't know of many divorces that are *upbeat* experiences, Ioan. I think it's probably best to make a clean break as soon as possible. That will mean that you and the kids can begin to heal, and the constant sense of insecurity is gone if they understand that things are never going back to how they were." She paused. "It also means that perhaps, in time, you can find happiness again."

Ioan looked at her once more, his face taut with pain. "I can't imagine that right now, but I guess it's comforting to think it might happen one day. I hope it happens for you too."

"It might, and I think we both deserve it to," Beth replied.

As they drove on, both of them knew that, beneath the surface of their brief conversation, something very important had not been said, but had been felt.

The art gallery was bathed in spring sunshine, and the cherry blossom trees below it were just daring to bloom. Set atop a gentle hill, Beth spotted a derelict grain mill in the middle distance.

"It's such a shame, when the old windmills fall into complete disrepair like that," she said, pointing at the crumbling tower. "Did you know that there were once nearly fifty fully operational windmills on the island, but many are now just ruins? I know they'll never work as part of the island's economy again, but they are so much a part of its history."

"You hated growing up in one, I seem to remember," Ioan said. "I think your favourite description of it was 'draughty, dark, dingy and dreadful' in fact. Typically alliterative."

Beth smiled. "Ah yes, I did say that a lot, but I was a sulky teenager then, and Mum and Dad had no money to restore it, remember? And it *was* all those things, but now, I can see how magical a home it is too. How many people have circular kitchens, I ask you?"

"Hopefully not many, because I remember how much Cai Hughes used to swear about having to design and make one for your parents!"

They headed straight for the large, warmly lit room in which Kyffin Williams' paintings were all displayed. As they entered, the only sound was the creak of their footsteps on the wide, wooden floor, as the gallery was empty.

"Wow, we have him all to ourselves," Ioan murmured.

The size and subject of each canvas differed, and the tones and textures of paint the artist had used were as varied as the landscape and the weather in North Wales, but every one of them reflected a familiar mood of the area, of which there were many. Craggy stone cottages nestling at the foot of a rock face spoke of a bleak life and hardships endured; alert Welsh sheep-dogs were caught in a moment of beautifully poised anticipation of the task at hand, to gather the sheep, and Beth sensed the endless, ever-changing movement of the sea in every one of Williams' paintings of the beaches and coves around the island's rugged coast. Finally, they both stood in front of a painting of a gaunt, flat-capped old hill farmer, leaning into the wind with one hand on a walking stick as he surveyed his rocky kingdom, a faithful sheepdog crouched by his side. Smears and streaks of thick paint stood proud of the canvas – a limited, dour palette of greys, browns and blacks with a solid, snow-white sky.

"He captures it all, doesn't he, as nobody else could?" Ioan whispered. "The wildness of this place, its lack of *finesse*, some-how. Like the people, I suppose. Rough-hewn, but glorious."

Beth said nothing, lest she embarrass him, but wanted to tell her companion how perfectly he had just described himself.

They moved slowly around the room, in unison, as if in a measured dance. Sometimes, one of them made a brief comment, or pointed out something particular, but for most of the time, they were silent and moved forward as one. It was a contented, easy hour, which both knew was a rare gift indeed.

Afterwards, in the café, over creamy leek and potato soup and local sourdough, Beth decided to broach the subject of Megan's baby. She poured them both a cup of tea, her heart thumping in her chest – but she had vowed to herself that she would do this, so she had to keep her promise.

"I need to ask you something a little... difficult," she began. "Megan told me about her baby boy, and that your parents arranged for him to be... adopted."

The atmosphere changed, and all warmth between them vanished in an instant as if the sun had disappeared behind a dark cloud. "I'm very surprised she told you that," he snapped. "Especially as I expect you know who the father was. He played you both for fools back then."

Beth flinched and focused very hard on her teacup. He was angry, but why was she surprised at that? Of course he would still be angry with her about Dylan if she prodded that old wound. Her infatuation with him had hurt him deeply. But she went on, for Megan's sake.

"Well, she did tell me. She said that she went to some of your mum's relatives up in the hills to have him, and that the baby stayed up there when she left to come home after she'd recovered from the birth. Is that true?"

"Yes, that's true, but she never really came 'home', of course. She wasn't welcome there, so she went to live in that awful cottage instead," he said bitterly. "Why are you asking me these things, Beth? We'll get on just fine if we don't go there. I'm not comfortable talking about how my sister's life was ruined, to be honest, especially as you were partly the cause of it."

Stung, Beth hesitated again, before mumbling, "I know, and I wish none of it had happened, as you do, and I can never undo the... things I did... and I want you to know that I had no idea she was pregnant, or had a baby after I'd left."

"I know that, but she *loved* Dylan, Beth, and you took him away," Ioan said.

Beth paused. "I know, and I have regretted it ever since, but she has forgiven me, so I hope you can too."

Ioan stirred his tea for a long, long time. "Well, perhaps if she can, then I should," he said eventually. "I'll try my hardest, for sure."

"Thank you. That's the past, and we can't change it, but we can make things better for Megan now, and I would give anything to do that," Beth said, adding, "I feel, no, I *know* that Megan wonders where her son is, how he is, if he's happy, and I owe it to her to try and find out. Does that make sense to you?"

A pause, a clattering of dishes and a slow sipping of tea. Ioan's eventual answer was so astonishing that Beth almost dropped her cup.

"It does. I have wanted her to let me do that for years, but she's always said that no good would come of it. Like you, I think it could."

"You do? Oh, thank goodness!" Beth said breathlessly. "Do you know who took him in? Megan said that she didn't think it had been official, as your father wanted it all kept under wraps. Someone local, was all she knew."

"I don't know, no, and I can't ask anyone who might," Ioan said, "but I remember where Aunty Medi and Uncle Alun lived. On a farm right up in the hills, beyond Rhydd Ddu. They'd be pretty old now, mind, but they had two sons, so one of them will probably still be farming there if they're both gone."

Beth reached across the table and took his hand, and he let her. "We need to find out. Shall we do this together – try and find Megan's boy for her?"

"We'll have to be very careful not to raise her hopes."

"I know, but I think she wants us to do this," Beth replied. She had to convince this man to help her, to believe that she could make amends.

"I need to be sure, before we begin rattling any cages."

"OK. I can try and find out how she really feels, but it won't be easy."

Ioan looked at her. "No, it won't, but if anyone does it, it should be you."

TWENTY-EIGHT

Spring warmed into early summer with surprising stealth. The changes each day brought were subtle, but everywhere: the island seemed to reveal a little more of its beauty every day as sunshine set its rich array of colours ablaze.

Beth looked and felt better than she had in all her years of gyms and expensive facials. She now actively looked forward to sea-swimming with Megan, and they met at least twice a week, often in tiny coves that were so hidden from sight that they even risked skinny-dipping a couple of times. The experience of her entire body making unhindered contact with cold, pure water was so exhilarating that Beth yearned for it as she sat in the stuffy shop, or the gloomy mill, whose tiny windows let in so little light. Megan also delighted in their regular meetings and she, too, was blossoming. Her skin began to glow, her hair to grow again and her body, when released from layers of baggy clothes, was strong and toned. The dark cloud that had enveloped her for so long was lifting.

One sunny, windless morning, as they sat munching biscuits on the shore after their dip, Megan turned to Beth with an expression she recognised.

"I know that look. You're about to quote some Emily Dickinson at me, aren't you?" Beth said, grinning. How wonderful it was, that they were so close again, almost as close as they had always been. Perhaps now was the time to ask whether she had her blessing to look for her son?

Megan smiled, but when she spoke, her voice was low, and subdued. "Just listen to her words:

"Are friends delight or pain?
Could bounty but remain
Riches were good.
But if they only stay
Bolder to fly away,
Riches are sad."

"You're worried that I'll leave you again, aren't you?" Beth said quietly.

"Yes."

"What do I have to do to prove that I won't abandon, or betray you, ever, ever again?" Beth asked. "I'll do anything you ask."

The moment she looked into Beth's eyes, she knew what the answer would be.

"Find my son for me," Megan whispered.

"I thought you would say that. I hoped you would. I will try my absolute hardest," Beth replied, wrapping her arms around her. "And you know that Ioan wants to help me, don't you? I can't do it alone. It's too great a responsibility."

"Yes, I do. *Diolch o galon*/Thank you very much."

On the rocks beyond the beach, a curlew's cry floated over the water, and its distant partner responded seconds later. The aptness of this, the loneliest of calls, and the immediate response it was met with, was not lost on either woman.

. . .

The day Ioan and Beth visited the farm where Megan had given birth and left her baby, was very wet indeed. Horizontal sheets of rain lashed the rocks on either side of the small, winding road as they drove up into the mountains, slicking them and the ribbon of tarmac with an oily sheen. A few sheep hunkered next to stone walls or windblown hawthorns in a vain attempt to stay dry, but their faces told of many such days, and many unsuccessful quests for shelter. They were the hardiest of animals, nimble and resourceful, but this comfortless terrain with its unpredictable weather was often merciless, even for them.

Ioan had rung his relatives and told them he was coming to see them, but he had not said why. His uncle had sounded delighted, but slightly suspicious.

"Uncle Alun hasn't had anything to do with our family for years. What with all the upset about Megan and the baby, and Dad's conviction shortly afterwards, he decided to keep well away, even though Mam's his only sister. I wasn't sure he'd welcome me today, as he's a *dyn parchus iawn*/very respectable man," Ioan said. "I suspect he's wondering why I'm contacting them after all these years, but he's too polite to ask – and too kind."

"Do you think he'll tell us what happened to Megan's baby if he's so proper?" Beth asked, feeling the first flicker of worry that he might not.

"I'm really not sure. Secrets are kept close on that side of the family, and many of them are very religious. That's why my parents sent Megan there, I suppose – because Uncle Alun was a good man, and they could trust him to keep her safe."

"And keep any potential scandal quiet, which was Twm's main concern, of course, rather than Meg's wellbeing."

Ioan winced, and shook his head sadly. "My father was a shit, but I spent many happy days with Uncle Alun when it was the time for the gathering, and a team of us had to get all his sheep down off the mountains. He won't have forgotten that."

When they pulled into the farmyard, Beth's doubts about the success of their mission grew stronger. It was a bleak spot, sheltered inadequately sheltered by a mountain that reared up behind the farmhouse and cast its long, dark shadow over everything beneath it. When a pair of whippet-lean sheepdogs charged over to their car, barking, Beth pulled her legs back inside and closed the door. A minute or so later, an elderly man emerged from the house, leaning on a stick with his right arm and waving his left enthusiastically at Ioan.

"*Croeso yn ôl, Ioan*/Welcome back, Ioan," he said. "*Mae'n fendegedig dy weld di*/It's wonderful to see you."

He put two fingers in his mouth and whistled. Both dogs ran towards him and lay down on the ground in an instant, trembling with pent-up anticipation of visitors to greet. Then the farmer beckoned Beth to come out of the car, his weather-beaten face wreathed in smiles.

"*Helô. Alun, dw'i. Dach chi'n siarad Cymraeg*?/Hello. I'm Alun. Do you speak Welsh?" he said, reaching out for her hand and pumping it with a vigour that surprised her, given his age.

"*Beth dw'i. Ddim yn da iawn, dweud y gwir. Gawn ni siarad yn Saesneg, os gwelwch yn dda*?/I'm Beth. Not very well, to be honest. Could we speak in English, please?" she replied, returning his smile.

He laughed, a rich sound that reverberated off the stone buildings around the yard and spiralled up and into the rocky crags above. "*Wrth gwrs, cariad*/Of course, love. *Ond unanfoddus, dw'i ddim yn siarad Saesneg yn dda iawn*!/But unfortunately, I don't speak English very well!"

Beth liked him already.

Alun led them into the old stone farmhouse, which was so dark that they could hardly see anything for almost a minute. As their eyes adjusted, however, she managed to make out a shadowy figure slumped in a chair on the far side of the room – an old woman, a frizz of white curls on either side of her face.

"Aunty Medi!" Ioan exclaimed, moving quickly towards her. "*Sut wyt ti?*/How are you? *Dyma Beth, ffrind i mi*/Here's Beth, a friend of mine."

"*Paid!*/Stop!" Alun said sharply. "She's not been up for surprises since her stroke, but she'll be pleased to see you. She can't talk, but see – she's smiling at you."

Ioan stopped short, shocked. As both he and Beth looked at the woman more closely, they could see that one side of her face was indeed smiling, but the other was not. One of her hands was held close to her body, tightly clawed; Beth wondered when she had last been able to stretch her fingers freely.

Moving nearer, Ioan hugged his aunt very gently. "It's wonderful to see you again," he murmured with feeling in his voice. "I still remember the post-gathering suppers you used to do for us all. Feasts fit for kings, they were."

Alun cleared his throat. "*Reit 'ta*/Right then. *Amser panad, dw'in meddwl*/Time for a cuppa, I think. And then time for you to tell me how things are with my little sister Nia, and why on earth you're here," he added with a wink.

Over a pot of very strong tea and some rather stale Welsh-cakes, Ioan started by telling his uncle his main reason for coming. News of Nia's fragile health would have to wait; he knew Alun would be upset about it.

"We're here to talk to you about Megan," Ioan began nervously. "She's never fully recovered from losing her baby, and Beth and I think that, if she could know that he's well, that he's leading a good life, she'd feel more... *at peace* about it."

Beth spoke next. "Since she left you, Megan has lived all these years on her own, an outcast, because her family didn't want her back in their home."

Alun shook his head. "She was distraught when the baby was born, because she knew she couldn't keep him for long. It broke our hearts, but Twm, your idiot of a father, told us that we had to arrange for someone to take him in, in case any shame fell on his family. Ironic, we thought, that a man like *him* made his daughter feel ashamed. She was such a lovely girl."

"She still is," Ioan murmured.

At this, Medi wriggled forward in her chair, and it was clear that she wanted to say something. The strange sounds her mouth produced made no sense at all to Ioan or Beth, but her husband understood them.

"Medi agrees. She says she wants you to say sorry to Megan from her, for what happened. We had no choice, though. Your father made that very clear, and he was not a man you wanted to cross."

"No indeed he wasn't, the bastard," Ioan said with a deep sigh.

"We came to ask if you remember where Megan's son went when she left here? There was talk of a local family..." Beth said.

Nobody spoke for a few seconds, so the only sound in the room was the low tick of an old grandfather clock and the breathing of the two sheepdogs dozing by Alun's feet.

"We kept him here," the old farmer whispered, casting his eyes up to Ioan as if pleading for forgiveness. "Medi, well, she couldn't do what you father had asked us to, Ioan. The couple he wanted him to go to were not good people. The boy stayed with us, and we didn't tell Megan or your parents. We told nobody."

Ioan paled, and his hands were shaking. "No, you didn't. In fact, we never heard from you again, which caused Mam so much pain, especially after she lost my little sister Eirlys as well. And the boy was here, all these years. Poor Mam."

When Alun's eyes began to mist with tears, Beth knew she had to keep him focused on answering their questions or the moment to do so would have passed. Guilt, details and apologies would have to come later, however urgent they seemed now. "So, he grew up here, with you?" Beth said.

The old man put a finger to his lips, and glanced quickly at his wife, who was drifting into a doze. "Sssh! It upsets her to talk about it all. Come into the barn with me and I'll tell you more, but it won't be easy listening, I'm afraid."

The rain had stopped when they followed Alun and his ever-faithful sheepdogs back outside and the air felt washed-clean as it could only do after such a downpour. Swallows were nesting under the eaves, as they did every year, and they looped and dived above them in a lightning-fast display. Sitting nervously on a wooden feed-trough, Ioan and Beth waited for Alun to speak. Beth put a hand on Ioan's arm to calm him, and she could feel the tension in his body like an electric charge.

"He was a lovely little boy. Caleb, we called him. Lots of blonde, curly hair he had, as bright as sunshine and a smile that took your breath away," he began. "But things changed, *he's* changed, this past year or so. We watched it, as we watch the dark clouds gather over the mountain and know what lies ahead."

"Do you mean he got ill?" Ioan asked.

"He got *different*, is the best way I can put it. The cheerful, helpful lad we'd always known became someone brooding and melancholy, someone who couldn't sleep at night but wouldn't get out of bed of a morning. And we can't seem to find a way to reach him. He's just not himself."

"When did this all start, Alun?" Beth said.

"It was gradual, really. We knew he was a gentle soul, very different to our own two lads, Llion and Osian, who were well able to return a punch and sink a pint: they always looked out for him when he was little, and still do. But the louts at school teased Caleb cruelly once his big brothers were not there to protect him, and he started saying he wouldn't go. Medi was firm, as she knew that an education was his best chance and he's a clever boy, but he never went again. He left school with nothing, but he's so bright and I can't see him farming. What on earth will become of him hiding up here, with us?"

"Is he still living here, with you, or did he leave?" Ioan said.

Alun paused, and lowered his head sadly. "He's still here, but he's *not* really here, if you get my meaning."

"*Be*?/What?" Ioan said, a flicker of anger in his voice. "Please, Uncle Alun, no more riddles."

"He's upstairs in his room now, but he won't see you," Alun said. "He won't see anyone. Sometimes, he only comes out at night, when we're asleep, to wash. I have to put food on a tray outside the door, and he leaves the empty dishes for me. He walks a lot, I know, in the hills, but it makes me sad to see him so lonely. School was bad, but Medi's stroke was the final straw, I think. They have always been so close, the two of them, and she doesn't have long now, the doctors tell us. Caleb said he knew that before I even told him."

"Does he know he's not actually yours?" Ioan said, because it had to be said.

Alun winced at these blunt words, and Beth reached over and put her hand on top of his, in reassurance. "He knows, yes. We waited until he was old enough to understand, once that scoundrel Twm was out of the way, but I think he's always known, really. He's so much younger than our boys, and looks nothing like them, or us."

"Did he ever ask about his real mother?" Ioan pressed.

"No, never. He seemed to understand that it was best not to, but perhaps he needs to know more now. It's awful, I know, but as we don't even have his birth certificate, in a way, Caleb doesn't exist."

"Megan has that, I think," Ioan said. "She showed it to me once."

"Medi loves him, and he loves her, but I think he's always sensed that he had another mother out there somewhere, and we would dearly love him to meet her. He told me once that he felt her longing for him as much as he longed for her. I always think he's sort of like a harp being played, vibrating, humming. He feels other peoples' feelings like his own, you see."

"He does have another mother, and a *nain*/grandmother, too, though she won't understand any of this," Ioan said. "I must tell you that my mam's not herself anymore either, Uncle Alun. Life was too much for her, and too many bad things have happened to her. She's safe, but sad – yes, that about sums it up."

The old farmer shook his head. "Poor Nia. My little sister."

The sheepdogs stretched and opened their mouths in a yawn. Alun stroked both their heads gently, until he felt able to continue:

"Do you think that knowing where he came from might help Caleb recover from whatever it is he's struggling with?" Uncle Alun asked. "We have prayed for him, so often, but it's no good. We can't help."

"It sounds like depression, which is common, and can be hereditary," Beth said, immediately thinking of Megan, Caleb's birth mother. "The 'invisible illness', they call it, but it can ruin your life just as well as an illness you can see. People can make a good recovery, but they need help and support." She thought of Megan, weighed down with exhaustion and sorrow all these years.

In the stalls near them, a cow started mooing, a deep, mournful sound.

"She's sad too. Lost her calf last night, and she's grieving," Uncle Alun said.

Suddenly, he pulled a very basic, mobile phone out of his pocket, pressed a button or two, and then showed the screen to Beth and Ioan. "Look, this is Caleb. Handsome boy, isn't he? 'Face of an angel,' Medi always says."

"I can see why," Beth murmured, feeling a ripple of shock pass through her whole body. The lad in front of her was indeed angelic, with his fine features and glossy blonde hair, but what struck her most, and made her stomach lurch, were the similarities between him and Lewis. She reminded herself that they both had blonde hair, and were both young men, and her thoughts quietened a little, but she could not forget her mother saying that Lewis reminded her of someone *other* than her, and Ziggy very quickly crossing Hugo off the list of candidates. She dismissed the dreadful possibility these thoughts aroused, as she had done for many years, but they had unsettled her deeply.

Ioan stood up and walked quickly to the other side of the barn. Beth knew he was also disturbed by what they had seen and heard, but for different reasons. She could only imagine how hard it would be to realise that his nephew, the child his sister had thought she would never see again, and had grieved for terribly for years, was only a few hundred feet away from him right now.

"I don't know what to do," he cried out. "I can't leave Caleb here, depressed, and thinking he's alone in the world, but I don't want to distress him even more."

Beth went over and gripped his elbows to hold him steady. "We know much more than we'd expected to today, Ioan. We know that Megan's son is alive, and cared for, and with family. Those are things to be thankful for. What we do next, we need to talk about, and think about, very carefully indeed."

Ioan nodded. "You're right. And I don't mean to seem angry, Uncle Alun. You took him in and loved him, and that was a good deed. It's just the tragedy of so many missed opportunities that's eating away at me. That, and worry about what to do now. We can't tell Megan anything until we're sure it's the right thing to do, though."

"*Dw'in cytuno*/I agree," the old man said.

"But don't feel bad about being kind, Alun," Beth said as they prepared to leave. "You did what you felt was best, and it probably was, at the time. Who knows what Twm would have done if Megan had come home with her baby."

"It's also the secrecy that I'm wrestling with, *dweud y gwir*/to tell the truth," Ioan added. "If Mam and Megan had only *known,* things could have been so different. Perhaps they could have visited, at least, not lost him forever."

Ioan went inside to say goodbye to Aunty Medi for what he now knew might well be the last time. As Alun and Beth stood by the car, their eyes met.

"I've worried about what we did for so long, Beth. I must confess to feeling relief in sharing it with you both," he said, adding, "I remember you as a tiny girl, you know, when I came to 'Berffro/Aberffraw to see my sister. You and Megan, thick as thieves and bright as buttons, you were, even then. *Neis dy gyfarfod di eto*/Nice to meet you again."

Beth smiled and put an arm around the old man. "I think I remember you, too, now you remind me. You always secretly gave us boiled sweets! Please, ask if you need anything for Medi, and I promise we will get some help for Caleb when the time is right. We'll take our lead from you, on everything."

"Medi will be very, very happy that you came today, and why you came," the old man said. "I know she will, but it might also upset her a little to know that, when she's gone, Caleb will have another mother."

"Nobody will replace her in his heart, I feel sure," Beth said.

"Do you feel we should wait to tell Megan about Caleb, so that he can focus on the time he has left with Medi?" Beth said softly.

"I would be grateful if you would do that, yes. It might be too much for him, coming now, and difficult for Medi, too, in some ways."

When Ioan returned, wiping his eyes roughly, he hugged his uncle warmly before getting into the car.

"Wait!" the old farmer shouted as they began to drive out of the farmyard. Ioan stopped the car and wound the windows down. "There is one thing I haven't told you! He writes poems, you know, Caleb does. Beautiful, they are."

Neither Beth nor Ioan said a word, but both of them smiled at the old man to let him know that this was no surprise to them at all.

When they drove away along the rutted track back down through the mountains, Beth was buffeted by so many emotions that she was silent all the way back. Most of her thoughts centred on Caleb and how they could help him; some were based on Megan, who longed to know him, and a few on her mother Nia, who might understand who her long-lost grandson was if she met him on a good day. But the rest of her thoughts were of Lewis, and how alike the two boys looked. She also recalled how low her son had been, how unusual he was, how very down he had been when she'd rescued him, but how he was flourishing where he felt he belonged, where he was valued, fulfilled and loved. Perhaps the same could happen to Caleb if he met his birth mother, the missing piece in the puzzle of his life? She could only hope it would.

TWENTY-NINE

Unfortunately, any possibility of taking matters further with reuniting Caleb and Megan was shut down within days of returning from Alun's farm, when Tabitha had what the doctor called "an acute nervous collapse". She was found one afternoon by Dafydd Owen, the postman, as he walked his dogs, curled up on the beach below the windmill wearing only her nightdress and sparkly necklace and shouting at an uncaring sky.

Lewis was beside himself when she was delivered home. He had been caring for his grandmother a great deal since the shop opened. Beth was busy and Tabitha responded well to his gentle manner and endless patience with whatever she said and did. He had not heard her open the new latch or the security chain on the windmill door, both designed to keep her safe, and he had not noticed that she was not sitting in her Parker Knoll armchair for almost half an hour. He made sure she was calm, warm and comfortable in bed when she was brought home, and then burst into guilty tears and ran up to his room, followed by a concerned Zebedee.

Beth and Ziggy rushed home from the shop within

minutes, leaving Megan and Cai in charge. They found their mother lying on the bed, eyes wide open despite the strong sedative the local GP had given her. He told them that nervous exhaustion was the probable cause, and also talked of there needing to be a thorough review of her ongoing care, given her diagnosis and the many other commitments of her family members. They could not possibly watch her 24/7, he said gravely. Beth knew what this could mean, and how Tabitha would hate residential care. Her heart sank at the very possibility.

When the doctor had gone, she and Ziggy went up to Lewis's attic room, where he was sitting, red-eyed, staring out of the window and hugging his knees.

"Lewis, this isn't your fault. It was always going to happen, and we all knew that."

"We did, old bean, and you aren't to blame at all. You did your best," Ziggy said.

Lewis shook his head in silent misery. "But my job was to keep her safe."

"She's safe now, love. And we do need to ask whether you have got any idea *what* was she shouting, down on the beach? Did Dafydd tell you?" Beth asked gently. "If you could tell us anything, it might help us understand what she needs."

"He thought she said Dad's name, but he couldn't make out the rest of it," Lewis murmured, rocking to and fro on his bed. "She's always saying strange things now. What's with the 'white feathers', for instance? She mentions them in nearly everything she says these days. I don't understand at all."

"Feathers, or Featherston*e*, perhaps?" Beth said quickly.

"Not sure: her speech is pretty unclear now," Lewis replied. "But she's so agitated all the time as if she's desperate to go somewhere she can't get to. I know it's part of her illness, but it's so hard to witness."

"I think she's desperate, love, and I think we need to take

her where she wants to go as soon as possible, don't you, Ziggy?" Beth said, her brow furrowed with concern.

"But where the hell *is* it that she wants to go?" Lewis said.

"I think it's to her childhood home, *Featherstone Park*, which she ran away from with *Taid*/Grandfather, and came here. That's about all we know for certain yet, but her old memories are breaking through so often, and making her so upset, that it's time to take her back now, before it's too late."

"But we can't leave the shop, can we? Some of the fresh stuff will go bad, and be wasted," Ziggy said.

"I can sort out an emergency rota for a few days in the shop. We've got plenty of people to ask for help now, when we really need it."

"It won't be easy, but yes, I agree that if we can do this, we must. The sooner, the better," Ziggy said, looking at his sister in admiration.

"I'll finally ring Flora too. Mum can't tell us anything of course, but she might be able to shed light on some events."

Ziggy smiled. "Good to know that The Management Queen has not quite left the building."

At just after 10am two days later, Beth, Ziggy and Tabitha set off for Sussex in a four-berth campervan they had borrowed from Dafydd Owen.

"Happy to help that poor woman in any way I can, but you need to be with her all the time," he'd told them. "It frightened me to see her like that on the beach."

The distance, plus the difficulty of getting the campervan down the narrower roads, made the journey a long one, and it was almost seven hours later when they trundled through Shoreham towards the mobile home park they had booked for the night. *Featherstone Park* was only five miles from this coastal town. It was, so Ziggy read aloud from his phone, "...*a stately home established over 450 years ago and set in several thousand acres of rolling arable land, bordered with mixed woodland and a small river, locally renowned for freshwater fishing. Owned by the Acaster family, who were honoured by Queen Victoria for their charitable works and the promotion of safer working conditions for farm labourers. Sold at auction in 1961, due to the prohibitive death duties on the demise of George Acaster without a living male heir. Purchased by an anonymous overseas buyer for an undisclosed price. Open to the public 11am-4pm, weekdays only."*

"Bloody hell," Ziggy said. "All this is something to be proud of, isn't it, however it all ended?"

Beth glanced back at her mother, who was sleeping in the back seat, wrapped in a thick Welsh blanket. She was not wearing her necklace today: losing it would cause her such immeasurable distress that Beth quietly insisted it was left safely at home.

"Well, whatever luxury she came from, it's long gone," she murmured. "I do hope we're doing the right thing, and not stirring up memories that will make things worse. All Flora said she remembers is how much Mum was unhappy at home, and disliked most of her family, despite their wealth and fabulous parties."

"I still feel that Mum needs to see this place, so that all those memories stop being like a snowglobe that someone's shaken, but form a pattern she can recognise and come to terms with," Ziggy replied.

"That's really poetic, Zig. I hope to God you're right."

Tabitha was terribly restless that night. She got up numerous times, bewildered by the unfamiliar confines of the campervan. All three of them were exhausted by the morning, and their mother was gabbling incoherently when they drove through the

elaborate wrought-iron gates of *Featherstone Park* just after
11am. They were so focused on looking for the right car park
that they did not notice the sudden quietening from the back
seat. It was only when they undid their seat belts and looked
behind them that they saw Tabitha's face alit with joy, a stream
of silent tears rolling down her wrinkled cheeks.

"Home," she mumbled. "Tabby has come home."

Ten minutes later, both with one of their wrists gently
joined to one their mother's by the soft, toddlers' wrist reins
Beth had found on Amazon, the siblings led Tabitha towards
the main entrance of the house. She did not utter another word,
but her eyes darted everywhere, taking in both the remembered
and the new. Much had obviously changed since her family had
lived here, but Tabitha's face reacted to a worn patterned
carpet, or an ornate vase, her eyes caressing them soundlessly
and her fingers twitching as if she longed to touch them. Few of
the rooms were open, and in those that were, visitors had to
follow a pathway delineated by thick rope that hung from brass
posts. When they entered one of the bedrooms, a swagged four-
poster bed resplendent in its centre, Tabitha gasped and her
hand fluttered to her mouth.

"Was this your bedroom, Mum?" Beth whispered. "Did you
sleep in that bed when you lived here when you were a little
girl?"

The old woman looked at her daughter but did not see her.
Her eyes were cloudy and wet with tears. "Luci," she said.
"Where is Luci?"

Ziggy was upset. "Oh no. This was her sister Lucinda's
room, and look, she's crying. She remembers her. Let's move on
quickly. I can't bear it."

But a few minutes later, as they shuffled through an
adjoining bedroom, he stopped, and began extricating his wrist
out of the reins that bound him to his mother. There was a
determination in his expression that Beth had rarely seen.

"Beth, you take Mum. I'm going to try and find out if her sister's still living in that cottage on the estate, like it said in the paper. We'll probably never be here again, and she certainly won't. I have to try. She needs to know."

Beth nodded quickly, and watched Ziggy vanish down a stone stairway towards the entrance hall where they had both spotted an information desk.

It was almost half an hour before he found them both sitting on a sun-warmed bench in the kitchen garden, watching bees buzz from flower to flower, spreading life as they did so. Beth could see instantly that he had news. He sat next to her and spoke in a low voice to her alone.

"Lucinda Acaster is alive and well, and she still lives in *Farrier's Cottage* on the west side of the park. One of the staff is going to bring one of those golf-car things and take us there this afternoon. He was beside himself when I said who Mum is and said that her sister will be too. Let's hope he's right."

Beth felt a spasm of panic. "But we can't spring this on either of them. The shock might be too much. And remember, the last time Mum was here, she may well have witnessed her brother's death."

"Whatever she saw, it's been eating away at her for years, and we've seen it affecting her peace of mind more and more each day. We brought her here to see if it would lay some ghosts, but perhaps she has to *acknowledge* them first. We've got a few hours to try to get her to understand what's happening."

Beth nodded reluctantly. "OK, I get that, but she might *never* understand, however hard we try. Are you quite sure this is the right thing to do, for Mum, I mean? You know her better than I do, after all the years together you've cared for her and Dad." There was a pause, before Beth added, in a quieter voice, "And I have to ask you this, Ziggy. Are you doing all this in the hope of getting some money? Because if you are, I want nothing more to do with it."

When her brother turned to face her, she saw the hurt in his eyes. He was once more the little boy whom nobody truly listened to, because her louder successes had drowned out whatever quiet, kind things he had done. In that instant, she realised that, although her parents had supported him, bailed him out of trouble, and been hurtfully scant in their appreciation of all *she* had achieved, they had never, ever been *proud* of him. Ziggy had their mother's well-being at heart, in all he did. He always had done, in the years she had been away, living her very different, very selfish life. She kissed his cheek.

"I'm sorry. Forget I said that," she murmured. "*That* Beth, the jealous, self-centred one, full of herself and incapable of seeing true value in people, has gone for good, as of *right now*."

"Thank goodness for that. I never liked her much, to be honest," Ziggy replied, kissing her cheek in return. "OK, let's find somewhere quiet to talk to Mum. I know this could go badly wrong, Beth, but I feel it's worth a try."

"So do I," Beth said. "And if not now, when?"

THIRTY

The route to *Farrier's Cottage*, where Tabitha's sister Lucinda now lived, took them through the most established parts of the beautifully landscaped grounds of *Featherstone Park*. Mature cedars and avenues of oak were in full leaf, and they seemed to have been born of the landscape, so perfectly were they blended with the dips and folds of it. Tabitha was very quiet during the fifteen-minute ride, but she was alert, and not as agitated as she had been at times when inside her former home.

"Does Lucinda know we're coming?" Beth hissed to Ziggy, who was chatting animatedly with Lenny, their driver. "I hope so."

"Yes, the staff rang her, and they told me that after the initial shock, she seemed delighted," he replied. "But very emotional, of course, so we'd better brace ourselves for a tsunami of tears."

"I'm braced already. I just hope Mum is. I told her where we're going, and why, but I'm not sure how much she took it in," Beth said.

"Let's hope it's enough," Ziggy replied.

.   .   .

The approach to the cottage was dark, as a tunnel of overhanging trees formed an arch above the narrow lane, rutted with tractor tracks and stones.

"This is an 'unadopted road', as you can see," Lenny said as they lurched and bounced between potholes. "And Miss Lucinda says she's too old to maintain, or 'adopt it' now. She doesn't drive, so she doesn't care, she told me."

Beth winced. It sounded as if her long-lost aunt was as acerbic as her mother used to be. How would the meeting of these two strong siblings go?

As they passed a beautiful, willow-fringed expanse of water to their left, she felt her mother stiffen and move her lips as if she wanted to speak. This was where she had last been seen, they had read in the newspaper, before her flight from everything she had known. It was also where her brother Henry had drowned. Beth stroked Tabitha's arm gently as they drove past the lake, and she felt some of the tension slowly leave her. Questions could come later, but now, meeting her sister was the only priority.

Farrier's Cottage was far larger than the term "cottage" implied, with its double-windowed frontage telling of a substantial home. The oak door opened the moment they stopped, and a stooped, elderly-looking woman appeared in the doorway leaning on a metal Zimmer frame. She was wearing a blue sweater, tweed skirt and very sensible brown brogues. Her hair was like a ploughed field of rippled grey. Beth heard Tabitha gasp and saw her begin to scrabble at the seat belt in the buggy.

"Do, please, come nearer," the elderly woman said. "Quick, quick! I can't come to you, with this bloody frame."

Beth and Ziggy helped their mother down and let her walk towards her sister on her own. As the two women neared each other, the resemblance between them was startling. Both had strong chins, high cheekbones and a mane of soft grey hair, but what Beth noticed most about them was their poise, their simple *elegance* as they moved towards each other, and slowly, gently, embraced. Neither rushed, or grabbed at the other or cried aloud, but it was almost balletic, like watching two halves of one, long-separated, thing gently conjoin and form a whole once more.

Beth and Ziggy sat at the far end of Lucinda's living room as the sisters talked. It felt intrusive to do otherwise. They watched, in silence, as both women wept quietly and stroked each other's hands, but they heard very few of their words. At times, they saw Lucinda "tut-tut" as if in irritation, or with a puzzled expression on her face, but they knew it was best to let her see what remained of her sister without their explanation. She was who she was, and how she was, now, and they all had to accept that. Only when Tabitha beckoned them, her eyes bright and calm, did they move nearer the sisters.

"These are my children, Luci. Beth and Ziggy," she said.

"*Ziggy*! What kind of a name is that?" Luci said with a guffaw. "Jed's choice, I assume. He has a lot to answer for, that man."

As happened more and more, Tabitha drifted off into a reverie, without responding, and her face softened with a sleepy smile.

"Dad's dead," Ziggy said quietly. "Did Mum not tell you?"

"No, she didn't. To be frank, your mother hasn't told me much at all, and I am finding it tricky to understand a lot of what she's saying," she whispered. "She's not quite herself, is she?"

Beth shook her head. "No, but she looks so happy to see you again, Aunt."

"Aunt! Well, that's something I never thought I'd be called,"

Lucinda said cheerily. "I'm delighted to be given the appropriate nomenclature at last."

A light snore told them that Tabitha was fast asleep. The opportunity to ask questions that could upset her was now, Beth realised – so she took a leap.

"Aunt Luci – I hope I can call you that, rather than Lucinda?"

"No, you may not. My full name, please."

Startled, Beth continued. "Mum has never told us anything about her family, her home, er, Lucinda. So, can we ask you some questions about, well, why Mum left *Featherstone Park*? Might that be acceptable? It might be our only chance, you see." She felt very nervous now.

The old woman harrumphed and folded her thin hands in her lap. "I thought this day would come, and it's probably good that it has, though I'm sorry my sister is so... *removed* from us. We are both getting on a bit now, so it's to be expected, I know, and my health is not all it could be either, but it saddens me to see her like this. Tabby was so full of *joie de vivre*, once..."

"Mum took Dad's death very hard, and now she's ill, and declining more each day, but when she started talking about wanting to come home, we knew it was more than grief that was making her so anxious," Ziggy said. "It was secrets she had buried long ago, we think, ones that need to be resolved before..." Beth, seeing him stutter to a halt, stroked his arm.

But Lucinda looked unsure. "What good will it do now, to dig up skeletons from the past, as it were? And none of that mess was my doing, to be frank. I always looked after her, even when it got me into terrible trouble."

Ziggy looked at the old woman, sensing more, but she did not go on. The mood in the room had shifted. There was now a slight crackling of tension in the air.

"Of course, and we believe you, but we hope that coming here will bring her some peace, in the end... because she is not too far from that now, the doctors say. The progression of this illness can be cruelly quick. She has early-onset Alzheimer's, you see." Beth watched Lucinda's face as she said this, and was sure she saw a flicker of painful understanding at the name.

"And we want to know about her past, before she's gone and we can never find out, and we can't ask her," Ziggy added urgently.

"What exactly do you want to know," Lucinda said, her eyes sharp and prowling. She was very wary, and very proud.

"How did Mum and Dad meet, and why did they run away?" she said.

"And what happened to Henry, your brother?" Ziggy added. "If we know, the next time Mum gets upset about it, at least we'll understand, and perhaps be able to soothe her."

"It's awful, to see her yearning for places and people we know nothing about, you see," Beth said. "All we want is to help her."

"I know, my dears, and I do understand." She paused and took a deep breath. "Don't interrupt me, and I will tell you what you want to know, but if Tabby wakes up, I warn you that I will stop because it might upset her more. I will be as succinct as I can, but *don't ask any questions until I stop speaking*. Is that understood?"

Brother and sister nodded meekly, and Lucinda began to speak.

"Your mother was a fragile child, and often ill. As the youngest, and a girl, nothing much was expected of her, which should have made her feel safer than she did from the pressures that were on poor Henry from the day he was born, but it did not. She brooded about things, hated school and refused to be the pretty, uncomplaining child she was supposed to be. Our father, a mean-spirited man, did nothing but shout at her and our mother, Elspeth, was often sickly and miserable herself. We would call her a 'depressive' now, I believe. Whatever she was, she did nothing to help Tabitha get through life, so I acted as her mother in most ways. I never resented it, and it turned out to be the only experience of motherhood that I was ever to be granted, sadly.

One summer holiday, your mother could not come home from boarding school until August, as Daddy was away on business and Mummy didn't want her here as she was... unwell, so she went to a music festival instead, with some friends from school whose families were less *constrained by tradition*, shall we say. There, she met your father, Jed Thomas. He was what is now known as a 'celebrity', I believe, and 'played the guitar in a rock band', as she put it to me when she telephoned from a call box goodness knows where, full of excitement and begging me not to tell our parents about him. This was not what was expected of an Acaster girl at all, as I'm sure you can imagine."

"Jed *Thomas*?" Ziggy blurted. "But our surname is..."

"I said, don't interrupt me, so please don't," Lucinda said firmly. "He obviously changed his name, though it was typical of him to choose one quite so idiotic."

Beth smiled in agreement but said nothing.

"So, rather naively, she brought this chap, your father (as she was already pregnant at this point), to *Featherstone Park*. Unsurprisingly, it did not go well, and they stormed out, down to the lake. Daddy sent Henry to talk some sense into them, and I was sent along to act as the second in this 'duel of cultures', if you will. Well, things got very heated indeed, and Henry and your father started fighting. Henry lost his footing and fell into the lake. Despite his hugely expensive schooling, my brother was a poor swimmer, and he drowned, though to his credit, your father did dive in and try to haul him out." Lucinda was trembling with emotion, but she continued. "We panicked, and I told Tabitha and Jed, who were justifiably terrified about the consequences, to go. I had to explain what had happened to Henry to my parents and said that it had been a terrible accident. I also had to tell them that Tabitha had gone, knowing that it probably meant I would never see my sister again. It was terrible, everything was terrible, after that. Especially for me."

Lucinda paused again. The dimly lit, airless room suddenly felt full of regrets and resentments and long-held feelings, both good and bad, that had never been expressed. It was stifling.

"It broke my mother's heart, and she died in her sixties. We never had a diagnosis for what killed her, but I am pretty sure after today it was what Tabitha has and now I know what it's called. I remember her terrible agitation, the blankness of her face when I spoke to her." She sighed, and said nothing for a few seconds, lost in her own sad reminiscences. "All this left my poor father wracked with guilt and grief. The estate, without a male heir, and with Daddy so despondent, soon foundered and had to be sold. When he died in that terrible crash, a huge proportion of the sale went in death duties. I was given this cottage, a small income and I have lived here, alone, ever since." Lucinda looked at Ziggy and Beth. "In conclusion, you could argue that this family was effectively ruined by a teenager in love."

Beth could hardly breathe; these revelations had been so crisply delivered that it had shocked her. She could not help but be reminded of her own story in Lucinda's final words: a teenager in love was a dangerous thing.

"So, there you have it, in a proverbial nutshell. Tabitha felt responsible for Henry's death, and the price she paid was exile and a life with your layabout of a father. I never saw him on the television again, so he obviously left that band he was in. Where did they go, out of interest? We never knew." She took off her glasses and began to clean them with the edge of her blouse. Her hands were still trembling, Beth noticed.

"Anglesey, the island off North Wales," Beth replied. "A

village called Aberffraw. It's very beautiful, and right on the coast. We live in an old windmill, actually…"

"A windmill in 'Abbafrow', in the wilds of Wales? That sounds absolutely awful," Lucinda cut in. "But your father had Welsh links, didn't he? His parents disowned him, too, I remember Tabby telling me proudly. He refused to earn a respectable living, as his family had always done, and chose self-ishness and stardom over loyalty and honour. That says it all, really. He was a feckless, useless man who ruined my sister's life, and mine."

Ziggy stood up, his face puce. "My dad loved my mum and she loved him, which is clearly more than had ever happened in *your* family!" he snapped. "Mum chose him and felt guilty about a tragedy that was not her fault all her life. Don't you realise how much that's hurt her over the years – a wound that never, ever healed?" He started pacing around the room in his distress.

Beth stood up too. This situation was spiralling out of control. "Ziggy, please calm down. Thank you for filling in the gaps, Lucinda, but I think we'll take Mum home now. We'll walk slowly back to the house and to our campervan so that she can see everything one last time."

"Wait, please. As Tabby's son, Ziggy, you are entitled…" Lucinda began.

"I don't want anything, from any of you!" Ziggy said, his voice shaky. "Mum's been back, seen her old home and met you again, however little sense she made, because she's ill. I just hope she can relax now and have some peace at last. I don't think she's missing much, personally."

The older woman opened and closed her mouth like a fish on land, gasping for breath. "Oh, I, surely you understand that, under the circumstances…"

Beth stroked her mother's hand gently, to wake her up, and doing so calmed her racing thoughts. She had expected a fond reunion, a resolution of some kind, but this meeting had been far from either of those.

"I think it's fair to say that our family doesn't function quite like yours, Lucinda, which is obviously why Mum left here and stuck with Dad, for all his flaws," she said calmly. "It's been... good to meet you, but I think we need to go now."

Lucinda stood up quickly, and then winced with pain. "Wait! Please don't judge me too harshly. My family have always done good works and supported others!" she called as they walked towards the door, before adding in a plaintive tone, "And I loved my little sister, when nobody else did."

"Dad did," Beth said softly. "Goodbye, Aunt Lucinda, take care of yourself and thank you." . Yes, this woman was brusque, but Beth, more than anyone, knew how easy it was to misjudge others.

"But tell me, please, before you go – does she still have the diamond necklace I gave her, when I thought she might need it at some point? It's worth a great deal of money, so sell it and use the money to make her as comfortable as she can be..." Lucinda said, adding in a murmur, "Promise me you will."

"She does still have it, and we will," Beth said after an intake of breath.

With one arm under each of their mother's, the siblings guided her out of the cottage, and they set off slowly back towards the way they had come. Tabitha looked at the view, the lake, the trees, but they could almost see brief memories return-ing, being acknowledged and then almost immediately vanishing again like a ripple in water. Both her children felt that this was the kindest outcome of all. Their world had shifted on its axis in the last hour, but they wanted nothing more to do with this place, or this family.

On the long drive back to Anglesey, they spoke little, but were all deep in thought. Their tension gradually dissipated as they got further north, and Tabitha slept almost all the way, her face a picture of tranquillity.

"There's just one thing that still bothers me," Beth said as they neared Snowdonia, and the last leg of their trip.

"Just one? There are thousands, aren't there?"

"I can understand why Dad had to change his name, to make sure the Acasters never tracked them down, but he had to go and bloody well choose *Tonks,* didn't he? That name was the bane of my childhood."

Ziggy threw his head back and laughed. "I know, but I guess he did it for the same brilliant reason he called me Ziggy. To make us stand out from the crowd, sis."

THIRTY-ONE

Tabitha was a lot calmer after they returned from their road trip. The GP was satisfied that she could stay in *Melin Arian* for the time being, but Beth, Ziggy and Lewis watched hopelessly as she retreated more and more into herself. They drew up a rota to ensure that she was never left alone, but this was tricky when the shop was busy with customers, orders to deliver, or new stock to mark up. A few times, they even wheeled her down to the village in the wheelchair social services had lent her, and she sat happily in the shop as people came and went, many of them greeting her warmly as one of them. All of them had heard about Dafydd Owen finding her on the beach. Whatever Tabitha Tonks had been in the past, however different she still was in many ways, she had lived amongst them for years, and so they cared about her.

She no longer shouted about her home or asked to return there: she seemed to understand, somehow, that she had done that. Occasionally, she still mentioned Jed, but her grief seemed quieter, like a wave slowly ebbing out to sea. As the weather was warm now, she spent much of her time outside, lifting her face to the sun with her eyes closed in bliss. Every morning, Lewis and Ziggy carried her old Parker Knoll armchair outside, and each evening, they carried it in – earlier, if a shower threatened. Children waved to her on their way to school, and on their way home, and she waved back gaily with no idea who they were. Ioan's kids brought her a small branch of frothy white cherry blossom from a tree in their garden that had been battered by strong winds, and she put it to her nose and beamed at them. Megan sat with her and read poetry that she probably didn't hear or understand, but produced a smile every time she heard the musical voice that read them.

As summer drifted past, and the village was awash with visitors, whole days passed without Tabitha speaking at all. Her family learnt to interpret every gesture, every flicker of feeling, without her needing to, as Uncle Alun understood his stricken wife's strange sounds. All of them felt as if they had pressed "pause" on everyday life, because watching and waiting for Tabitha to need them was all-consuming. One evening, after they had settled her in bed, Beth and Ziggy sat outside the mill to watch the sun set. Lewis had laid a fire in an old compost bin, fuelled by offcuts of wood from his latest project – making curved window boxes for the ledge outside his *nain's*/grandmother's bedroom window so that she could always see some flowers. They were proud to see him attempt the tricky technique of steaming the wood to make it bend and curve with hot water and various clamps. The results were never as he hoped, which left him pacing up and down in his room in frustration. He'd refused to join them that evening as he was experimenting with making kefir, now doggedly convinced that Tabitha's "poor gut flora" was the source of her illness. Beth did not want to alarm him with the true diagnosis, or the likely prognosis, until she had to, as she had no idea how he would react.

That evening, as the flames danced and tiny bats began to flitter above their heads, she began the conversation with her brother that they had not had since their return from Sussex, but knew they needed to.

"How hard it must have been for Mum, to leave her whole life behind so suddenly, and after something as shocking as that," Beth said. "She's spent most of her adult life thinking she was responsible for her brother's death, when she wasn't. It was an accident."

"And Dad gave up his music career for her, don't forget," Ziggy said. "He was very good, but he never really found his way again after that, did he?"

"No, he didn't. It's so strange, putting all the bits of their history together, now that we know what happened to them in the past."

"No wonder they bloody argued so much and found it hard to bring us two up. They'd never seen any good parenting to know what to do!"

"They did their best, which is what I'm trying to do now. She wasn't the best of mothers, but it's lovely to see how close Mum and Lewis have become over the months he's been here," Beth said. "He's missed out on so much family stuff..."

"Not really, Beth," Ziggy said firmly. "Whenever he was allowed to come here, he was right at the heart of the family. Fishing with me and Dad, trawling the charity shops with me and my mates, nicking chocolate mice from the shop with me and Ioan."

"What? Stealing! I knew you'd lead him astray!" Beth exclaimed, trying not to smile. "And I would never have thought Ioan could be so *naughty*!"

"Rite of passage here, to see if you can nick something from the village shop," Ziggy replied with a wink.

"Right, no more unaccompanied kids allowed in from tomorrow onwards," Beth said.

"No, but seriously, Lewis has always fitted into this family, weird as we all are. Mam used to make sure the biscuit tin was brimming for him, which it never was for us two! You just didn't bring him here often enough."

Beth said nothing but watched the flames lick around the wonky offcuts of wood Lewis had put in the fire. She felt the truth in all her brother's words, and they made her ineffably sad.

"Luckily, we've both been given another go at 'family life chez Tonks'," she said. "Mum has got to know my son almost as well as I now do!"

"Then she's had some very good luck indeed," Ziggy replied.

Tabitha died in August, on a bright, azure-skied day that was so hot that even the seagulls sought shade from the sun. Beth found her looking very peaceful in her armchair outside the windmill she had lived in for over forty years. She knew immediately that life had left her as all the wrinkles on her face seemed, miraculously, to have been smoothed away as her body relaxed in death.

Telling Lewis was hard, very hard, as he had grown to love his *nain*/grandmother so much, but his response was calmer than his mother had feared it might be. He decided that she was now with *Taid*/Grandfather, whom he remembered with huge fondness, and that consoled him a little.

Tabitha's funeral, within a few months of her husband's, was far better attended than his had been and this was largely due to her daughter. Beth had endeared herself to everyone in the village through her work at the shop and the way she always treated people with equal respect and kindness. Her devotion to her mother had not gone unnoticed either, in a community that traditionally cherished its elderly, and shared their care whenever they could. The chapel was nearly full, which meant that the hymns were sung so enthusiastically that Lewis clapped his hands over his ears at one point, as the wall of sound stressed him. Beth watched as Ziggy gave an emotional, very personal, tribute to their mother, but instead of cringing at his stumbling delivery, as she had at her father's funeral, she saw only the wave of support that surrounded her brother when he tripped over his words, and how genuinely he was cared about in this community. It was both a humbling and an uplifting experience.

Flora came from Hampstead on the train and was picked up by Cai Hughes to save one of Mrs Tonks's old friends having to risk the bus. She stayed for four days, and struck up an almost-immediate close friendship with Cai, largely based on their mutual interest in butterflies. Their newfound happiness was palpable, and Beth was glad of it, because both deserved to love and be loved after years of loneliness.

Tabitha was laid to rest next to Jed in the churchyard, with the sea laid out like a glistening carpet before them. Lewis planted the perennial plants he'd carefully selected for her window boxes around their headstones instead, where they would bloom each year, and be just as colourful as his grandparents had been.

Beth debated whether to inform Lucinda of Tabitha's death, as she had seemed rather critical of the woman her sister had become. In the end, Beth did so, as she had seen how much she had still cared for her. She wrote to *Farrier's Cottage* with the news that Tabitha had died peacefully, sitting outside in the sunshine listening to the waves hit the shore below. She also told her aunt that, to a large extent, she felt that this was because she had returned to *Featherstone Park,* and seen her again, before it was too late. When she asked Megan for help with the wording of her concluding sentence, her friend brilliantly suggested:

"The circle of her long life had become one continuous whole, with its mixture of joy and sadness, happiness and regret, as all lives are."

When Ziggy had read Lucinda's reply, which arrived a week later and was addressed to *"The Head of the Household, The Windmill, Abbafrow, Anglesey, Wales,"* he yelled so loudly that Zeb's ears flattened against his head in alarm. Beth was upstairs, cleaning.

"Beth, come here! The old bag has put me in her will!" he shouted. "She's sort of apologised and says how lovely it was to see her sister again and to meet us. Seems she's not long for this world either – bone cancer, she says. That's sad, but she was a piece of work, wasn't she?"

"She was a product of her background, I think, poor woman," Beth replied, sitting down opposite her brother, who was pacing around the table tugging at his hair. "But she loved Mum, when nobody else in her family seemed to."

When Beth read Lucinda's handwritten letter, she was as shocked as he had been. It stated that, as the only male Acaster heir, Ziggy would, "when my time comes, which I am reliably informed should not be too long", inherit what remained of her funds. What he chose to do with them was his decision entirely, she wrote, but she trusted he would do good things with it, "as our noble-blooded ancestors did in the past". She ended by saying that she "felt assured, from the loyalty to my sister that I witnessed from him on the day we met, that my money will be in good hands."

"Wow. I bet just the sale of her, massive, 'cottage' will raise quite a bit. I'll go halves with you, if you're nice to me," Ziggy said, nudging her.

"I don't need it, Zig, and Lucinda wanted to give it to you. Just think what you could do if you had some money at last? Travel, buy yourself a car, train in something perhaps..."

"I think I'd do exactly what I'm doing right now, actually, with you and Lewis, in our beloved *'Berffro*/Aberffraw!" He paused. "Mind you, I suppose it would be good to do something with the old tearoom. That would give your boy his chance to be a part of something big and focus on it too. He's frittering his energy away trying to do too many things at the moment."

"When did you become so wise? I think exactly the same thing, almost every day," Beth said with a wry smile. "Zig, Megan was right about you, when she quoted this at me:

"He doubtless did his best."

"Did you ever really doubt me?" Ziggy replied, wrapping an arm around her.

PART 5

TO HAVE AND TO HOLD

THIRTY-TWO

At the end of August, the island seemed to empty of visitors almost overnight. Everyone in "The Village Shop Team", as they dubbed themselves, was exhausted as they had been so busy. Not only had local people embraced what it now offered them (which saw the bike-deliveries Lewis had to make doubling in a month) but many tourists, who had popped in for an ice cream or a snack, were pleasantly surprised that they could buy what they needed for that night's meal at a pretty reasonable price without having to drive to a big supermarket. They loved the "retro" brown paper bags Beth had chosen, the vases of wildflowers that always dotted the shelves, the breadth of local products they could buy and find out about. Megan, in particular, loved telling people exactly where a jar of honey was from, or the provenance of a creamy cheese made up in Snowdonia. Ioan told Beth that he had not seen Megan this happy for years.

"I asked her if she's still writing poetry, as I felt so guilty for not having done so for a while, and she says she's almost got enough 'good' poems for a small anthology now. I doubt she'd ever let us help her publish it, but you never know. I see more and more of her old self every day..."

"Me too, and part of me is longing to tell her about Caleb, take her to meet him and let her know that he's writing poetry too," Beth said earnestly. Seeing her old friend happy again filled her with enormous joy, but she knew there remained one yawning gap in her life. "Taking Mum back into her past was a risk that paid off, but if it goes wrong, and if Megan finds the whole thing too much, it will be our fault. We promised Uncle Alun we'd wait, anyway, until the time was right for Caleb."

"I know it's risky, but real friends take risks for each other, Beth. And she *asked* you to find him for her, didn't she?" Ioan said quietly.

"Yes, but I'm just frightened about what it might do to her, to see him now and realise what was taken away from her." Beth frowned, and her face clouded with worry. Megan had indeed missed so many birthdays, so many milestones.

"At least she would have the chance to make some memories now. I think it could be the final part of her rejoining the world again," he replied.

Ioan had dropped some of his hours at the hospital so that he could spend more time with his children and feel more in control at home as the single, working parent he now was. His divorce came through quickly, and he seemed to accept his changed circumstances better as time passed. A growing part of him was glad of them. Ceri had the children every other weekend, but when she called to collect them in the white Range Rover she now drove, he hardly recognised the uber-groomed, heavily made-up, Botoxed woman she had become.

"If I ever loved her, I certainly couldn't now," he told Megan. "She looks like a bloody monster."

"She was always a bloody monster," his sister replied. "You just didn't see it."

Now that the shop was quieter, Ioan and Beth started to meet regularly on their days off. They sometimes went out on the water in his rib and fished together in companionable silence. On fine days, he took a small watercolour palette and a sketch-pad, and painted whatever was laid out before them while Beth dozed, after eating their simple picnic. It made her happy to see him doing what he loved, and she could see his respect for the landscape in every sweep of colour on the page. They walked the majority of the coastal path in short, manageable sections, taking Jonah and Whale, who loved the variety of the walks and had both discovered a new lease of life since a young and bois-terous Zeb had joined their ranks. Ioan knew the quieter parts of the coast, where the only people they would encounter would be a few other walkers, and probably, nobody at all. One glorious morning, they set off from Rhoscolyn to walk along the cliff path, past the spectacular rock arch that saw the sea crashing under it and out the other side, and then on to Trearddur Bay. There was a warm breeze which whipped up meringue-white peaks on the waves and saw seabirds riding the thermals above the water in undisturbed bliss. A few black choughs accompanied them, their vivid red feet and beaks flashing in the sunshine as they performed astounding aerobatic feats above. Their strange, grating call felt like a warning as Beth and Ioan walked past.

"It's like they're saying, 'we rule the skies here, so leave us alone'," Beth said.

"They do, and we will," he replied.

In a couple of the tiny, rocky coves they had to walk through, groups of seals were basking on the warmest rocks, their fat, slippery bodies completely relaxed. They looked well-fed after a summer's gorging on fish in these fecund waters. They would need to be to survive the long winter that lay ahead.

Beth started to struggle on some of the steeper parts of the path, as the midday sun beat down on their heads. She had started having the occasional hot flush lately and her forty-third birthday was not too far ahead, and she dreaded that she was entering the menopause proper. Tabitha had never discussed such things, so Beth had no way of knowing if this was likely to be true. She would be young for it to happen, but it did, to many, many women. The thought triggered waves of grief, because it meant that the door to her fertility might finally be closed.

Ioan was far fitter than she was, and often bounded ahead on their walks, which exacerbated her feelings of inadequacy.

"Wait for the old lady," she panted as she skidded on a scree of rocks. "I'm a few years older than you, remember!" She was laughing, but one look at Ioan's face told her he had not found it amusing, and that she had touched a nerve.

"I remember you being very focused on our age difference once before. It didn't matter then, and it matters even less now," he said in a sour voice Beth had never heard him use before.

For the next quarter of an hour, she concentrated on her feet and on trying not to cry.

Life at *Melin Arian* had changed since Tabitha's death: above all, things had got a great deal noisier, because nobody had to tiptoe around for fear of waking, disturbing or upsetting her any longer. Beth invited Ioan, Megan, Gareth and Envys to supper once a week, and Lewis delighted in sharing his latest culinary creations with an appreciative audience (even though the kids told him that "anything is better than Dad's cooking"). His new dishes were a vast improvement on the ones he'd created when he first started cooking in the windmill, only a few months earlier. As a person who disliked chaos, and too much muddling detail, he applied his own need for the straightforward to his cookery. He started to follow recipes, and learnt to tone down his seasoning and moderate the spicing; now, he let the flavours of his ingredients sing for themselves, often cooking some fresh local fish to perfection in only butter, freshly picked samphire and lemon juice, or roasting some Welsh lamb with rosemary from the garden and all the trimmings. His ability to create something simple but wholesome and tasty, out of very few ingredients, was a real gift, Beth and Ziggy concluded, and they encouraged him wholeheartedly.

"We need to foster this interest, I think," Ziggy said. "He's a natural at cooking, and he wants to learn more – he told me. When the bequest from Lucinda comes through, let's think about a business plan for the big room next to the shop, Beth. With his skills, your management know-how and my all-round excellence, we'd be an unbeatable team!"

"No way," Beth said without hesitation. Containing her son's passions and her brother's wacky schemes was enough of a full-time job for now, she told him firmly. But despite herself, in the quiet of her bedroom, she began to mull over ideas. Lewis did need a plan for the future, as he would never return to Oxford. She needed to talk it all through with Hugo, of course, but could this, perhaps, be it?

One Sunday evening, as the sun slowly set over the sea, casting a golden strip across the horizon, the conversation with Megan about Caleb, that Ioan and Beth had been postponing, took place. It could not wait any longer. They had eaten outside the windmill, as the evening was a warm one, but Megan was out of sorts, restlessly picking at the seafood linguine Lewis had cooked and picking at her fingernails rather than joining the lively conversation around the table. When Ziggy, Lewis and the kids went into another room to play PlayStation, she relaxed a little, but something was on her mind. Beth was almost certain she knew what it was, and braced herself for revealing news she knew would have an earth-shattering impact on her friend.

"I need to know. Have you two found out what happened to my baby, yet?" Megan said, her eyes fixed on Beth's face. "I know you'll have been trying, or at least talking about it, with all these days you now spend together. Tell me, please, if you know something."

The pause that followed lasted only a few seconds, but it felt like hours. Neither Ioan nor Beth wanted to speak first, and they looked at each other long and hard before Ioan took the plunge.

"Yes, Meg, we know where he is, and where he's been all these years as well," he said, his voice wobbling slightly. "We've known for a while, but so much has happened in between, to him and to us, that we were worried that, if we told you, it wouldn't bring you any peace of mind, but make you angry and sad."

"Angrier and sadder, you mean. Tell me, whatever it is, and stop being such wimps, the pair of you! Knowing has to be better than guessing, and I've been guessing long enough."

Beth shifted in her seat. Megan was right, and she felt bad about having kept something so important from her, however well-meaning their motives. The truth, when revealed, would be agonising, but there was no avoiding it.

"He stayed on the farm with your Uncle Alun and Aunty Medi," she said quietly. "They took him in and loved him, Meg, but they couldn't tell your family, as your father would never have accepted it, and would probably have taken him away from them."

Megan made no sound, but her mouth moved as if she was trying to speak. She turned her face away from them to hide the tears that flowed, silently, down her cheeks and onto her clothes. When Beth reached out to hold one of her hands, she did not respond, or look at her, but sat, motionless, as the room and everything in it seemed to hold its breath.

"Good," she whispered finally. "They were kind people."

"They still are, and his stepbrothers have looked out for him too," Ioan said. "He's been with family all this time."

"Just not with me, or my family. I can understand your hesitation in telling me now. It's a bitter pill to swallow." Megan slumped forward and put her head in her hands. "Oh God, I don't know how to *feel*. Everything and nothing – joy, grief, anger, longing, relief..."

"All entirely understandable, I'd say," Ioan murmured. "We knew it would upset you, and it will take time for you to take it in, as it did us."

Megan looked at him, her eyes wide, but unseeing. She was clearly in shock. "Have you seen him, my son?"

"No, we haven't," Beth said. "He, isn't... *well* at the moment."

Megan took a quick, deep breath. "What do you mean? Tell me straight, don't patronise me please."

"He's... depressed, and doesn't come out of his room," Ioan said. "Alun isn't sure how to help, but he wants to help him get better. There's good treatment he can have, and therapy. We can organise that for him."

"He's like me, then. Trusting, and easily hurt. Does he see Aunty Medi as his mam?" Megan blurted. "Does he love her?"

A pause, before Ioan said, "Yes, he does, very much, and she loves him, but she's poorly herself now, as she had a serious stroke last year. She can't talk and isn't the same woman he's always known. Alun says Caleb's so sensitive. He's worried he's going to lose her, which of course, he will. Meeting you for the first time too soon, might be too much."

Megan sighed deeply. "Poor boy. He's suffered a lot in his short life. Does he know he's adopted?"

"Well, the thing is that he isn't, not formally, anyway. They don't have his birth certificate and never went through all the hoops to adopt him, which is worrying now that he's an adult."

Megan stared at him, as successive emotions scudded across her face like clouds on a summer's sky. "I see. Bloody hell. But I suppose it was easy enough to do that, up where they live. Nobody visits, so nobody would know he wasn't... theirs. And he was *family*, after all."

"They told him that they had taken him in when he was old enough to understand, but Uncle Alun thinks he'd guessed long before that, as he's so different to their other sons. How did he put it?... 'the boy feels that a part of him is missing', I think it was."

Twilight was deepening now, and they could hear the chattering of the swallows above their heads as they prepared to roost for the night.

"It is: *me*. And that's how I've felt for over twenty years, that he's missing from my life. Oh, when can I see him, Ioan?" she blurted.

Ioan looked uncomfortable. "I... well, it's not easy..."

"...because we need to take things slowly, for everyone's sake, especially your son's," Beth said. Her heart was pounding: it would be so easy to get this wrong, and make things worse. "I think we should ring Alun first. He's expecting to hear from us again, and to speak to you. He feels terrible about having to deceive you when you left your baby there. He just did what he thought was best for Caleb."

"Caleb? His name's Caleb?" Megan whispered, putting her hands together as if in prayer. "That's nice. I like that name. Thank you, both of you, for finding him."

Ioan looked at Beth, relief writ large on his face, and she returned his smile with warmth. They had done it. She knew the truth. A rough road inevitably lay ahead, but the worst was over. Now, Megan knew that her boy was alive and cared for, and that had to be a good thing.

"How do you feel about it all, Meg, now you know what really happened?" Beth asked gently. "We were so worried, about how you would react."

Smiling, she replied, "I'm over the moon in the main, because my son's future includes me in some way, and mine includes him, whenever it happens. It must be the right time, as you say."

"That's wonderful," Beth said, and then caught a glimpse of a very familiar expression on her friend's face. "Uh-oh, Emily Dickinson quote incoming!"

Megan stood up, wrapped a towel that was drying by the range around herself as a dramatic mock cape and declaimed, with a huge smile on her face:

"Going to heaven!
I don't know when,
Pray do not ask me when,
Pray do not ask me how,
Indeed I am too astonished
To think of answering you!"

When she had finished, the others stood and wrapped their arms around her and squeezed until she squealed for release, her eyes full of joy.

THIRTY-THREE

Three days later, Alun rang Ioan to tell him that his wife Medi had died the night before, having slipped away in her sleep. Ioan let him talk, uninterrupted.

"Luckily, Llion is here, and farms the land with me, and Osian lives nearby with his wife and kids, and Medi is not suffering any more, which are all good things... but the place feels so empty without her," he said, his voice choked with grief.

Ioan listened and expressed his deep sympathy. Alun and Medi had married at sixteen and lived and worked alongside each other for over fifty years, so her loss would be huge. After a while, however, he could not help his thoughts moving to Caleb, and wondering how he had taken the news. To ask seemed inappropriate, so he was relieved when Alun mentioned it unprompted.

"But there is some very good news. Caleb seems to have turned a corner. Llion and I went into his room to tell him that Mam had passed away, as we were so fearful about how he would take it, but he surprised us, as he often does. In fact, he said something that will always stay with me. He said he knew she'd gone, because he'd *felt* it, and he knew that she was at peace now." A pause. "What an amazing boy he is. We're so lucky to have him in our lives."

Ioan breathed a sigh of relief. "So, he's not always in his room anymore?"

"Much less so since she went, honestly. He got up this morning and made me tea and toast, which he's not done for months. He says it's because he knows I need him – and I do, Ioan. The way he feels things so strongly, and feels for others so deeply. I know it sounds odd, but I am almost gaining strength to carry on from him, and the love he's giving me right now." His voice broke again, and Ioan heard his snuffling tears.

"He loves you very much, and he loved Aunty Medi, and because of that I'm not sure it's the right time to introduce him to Megan," Ioan said. "You need to grieve as a family, *your* family, before Caleb has to deal with meeting the one he lost."

"*Diolch, Ioan*/Thank you, Ioan," Alun said. "I hoped you'd say that. Let's wait just a little bit longer, for the boy's sake."

Just as Ioan was about to end the call, he heard another voice in the farm kitchen, as well as the old man's – a younger voice, with a mellifluous, almost-musical tone he recognised.

"*Dad, wyt ti'n iawn?*/Dad, are you OK?" the voice asked.

"*Ydw. Dw'in da iawn, Caleb*/Yes, I'm fine, Caleb," Alun replied. "*Wyt ti isio mynd am dro yn y mynyddoedd efo fi rwan?*/Do you want to go for a walk in the mountains with me now?"

"*Oes plis. Mae'n diwrnod braf*/Yes, please. It's a lovely day."

When Uncle Alun then ended their call, Ioan sat, trembling, for a few moments.

"He sounds so like Megan, his mam," he murmured.

However his nephew had come into the world, and however many years he had not known his birth mother, or her family, the time lay not too far ahead when he would do, and that made Ioan's heart skip a beat.

. . .

Medi's funeral was a small affair, with a short service held, following her strict instructions, in the "new" chapel in Drws-y-coed. She had been deeply proud of the fact that her forefathers had helped rebuild it almost 150 years earlier, after the original place of worship in the little village was wrecked when a massive boulder had rolled down the mountains and crushed it. A photograph of the renegade boulder took pride of place on her kitchen wall.

Ioan went to represent his family, but Beth could not face the third funeral of a much-loved parent within a year. She knew how it felt to lose a mother, and her heart ached both for Alun and his three sons. But when she spoke to Megan about it, she was comforted by her friend's acceptance of such things, having lived amongst the unceasing cycle of nature all her life.

"The death of a parent is sad, terribly sad, but it is also a continuance of life, as the children they bore mourn, but then have children of their own, and thus the rhythm of it all goes on, as it was always meant to do," she said.

Megan did not go to the funeral either, though she remembered Medi fondly. It would be too difficult not to react to seeing her son for the first time under such circumstances, and she agreed that it was Caleb's day to mourn the mother he had known, not meet the one he had not. Ioan shook hands with Llion and Osian, his cousins, on their way into the chapel. He had not seen them since their teenage years, as his last visit had been before Megan's pregnancy and the end of any contact between the two branches of the family. They were delighted to see him, but with their broad shoulders, strong jaws and thick, dark hair, Ioan could see how different his nephew must have looked, and felt, having seen the photo of him on Alun's phone.

"I remember you coming up to help us with the gathering every year," Osian said, his two small daughters huddling around his legs. "Dad has to ride on a quad bike across the *ffridd*/mountain pastures now, which he hates! We still have to do it the old-fashioned way, on foot, with the dogs. It's knackering, but great."

"Dad says you work at the hospital. Must be tough there. Always too busy, I hear," Llion said.

Ioan nodded. He tried not to let work enter his head when he wasn't there these days. Even the thought of it sent a shot of acid into his stomach. Now that he was only working four days a week, he treasured his free day. This was the one precious day when he could get sorted in the house so that the weekend was free to spend with Gareth and Envys. He might walk with Beth, and, if he was lucky, spend an hour alone on the cliffs as the sun set, revealing more about himself with a paintbrush than he could never do with words. He showed his efforts to no one, though.

Ioan sat near the back of the church, and watched, holding his breath, as his Uncle Alun came down the aisle proudly bearing one of the front corners of his wife's coffin, despite his age. His two sons took most of the weight at the back, but the fourth corner was held aloft by a young man with a shock of blonde curls, and hands delicate enough to be those of a pianist. Ioan knew this was Caleb, Megan's boy, bearing the body of another mother who had loved him all his life.

The tiny chapel rang with sound as they sang the hymns Medi had requested, and Ioan could clearly hear his nephew's pure tenor voice rising above the deeper baritones and gruffer basses of the farmers in the congregation. When Caleb stood in the pulpit and read a short, incredibly poignant poem he had written "*I Mam*/For Mum", there were tears in everyone's eyes. He had captured Medi, their simple life and the relationship they'd shared, so perfectly. As Ioan looked at his nephew's face, a memory stirred, buried deep. Who did this boy resemble most, he asked himself? Megan, slightly, perhaps. When Lewis's face floated into his mind unbidden, however, he suddenly knew the answer to a question that had been at the back of his mind for months, nagging at his peace of mind.

He looked out of a window at the sky, a brilliant blue, and the turning colours of the leaves on a rowan tree, a presager of the autumn ahead. Like his sister, he was always aware of the inexorable rhythm of each year, both punctuated and governed by the seasons, in all their glory. The past was the past, and the mistakes committed there, belonged there, as life surged ever onwards, and beyond it, he decided. He would wait to be told what he already knew.

Although it had been a sad occasion, Ioan was full of hope as he drove back to the island. In fact, he looked forward to telling Beth and Megan what a truly wonderful funeral it had been.

THIRTY-FOUR

In October, Anglesey settles into the strange limbo that lurks between seasons. Some days are sunny and relatively warm, but many are grey and rainy. The first of the storms that would punctuate the months ahead have yet to arrive. There was no frost yet on the grass when Beth and Zeb walked each morning, but there was a chill in the air and the trees were losing their leaves: nature had begun to slow down before the unavoidable stasis of winter. The sea was getting colder, too, but only gradually, so Beth and Megan still swam regularly, even though their fingers and toes were white when they came out. Beth found it hard to believe that it was almost a year since she had come home to the island. Her life was so utterly transformed for the better, despite the people she had lost. She, too, now began to sense the unstoppable forward rush of life, towàrds new, and better, things. It surrounded her every day.

When she began to think about Christmas preparations, both at home in *Melin Arian* and in the shop, she tingled with excitement. Business was steady, but she had plans to make the midwinter festival a real community event in the shop, with mulled wine and perhaps some Welsh carols, ones she remembered from childhood. She imagined Ioan, Ziggy and Lewis singing together, as all had good, strong voices and she saw herself and Megan glowing with pride. In some of her imaginings, she even saw Caleb, Uncle Alun and his sons Llion and Osian joining them, the whole family reunited once more and Megan's face glowing with happiness. There were many hurdles to overcome to make it happen, but she would try, she vowed once more.

There was an air of change in the windmill, too, as Ziggy announced that he and Lewis were drawing up a master plan. He refused to share any details with anyone else until he knew the parameters of what he was dealing with, which Beth assumed was Ziggyspeak for how much money he had inherited from Lucinda Acaster in her will. For weeks, she overheard them both muttering about overheads, load-bearing walls and ball-park figures to random people on mysterious phone calls, but both her son and her brother rebuffed her gentle enquiries, telling her to wait and see.

Lewis had now completely jettisoned screenwriting, birdwatching and carpentry and was mainly focused on cooking and sourcing ingredients, often going on foraging trips in the early morning, cycling to visit dairy farmers, fruit and vegetable growers and local meat producers to learn more about what they reared, grew or sold. He applied himself to learning Welsh, too, as, "a part of my heritage I need to reclaim". His stumbling efforts went down very well with everyone he came into contact with, especially his elderly customers. He even forced Beth to brush up on her Welsh, so that he could practice with her. The windmill was full of chatter, busyness and the aroma of delicious food, and the biting draughts of December and freezing bedrooms of January still seemed far, far away.

The weekly meal became a firm fixture and Ioan, Megan and his kids looked forward to whatever Lewis would cook for them. When, one evening, Gareth expressed an interest in learning how to cook, he became Lewis's "sous chef", instructed to arrive an hour earlier each week, with a clean apron. Megan wrote pretty name-cards for them all, Envys delighted in laying the table neatly for "The Windmill Family" as she called them (although finding enough clean, unchipped and matching crockery and cutlery always proved a bit of a challenge for Beth). These were happy times at *Melin Arian*, and everyone appreciated every single minute of them.

When, in early November, Ziggy finally found out the amount of money that Lucinda had left him, he was flabbergasted. The news came in a crisp, vellum envelope with a crest and the name "Callow & Noble, Jermyn Street, Piccadilly W1J 9LL" printed on the back of it in italic script. He yelled up the stairs to summon both Beth and Lewis immediately, and they found him sitting at the kitchen table holding the envelope in trembling hands as if it was a tiny fledgling.

"Open it, then, Uncle Ziggy," Lewis urged. "We've waited long enough to know what we can and can't do."

Ziggy hesitated. "I'm really nervous, folks. Lucinda was a tough cookie. What if she was kidding in that letter she sent, and has actually left me bugger all? I was quite, well, rude to her that day, *dweud y gwir*/to tell the truth."

Beth reached over and gently took the envelope from him. Her eyes sought his permission to open it, he gave it with a quick nod and then watched her like a hawk as she did so, and quickly scanned the letter.

"Well? Well?" he said after only a few seconds. "How much?"

Beth put the letter down, folded her hands on top of it and slowly smiled at him. "Almost a million pounds, Zig. You're finally even richer than *I* am, haha!"

Lewis let out a strange yelp and rushed over to hug his

uncle. Both men then danced in a tight circle, round and round, for several minutes as Zeb ran round them, barking as if to ask, "what the hell are these weirdos doing now?"

"We can actually do it all with that much money, Uncle Ziggy!" Lewis said breathlessly when they finally stopped. "We've made the plans, but we needed serious cash – and now we have it!"

Ziggy was too stunned to reply.

"That's great, boys," Beth said, "and am I right in assuming that these plans are all to do with the old tearooms? I'm still worried it would be another wacky scheme, to be honest. I'm thinking noodle van, and the beachside coconuts, Ziggy. I have serious reservations, I have to say."

Ziggy grinned sheepishly. "I know I don't have a good track record, but this time, we have some good, fully costed plans. You didn't sound very keen on the idea of developing that huge space. Well, you didn't sound keen *at all,* in fact, which I understood, so Lewis and I have made sure all our ducks are in the water, and, er, lined up. Isn't that what all you business hotshots say?"

"And you're used to big, glossy presentations, so we wanted to try and be as professional as possible from the off," Lewis added, his cheeks flushed. "Will you get the outline plans to show Mum now, Uncle Ziggy?"

Ziggy hesitated for a moment as if gathering his thoughts. "Yes, I will, as I think it's now the optimum time to share the operation we envisage coming to fruition at the end of the day. Er, soon, anyway."

Beth laughed out loud, and said, "So, going forward, you need clear blue water to facilitate the success of your ongoing strategy and ensure optimum payback, do you?" she replied.

The bemused expression on her brother's face told her that his knowledge of the corporate world still remained very limited. And she was heartily glad of it.

When he returned a few minutes later carrying a big sheet of paper, Lewis swiped all the folded washing, junk mail, local newspapers and random biros on the kitchen table onto a chair in one, dramatic, flourish. Ziggy spread the paper out and Beth saw what looked like an architect's drawings of a large room with exposed beams, a slate roof with two, large windows in it, a big central space and a kitchen area with one long bench at one end. The detail was incredible: tiny tables were outlined, there was a swatch of possible colourways in one corner and a ramp for disabled access through double doors that opened outwards. It was astonishing.

"My mate Gethin did these for us for free. He owes me one: well, several, actually," Ziggy said. "It's going to be a café, specialising in simple, hearty food and using as many local ingredients as we possibly can. It won't be anything like the restaurants you probably went to in London, but it will be ours, in our village, and we aim to open next Easter," he said, before pointing at Lewis. "And allow me to introduce the chef, who has already written the menu."

Beth, a huge lump in her throat, was lost for words. They had put a lot of serious thought into this. The fact that they were not over-stretching themselves to try and be something they were not, she found refreshing, as she remembered some of the pretentious eateries she had been to in the City.

"I am so proud of both of you," she said croakily. "I know you can cook, Lewis, and I know you can manage people and places, Ziggy. You've proved that to me, and to everybody else."

Both men started clapping their hands like kids on Christmas Eve.

"And, actually," she continued, "my absolute favourite restaurant in London was one that served just this kind of food. Full of flavour, filling and delicious."

The two men now whooped with joy and began their circling dance again.

"Hmm, enough of the odd dancing, please. You're upsetting Zeb, and worrying me," Beth said. "So, when does it all kick off? Easter's quite a tight deadline for all this to be up and running. This is a big project."

Ziggy cleared his throat. "Well, that's where you come in, sister dear. We'd like to ask you to project manage it, so that everything stays on track, on budget and on time. And before you say 'no', just stop for a minute, and think of us all working together on something for the good of this community and of the amazing island we all love," he said, to accompanying "hear hears" from Lewis.

"We've done some preliminary calculations, and should make a tidy profit too, when word spreads," he continued. "And in quieter times, your son wants to do cookery workshops and demonstrations. We could hold classes there, too, and events, like parties or even weddings. The sky's the limit, Beth. Come on – say 'yes'!"

After this outpouring, the silence that followed was deafening. Even Zeb sensed tension in the air and went to sit on Lewis's feet to keep him safe. Beth looked at her son and had a sudden memory of the desperately lonely boy she'd collected from Oxford, sentenced to a life that could never make him happy. This scheme was a huge undertaking, but its success seemed to rest mostly on his shoulders, it seemed to her. That was a big ask.

"Lewis, *cariad*/love. Is this what you want to do? Will this make you happy?" she asked calmly. "I need to know."

"Yes, Mum. This would be my dream come true."

"Oi, *Sant Lewis*/Saint Lewis! It's a joint dream, remember!" Ziggy said. "As a serial failed entrepreneur, this is my moment. I feel it, right *here*." He slapped one hand over his heart melodramatically.

Lewis blushed scarlet. "Sorry, Uncle Ziggy. Of *course* it's your dream as well – and it's your money that's paying for it, haha!"

"Too right, and if that doesn't show you how much faith I have in this lad of yours, Beth, nothing will. Right, it's make your mind up time."

Beth felt four eyes boring into her like lasers. An image of Hugo's face, aghast, flashed across her mind. She dismissed it as a problem to be dealt with later.

"Let's do it," she said.

She was immediately engulfed in a tangle of hugs.

THIRTY-FIVE

Work on the new café began almost immediately, as everyone was keen to make a good start before the winter weather made things more difficult. Ziggy seemed to be owed an awful lot of favours by an awful lot of people, as a constant succession of them willingly turned out to help him now. Whenever Beth wandered through the site with cups of tea and a packet of biscuits, she heard nothing but praise for her brother.

"Good lad he is. Saved my bacon when my wife was ill," a plumber told her earnestly. "Popped in to check on her when I was working. Even did her beans on toast for lunch!"

A man mixing cement said, "I'm happy to help The Zigmeister. He helped me build my garage a few years back and charged me nothing for it."

"Your brother doesn't blow his own trumpet, but he's always taken care of your parents and never been able to do anything much himself because of it," one man told Beth, who felt a familiar stab of guilt until he added, "He was always super-proud of his clever sister in London, though!"

"And we're all glad you're back where you belong now," a

man with a lethal-looking saw added. "Can't beat it, really, can you – home?"

"But we're hoping you can keep our Ziggy in check now he's a bloody millionaire!" the plumber said with a guffaw that made Beth's ears pop.

December arrived, and with it came the blasting cold winds she remembered from the previous winter. One morning, she and Ioan met for a blustery walk from Cable Bay to Rhosneigr. They had both been too busy to meet since the café project had begun and the hospital was struggling with annual winter pressures that now seemed to last all year. This was one of their favourite walks, taking them up over the hill that housed a Neolithic burial mound, round the rugged edge of the land and then down onto the huge stretch of shingly beach that led to Rhosneigr. As they walked, they talked, as they always did, and it was not long before the subject of Megan and Caleb arose. They had not broached it since Aunty Medi's death.

"Don't know if you've noticed, but Megan's not so good at the moment," Ioan said. "After all the excitement of finding out that Caleb is alive and living locally, I think this waiting to meet him is really hard for her. Can we contact Uncle Alun yet, do you think? I'm not sure what to do for the best, really."

"I had noticed that she's not as upbeat, yes, and her hair isn't as thick as it was a few weeks ago, which isn't a good sign, as it means she's stressed. Why don't we go and see Alun again and talk it all through, ask him how he thinks it's best to arrange things? It's a tricky call."

"OK, *grât*/great. He may think it's still too soon," Ioan said, but just as he was about to step down onto the beach, he heard a shriek from behind him. Beth was sprawled on the headland, with Zeb, Jonah and Whale licking her face frantically as she grimaced in pain.

"Oh no! I think I've broken my ankle. The dogs dashed in front of me and I couldn't see my footing. Ow, it really hurts!"

Ioan scrambled up onto the grass next to her, undid her bootlaces and gently eased her boot off. Then he peeled her sock down her leg and held her foot in one hand, feeling it gently with the other. Despite the pain, Beth could not ignore the effect his touch was having on her, and turned away.

"I'm going to try and move it now, very slowly, but shout if it hurts too much," Ioan said, adding, "and move back a bit, you lot," to the dogs.

"Look, it's swelling up like a balloon already!"

"It is, which is why I took your boot and sock off. Now keep as still as you can, and try and relax."

Beth closed her eyes, and the three dogs moved in close again, sensing that she was hurt and vulnerable. They watched, on high alert, as Ioan very tenderly moved her ankle back and forth, up and down. She gritted her teeth, as it certainly hurt, but she knew that this range of movement meant that it was probably not broken. Ioan confirmed this, his brow face riven with concern.

"Luckily, no broken bones, but it's a bad sprain and you need to ice it, elevate it as soon as possible and avoid putting any weight on it. By tonight, I'd say it will be a beautiful shade of purple," he said matter-of-factly.

"This is the last thing I need, with everything I have to do at the moment," Beth replied. "How am I even going to get back to the car? Oh bloody hell!"

When Ioan saw tears in her eyes, his tone softened. "*Mae'n iawn, cariad*/It's OK, love. I'll carry you."

And he did. He scooped her up in his arms and carried her back along the cliff path, over the hill past the burial mound and back to his car, with the dogs trotting behind happily as if on escort duty. When they arrived back at the windmill, Ioan rang Ziggy who came straight back from the building site within minutes to be given strict instructions on Beth's care when he had to leave to fetch the kids. He fetched a bag of frozen peas for her ankle and Ioan lowered Beth into Tabitha's old armchair before gently lifting her leg up onto a coffee table. Then he wrapped the packet around her ankle, finally putting the tiny brass bell their mother had rung to attract their attention on top of it.

"There, all sorted," Ziggy said. "If you need us, ring the bell just as Mam used to do before she couldn't remember how to. Worked a dream for a bit."

"I'll ring your phone, thanks, especially as you won't hear this thing from the café, where you're no doubt going to be all day," Beth said. She was fed-up. There was so much still to do.

"I can stay a little while, so you can get on, Ziggy," Ioan said, and Beth smiled gratefully.

When Ziggy returned to work, Ioan made them both a coffee and sat down on the saggy sofa usually occupied by a snoozing Zeb. Only then did Beth notice how exhausted he looked, and how his hair was, very slightly, receding on both sides. This past year had taken its toll on him, as it had on all of them.

"Thanks for being my knight in shining armour," she said. "Don't know what I would have done if I'd been walking on my own, as I often am."

"That had crossed my mind too. I'm glad I was there. I look forward to our time together so much, but what with work and the kids..." He lowered his head, and Beth also noticed a tiny bald patch amidst the thick brown curls. How quickly the years flew by, she thought. It seemed only a few days since they had sat together deciding which famous painter or poet they wished they could have been (and surreptitiously studying each other's faces and bodies with forensic zeal). They had wasted so much time.

"Is there any way you could drop more hours at the hospital?" she asked tentatively. "You look so tired, and I know how much the kids need you."

Ioan sighed. "No, I can't afford to. Money's tight. Gareth wants to go on Scout camp in Brittany in the summer, and Envys seems to grow out of her clothes in days." He paused. "I really want to be more involved with the shop and the café, and Ziggy was talking to me about perhaps giving some kids' art classes, which I would *love* to do, but I don't have the time. Perhaps one day. I have to put my family first, as we all do, and the bills go on and on."

"Of course, but that's a brilliant idea for the future. You know more than most how much joy creating something beautiful can give people," Beth replied.

Sensing that the subject was closed for now, she said nothing more, but a seed had been planted in her mind. If there was a way of helping Ioan feel happier, and more fulfilled, she would find it. She owed him that, and more, after all.

"I guess we won't be calling on Uncle Alun again for a while now," he said. "But I must admit I'm still not sure about the whole thing. What if Caleb rejects Megan, or reacts as she isn't expecting, as he may well do at the moment. I don't know if I could bear that."

"I had thought the same," Beth replied. "It's a lot to ask, of both of them."

"Perhaps what happened to you today gives us permission to take stock for a while longer, at least until you recover. More speed, less haste and all that."

"OK, let's wait. Part of me still isn't sure what Megan really wants, so let's tread carefully from now on."

"Especially *you,* peg-leg!" Ioan said.

THIRTY-SIX

As Beth was forced to rest her ankle, she had time to formulate plans for a much happier, livelier second Christmas on the island than her first one had been. They would host the main meal at *Melin Arian*, she decided, so that they could all celebrate the festival together. Megan's birthday would fall on Christmas Eve, so it was decided that they should have a big "Windmill Family" sleepover the night before Christmas. Gareth and Envys were beside themselves with excitement, especially as their mother was going to the Maldives this year, so they couldn't spend any time with her and Darren and their four French bulldogs, Trixie, Dixie, Pixie and Dex.

Beth and Megan decided to go to Beaumaris, a pretty town on the other side of Anglesey, to do some gift shopping together. Ioan had given his approval to Beth putting weight on her ankle once the bruising and swelling had subsided, but she took one of her mother's walking sticks, just in case. Every year, the little seaside town held a "Victorian Christmas" event, which saw the streets tastefully decorated, shopkeepers dressed up in period costume, various musical turns and local choirs singing carols filling the air. The two friends arrived just as darkness was falling, and the town looked like something out of a fairy tale, with twinkling lights festooned above the main street and the shop windows ablaze with candlelight. On the pier that led out into the sea, stallholders had set up tables selling crafts, sea-glass jewellery, cakes, hot food, mulled wine and all kinds of pretty gifts, so they headed there first of all. They recognised many faces and were enthusiastically greeted by several of the locals who supplied things to the village shop. Word had spread across the island that Beth Tonks offered a fair price for goods that she understood took time and love to make, produce or grow. She was a keen negotiator, but she kept her promises, so the word was: Beth was immensely proud as she walked from stall to stall. It felt good to be successful at something really worthwhile at last.

It was Megan who saw Dylan Jones first. The back of his head, crowned with a shock of blonde, curly hair, shone like a beacon under the fairy lights. He was wearing an expensive-looking camel overcoat and had a bright red scarf wrapped artfully around his neck. Manon, his wife, walked alongside him in a sweeping, black maxi coat, glancing at the little stalls but stopping at none of them.

"OMG, it's him! Look, over there – it's Dylan Jones!" Megan hissed. "I'd completely forgotten he lives here. Shit, shit, shit." She grabbed her friend's arm and held on to it tightly.

Slightly stunned, Beth stared at the back of a tall man in a smart coat with a lot of blonde hair, but it took her brain several, long, seconds to link these things with someone who had very nearly ruined her life and *had* ruined her friend's. When it finally did, she felt all the blood drain from her face in an instant.

"Christ, it *is* him," she whispered. "Thank goodness he's not looking this way."

"And thank even more goodness it's dark," Megan replied. "I would say 'let's run', but you can't, so 'let's hobble', OK?"

But just as they were about to try and weave through the crowds and escape, the man turned around and Beth gasped out loud. The face she saw before her, with its finely hewn features (though much-softened with age and good living) was almost identical to that in the photograph of Caleb that Alun had shown her. It was also undeniably, very, very reminiscent of her son's face. She began to shiver as a cold wave of dread spread throughout her body. As if in slow motion, she saw Megan turn to look at her.

"Are you OK, Beth? He hasn't seen us, so we're safe. Beth? BETH?"

But Beth was gone, all but shoving shoppers out of her way with her borrowed stick as she limped away from the crowd. Megan was behind her, she knew, but she did not once turn back, or respond to her cries of "wait", "please wait", and finally "stop!". All her worst fears now swirled in her head, round and round, stirring up memories, regret, guilt and dread she had fought for years to lay to rest. When she reached the car, she threw the walking stick away, slumped her body over the bonnet and wept, oblivious to the stares of passers-by and the distant sounds of festive bell-ringers.

When she felt a hand on her shoulder, Beth did not lift her head to see who it belonged to: she knew. Neither did she acknowledge it when she heard her friend's voice, low and gentle, making reassuring noises like those a mother might make to comfort a child, or when she felt a hand softly stroking her hair. She had no response, no reply to offer. All her assumptions about everything she had achieved, and had created, had been blasted to smithereens in an instant. Her worst nightmare, that Lewis was Dylan's baby and not Hugo's, had just come true. There could be no doubt about it at all. Megan could not know, as she would surely never forgive her, and yet her gentle voice was there still, implying that, perhaps, she might. But how on earth could she tell her *that*? When she half turned towards her oldest friend, her soulmate, she saw a face suffused with kindness, not judgement.

"I understand how you feel, Beth. I really do. That boy was our fatal flaw, a weakness we despised, but we shared. He was predatory, and we didn't love him. That's what nobody else can understand. We had no say in the matter: he bewitched us, trapped us in his web. He was Heathcliff, and we were Cathy."

Beth, still hiding her face, murmured, "Yes, he was toxic, for both of us."

"But he's out of our lives now, completely. We're our own women, remember? Things to do, people to see..."

Beth wiped her eyes roughly. Megan had clearly not guessed the reason for her hysterical reaction to seeing Dylan again: a large part of her was glad, relieved, but another part longed to tell her friend the whole truth. She had carried this secret like a dark incubus on her heart for too long.

When they arrived back at Megan's cottage late that night, they wrapped up in all the warm blankets they could find and sat outside on some old chairs, under a carpet of a myriad tiny stars, sipping warmed Welsh whisky to calm their jittery nerves. Beth, who had not drunk alcohol for months, needed its seductive charm to relax her now. The thick, dark silence of the night was interrupted only by a chorus of urgent peeping from some oystercatchers on the beach below. Beth knew that this was the time, the moment, to tell Megan the truth about who was Lewis's father. Taking a deep slug of whisky, she began.

"I need to tell you something that you might never forgive me for," she said.

Megan looked at her, steady and calm. "Go on."

"First, I want to tell you once again that *I had no idea* you were pregnant when I flirted with Dylan Jones at school, before I left for Oxford. I need you to believe that."

"I do believe it. You left, and I was sent away, before anyone knew."

"But there's more, Meg. I have never told anyone, *anyone*, this, but... I slept with Dylan on the night before I got married," she whispered. Now, the silence in the night air buzzed like white noise. "He was so, well, *romantic,* and I was angry with Hugo for not helping me with everything, and incredibly hurt that his snooty parents couldn't even be bothered to come to our wedding. I decided to take my stupid revenge on them all, by..." But she could not go on.

A pause followed, in which Megan's imagination filled the gaps.

"Did you love Hugo?" she said coolly. "If you did, why did you do it?"

"I think I did, but not in the same way as I did Dylan. We've said it before, but he had something, I don't know, something I always found impossible to resist. And he seemed like my last chance at real *passion,* Meg, like we'd always dreamed of if we ever got married." She paused. "That's not an excuse – there isn't one – but it was the reason."

"I understand. You know that he had that effect on me too. We were like marionettes to him. He tweaked our strings and we did his bidding, powerless," Megan said quietly. "Perhaps we read too many romantic novels back then."

"But why did he play with us like a cat plays with a mouse? I just want to know *why?*"

Megan hesitated. "His parents were pretty strict, I remember, so perhaps he just wanted to be able to feel in control of one aspect of his life. They despatched him to Cardiff, you know, when they found out about my pregnancy. He hated them for it, and they hated him right back. Still do."

"What a sad mess," Beth said. "But he was such a beautiful boy."

"Is Caleb beautiful too? I've been thinking about him so much," Megan said quietly.

"Yes, he is, but I'm still not sure it's the right time for you to meet him yet, to be honest," Beth said. "He needs to grieve with his... other family, Alun thinks."

"I know. I've been fretting about that, day and night. I want to *see* him, bask in having created him for a minute or two, but I feel I have no right to intrude in his life at the moment as a complete stranger."

"Then let's keep both secrets to ourselves for now," Beth said.

"Pinky promise, like when we were kids," Megan said, sticking her little finger out into the darkness to find Beth's, waiting for it.

"Sorry, but there's one more thing I need to tell you," Beth said, her heart pounding.

"Can it wait, Beth?" Megan said with a weary yawn. "It's late, and I'm absolutely shattered, and we have all the time in the world to bare our souls. As T.S. Eliot so succinctly put it:

"Humankind cannot bear very much reality."

Beth nodded. "It can wait, of course it can," Beth said quickly. Relief washed over her. Telling her friend that Lewis was Caleb's half-brother was too huge a revelation not to deliver in the right way, and at the right time.

PART 6

FULL CIRCLE

THIRTY-SEVEN

The windmill was full to the rafters on Christmas Eve, with everyone (including Whale, Jonah and Zeb) gathered to celebrate Megan's birthday, and then Christmas Day together. Every bed was taken, and Ioan's kids were happily sleeping on camp beds in a hallway. Beth felt a twinge of guilt at having a double bed to herself, so asked Megan to join her, and Lewis and Ziggy shared the new double bed in "The Garret". Another family member was supposed to be coming tomorrow, if she felt up to it. Ioan had visited his mother Nia at her flat that week. She had surprised him by saying she wanted to join them for afternoon tea on Christmas Day, promising to bring one of her famous *bara brith*/currant cakes. (Her son had little expectation of her actually doing this, as she had not baked for years, but he was deeply touched, nonetheless.)

Christmas Eve was a relaxed, but joyful, occasion. Lewis was in charge of co-ordinating the meal and ensuring there were no mismatched flavours or repeated offerings as there was an assortment of hot and cold dishes, to which every household had contributed. There were quiches made with eggs from the village, crunchy salads, local bread and cheese, freshly caught mackerel pâté and *stwnch ffa*/fried broad beans and potatoes (to absorb the alcohol). They all went down a treat, as did the chocolate brownies (made with "Siocled", an island brand) and "Red Boat" local ice cream for pudding. As Beth watched Lewis oversee the event with gentle efficiency, she almost wept with pride at how much he had grown up in the past year. He no longer flitted from fad to fad, and although he still struck some as a little unusual at times, he was more than happy in his own skin, which was a joy to see. There was no doubt that this was where he was meant to be, and what he was meant to do.

Christmas Day began too early, courtesy of Gareth and Envys, who could not contain their excitement until all the hungover adults felt ready to wake up. Once their gifts were opened, and Envys was blissfully cuddling her unnervingly lifelike baby doll, they settled down with the Isle of Anglesey version of Monopoly game that Ziggy had found on eBay. Megan was more than happy to be on veg prep duty, firmly guided by Lewis, and so Beth and Ioan were allocated the task of taking the three dogs for a long walk, to tire them out.

They decided to take Whale, Jonah and Zeb through the grass-covered sand dunes behind Aberffraw beach and to let them run off the lead for as long as possible. Very few people were out and about that morning, as there were far more urgent things to do, such as open presents and stuff turkeys. Small patches of blue sky peeped between thin drifts of cloud, and the dunes stretched as far as the eye could see, a strange, uniform landscape of so few colours and so little variation that they resembled the backdrop for a dystopian movie. Many birds nested in these grassy havens, safe from the crowds, and rare butterflies that Cai and Flora so adored fluttered between flowers that bloomed nowhere else on the island. They carpeted the ground with their delicate colours in spring and in summer, they filled the air with their scent.

"It's a limited colour palette here, but a stunning one, isn't it?" Ioan said as they strode behind the free-roaming dogs. "Kyffin painted these dunes several times and the greys, pale green and hints of blue seem to sum up the *feel* of Anglesey perfectly, in my mind. You need to look for colour, but it's always there somewhere."

Beth nodded her agreement, but she could not relax fully. This walk was the perfect opportunity to update him about Megan and Caleb. She had not yet had the chance to tell him of his sister's decision not to formally introduce herself as his mother yet, but she desperately hoped that he would be both relieved, and a little disappointed at the lack of a fairy-tale ending, just as she had been. Her mood was also clouded whenever she remembered her own recent discovery, that Hugo was not Lewis's father. That dark secret she was far from ready to share with him, and Megan needed to know it first. Beth was especially worried about how Ioan might react because both of them knew, but had not said, that they were now deeply in love with each other.

All began well. "I need to tell you that Megan and I had that chat about Caleb, and what she wants to do. It's not what we expected."

Ioan stopped walking and looked at her, his expression cautious. "Go on."

"She feels Caleb has lived his whole life without her, and he loved Medi as his mother. Like us, she's not sure it would be right to disrupt all he's ever known to make *herself* feel, well, more fulfilled. It might not be what's best for him, not yet. There's no rush, after all."

Ioan walked ahead for a minute or two, before turning to check that Beth was still behind him. "I can't say I'm surprised, but I am a bit sad."

"I know. Me too, but she's putting him before herself, typically," Beth said. "She wants to *see* him, but not to 'out' herself to him just at the moment, when he's grieving. Do you think we could organise that, if Alun agrees? I know it won't be easy, and she could still get upset about not meeting him, but it's a compromise."

"Yes. I agree, but you're right, it's bound to be upsetting for Megan, and perhaps for Caleb too," he replied, and Beth noticed that he looked preoccupied, even worried. He did not need this extra stress right now, and had mentioned money worries, but life was rarely fair in how it distributed such things, she knew from experience.

They had reached the end of the dunes and stood looking down over the wide expanse of sand and sea below them. The beach was almost deserted, and it was hard to imagine the hordes of holidaymakers who had picnicked, swum, paddleboarded, barbecued and sunbathed here only a few months earlier. They had been scoured away, as autumn and winter had inexorably reclaimed the shoreline until the following year. Ioan scrambled down onto the sand first, and turned to offer Beth a hand, in case of a repeat of her last disaster. But this time, when she reached him, he did not release her hand. Instead, he pulled her gently towards him, until their faces were only inches apart. She could feel his breath on her cheeks, warm and quick.

"Beth, I have thought long and hard about how to say this, but the right words probably don't exist unless you're a poet, which I certainly am not. So, I am just going to have to say the first ones that come out of my mouth," he said.

When she started to try and reply, he put a finger over her mouth to stop her.

"Let me say it now, the best way I can. I couldn't do it all those years ago and look how that turned out, for both of us. We both married the wrong people, for the wrong reasons, and had years of unhappiness," he paused to take a breath. "You knew how I felt back then, but we were young, and both so shy and awkward... and of course Dylan Jones was prowling like a jackal..."

Again, words formed on Beth's lips, but he stopped them.

"I tell you now, loudly and clearly, that I love you, Beth Tonks. I always have, and always will." He exhaled, took his finger off her lips and looked up at the sky. "*Iesu Grist*/Jesus Christ, it feels bloody good to finally say it as grown man, and know with all my heart that I mean it."

Beth's heart was beating so fast she worried that, if she opened her mouth, it would pop out, pounding and bouncing as if in a kids' cartoon. This compassionate, wounded man had just bared his soul to her, and she knew without a shred of doubt that she loved him too. But her secret, her shame, still lay between them like a river they could not cross. She would be unworthy of this man unless she was brave now. She knew what she had to do. She had to tell him everything, and risk everything, because not doing so meant she had lost it anyway. Emily Bronte's words floated quickly across her mind, like a banner of warning dragged behind a plane:

Honest people don't hide their deeds.

And she so wanted to be honest now.

"Ioan, I love you too, I do, so you must never doubt that, ever... I mean..." she said, stumbling over her words, "but there is something you must know, before we go a single step further towards wherever we're going."

A breeze had sprung up, and Ioan smoothed her hair off her face before kissing her, very lightly, on the lips.

"I know what you want to tell me," he said. "But I have known about it from the moment I saw Caleb at Medi's funeral, up in the mountains."

Beth started to tremble uncontrollably, just as she had done when she had seen Dylan Jones at the Christmas Fair. All her fear, shame and self-doubt seemed to be surrounding her, nipping at her heels like a pack of rabid dogs, spiteful and cruel. She had spent so long trying to deny what she had done, who she really was, and where she came from; it was terrifying to acknowledge all this at once, with no protective shell of money, jargon, influence or status.

"You know, then, that Lewis is Dylan's child?" she whispered.

"Yes. He and Caleb are the spitting image of the man, with a bit of you and Megan to temper the mix, thank goodness. Did you really think I wouldn't guess, eventually?"

Beth stepped back and stumbled. She felt a strong urge to run, to escape. When he reached out to grab her arm, she pulled away.

"But how does that make you *feel* about me? How can you possibly love me when I was so easily fooled by superficial things, by appearances?" she said, adding in a quieter tone, "And turned you down when you offered me something real because I wanted something fake instead!"

"*Cariad*/love, don't, please. We have all grown up, made mistakes along the way and have plenty of regrets: I married a 'monster', remember? And know this – if you choose to tell Hugo and Lewis the truth, I will still love you, and defend you, but that choice is yours and yours alone. I won't let you push me away again or tell me that you don't feel the same." He pulled her back towards him, and this time, she did not resist.

A few minutes later, when they parted, Beth saw a stillness, a peace in Ioan's face, that she had not seen in all the months she had been home.

"Does Meg know, about Lewis I mean?" he said. "I need to know that."

"No, no yet. We saw Dylan Jones in Beaumaris last week,

which was when I finally knew the undeniable truth, but I didn't tell her. She's no idea what Caleb looks like, remember, so she didn't make the connection," Beth replied.

"I won't tell her either. But you need to, and soon, for both your sakes."

He pulled her back to him once more, his mouth so close to her ear that she trembled at the low, reassuring timbre of his voice. "Lewis has a mother who loves him, a father, in Hugo, who cares about him a great deal, however hard he tries to disguise it, and family and friends here who love him. You need to think very hard about whether you want to shatter that relationship, for both father and son."

"I know. It's terrifying, to think how Hugo might react. And Caleb has his family, with Alun and his stepbrothers. I couldn't bear to risk that now, when they all need each other more than ever," Beth said, looking into Ioan's eyes. "But do you forgive me, for making us both waste the best years of our lives on people we didn't love?"

Kissing the end of her nose tenderly, Ioan replied, "Yes, I do, but only because the best years are yet to come, with people we *do*."

THIRTY-EIGHT

That Christmas Day in *Melin Arian* was one that was never forgotten, by any of the people who shared it. When Beth and Ioan walked in, holding hands and beaming from ear to ear, everyone in the kitchen erupted into cheers, whoops and applause, and a group hug commenced which included all three tail-wagging dogs. A few minutes later, when Ioan announced that he had asked Beth to marry him, and that she had said "yes", the hugging and cheering resumed. Ziggy immediately opened the two bottles of champagne he'd been given "by a mate" and been saving for ages, and everyone drank a toast and mmmm'ed in unison once they'd taken a long, delicious sip.

There was hardly room to move in the kitchen once every table in the mill had been put together to seat this magnificent gathering of friends and family. Beth was concerned that Gareth and Envys were a little quiet over lunch, but she knew that seeing their dad with another woman was something that would take time for them to get used to. She would take things slowly. As the host of all "Windmill Family" meals, she had already earned their love and trust, but what she wanted now, more than anything, was for them to see her as far more than their dad's new partner. This was her second chance at mother-hood, albeit step-motherhood, having, as she saw it, failed so spectacularly the first time around with Lewis.

"About time too," Megan said to Beth, once the celebrations had subsided a little and both friends sat down together with refilled glasses. "I don't say this lightly, but in the nicest possible way – you bloody well deserve each other!"

"He knew about me, er, flirting with Dylan, I mean," Beth whispered. "And he forgave me, straight away, just as you did. You must both really love me."

"We *all* love you, Wonkytonks. Always have, always will."

"I am so thankful for that," Beth said. She kissed Megan's cheek. Would her friend forgive the final betrayal, the one that had led to Lewis's birth? She could hardly bear to think about it. For now, she felt happier than she had in many years. As she looked at her friend, the expression on Megan's face was one she would always recognise. "Uh-oh. Quote coming up?"

"Yes indeed. Emily, let's sock it to her," Megan replied, saying:

"*A door just opened on a street—*
I, lost, was passing by—
An instant's width of warmth disclosed,
And wealth, and company."

"And what wonderful 'company' you all are," Beth murmured.

After lunch, the kids watched a movie, Ziggy and Lewis snored next to each other on the sofa and Beth and Megan washed up and then gave the dogs far more scraps than was good for their digestive systems. Ioan set off to fetch his mother Nia to spend the afternoon with them all. He was clearly nervous. His mother had not seen his children for a long time and had not been amongst so large a gathering for even longer. It could all go very wrong in a variety of different ways.

"When I bring her in, don't overwhelm her with noise or fuss," he warned everyone. "She's been having more moments of lucidity lately, but she's often so anxious that anything could upset her. Still, *dw'in wrth fy modd*/I'm over the moon that she wants to come and join us."

And when, half an hour later, he stood in the doorway with a smiling Nia clutching his arm, it was such a simple, moving sight that nobody even considered making any noise or creating any fuss. Nia nodded kindly at faces she knew but did not know, and was soon settled in Tabitha's favourite armchair near the range. Megan could not stop smiling.

"I have this for you, son," Nia said, her voice a little hoarse from lack of use. "My *bara brith*/currant loaf. First I've made for years. Famous it is, you know, in this place."

Beth poured everyone a *panad*/cuppa, Lewis cut thick slices of the cake for everyone, and spread them with local butter.

"Ooh, Mrs Williams, this is so good. Could I possibly have your recipe, for my new café?" he asked her after his second bite.

Nia glared at him, glasses on the end of her nose. "Over my dead body! It's been in my family for centuries, that recipe. If you want it, boy, you'll have to prove you're a good enough cook to make it."

Lewis gulped his tea. "*Chwarae teg*/Fair enough. Well, Mrs Williams, how about your coming along to the opening of the café? If you like what I cook, perhaps you'll reconsider."

"Lewis is a brilliant cook, Mam," Megan said quickly. "You might regret it!"

Nia was not listening but staring at Lewis's face as if fascinated by each detail she saw there.

"I know your face from somewhere. You look a bit like

someone who was around a long time back. He was handsome too, like you – but a bad egg. *Duw*/God, a very bad egg indeed."

Ziggy, Beth and Megan all held their breath, and Lewis blushed in confusion. What was this weird old lady talking about? Nia wriggled to the front of her chair as if poised to ask another urgent question, but Ioan quickly offered her a Welsh cake and she bit into it in bliss instead.

At around 5pm, Ioan gently took his mother's arm to take her back to her flat; she was still very cheerful, but clearly exhausted. As she passed Envys, who was still playing lovingly with her new baby doll, the old woman suddenly stopped and stared at it, her face pale and anxious.

"I had a baby like that, you know," she murmured, chewing the inside of her mouth. "But the ambulance took too long to come, and she died."

Ioan gave Envys a "don't worry, she's old and ill" look and Megan went to take her mother's other arm. "Come on, Mam. Let's get you home," she said.

But Nia would not move. She was studying her daughter now, her face inches from hers. "You had one too, didn't you – a baby? I remember now. Your father told me, but said I could never see it. You understand how terrible it feels to lose them, don't you, *cariad*/love? The most terrible thing of all, it is."

The deep silence that followed belied the fact that there were seven other people and three dogs in the room. Eventually, Megan managed to say:

"Yes, Mam, it's the most terrible thing of all."

THIRTY-NINE

By February, it was clear that the new café would be ready to open for Easter, which fell late, in mid-April, that year. In fact, thanks to Beth's organisational skills and Ziggy's army of willing helpers, all the structural work had been completed ahead of schedule and the new kitchen installed. One of Ziggy's mates had sold them a top-of-the-range eight-burner stainless-steel hob for less than a third of its selling price as it was slightly scratched, and Dai Evans, the village publican, had a contact in kitchens, which saw them getting an astonishing deal on units, sinks and gleaming worktops, and more than ten IKEA dining tables (which nobody liked to ask too many questions about). Elwyn Owen messaged from Tenerife, where he and Siân had now bought a time-share, to offer some old wooden pews from a chapel his uncle was renovating, which would be perfect for family seating in the new café. Beth drew the line at Ziggy's offer of an "off the back of a lorry" fridge and freezer for fear of leaking chemicals and half-defrosted food killing their customers. All that remained was to decorate the enormous space in a way that showcased it best. Beth already had an idea about how to do that but said nothing... yet.

It was decided that the wedding had to happen before the grand opening, as things would be full-on for all of them after that. Easter would see both the shop and the café very busy indeed if all went well. Neither Ioan nor Beth wanted a showy ceremony, presents or any kind of fuss, emphasising that this was second time around for both of them. They mentioned "close family only in Llangefni Registry Office", or even getting married on their own, on a Caribbean beach, but things were very soon taken out of their hands by everyone else, who had very different ideas.

"Look, this is the first time you've married *each other*," Megan said, leading the chorus of disapproval at their tentative plans. "And this is a wedding you deprived us of last time, remember. You owe us a big one, you two. The Full Monty."

So, one drizzly rainy Saturday afternoon in February, "The Windmill Family" sat down together to try and agree on a plan that suited everyone. An hour later, no progress had been made beyond a) Envys insisting on being a bridesmaid and wearing the red tap shoes she now even wore to bed and b) Gareth asking to be the DJ for the disco. Spirits were falling fast when Ziggy suddenly stood up, cleared his throat, put one hand on his heart and began to speak:

"Dearly Beloved, Lewis and I would like to make a daring, but spectacular, suggestion. We would like the lovely couple to plight their troth in the café, before it opens. It has the space, a kitchen ready to go and plenty of room for feasting and riotous dancing afterwards. Everyone from 'The Shop Team', and lots of other lovely villagers, want to come or at least contribute to your celebration. To refuse them this small sliver of ecstasy in our dark world of pain would, on this occasion, be churlish in the extreme. I rest my case."

Everyone burst into howls of laughter, which had all the dogs leaping up in alarm. Above the hubbub, Lewis shouted, "Hear, hear, old bean."

Ioan and Beth exchanged looks and small, resigned smiles; both of them knew that they had no chance whatsoever of successfully disagreeing with this plan.

"So, it's a community wedding now, is it?" Ioan said, grinning. "And there we were, Beth, thinking it was *ours*."

"I suppose it would be fun, and the space is ideal for a big wedding – whether we actually wanted one or not!" Beth said. "I still want it kept simple, however, and I refuse point blank to let Nesta and Mai design my dress, however many Nativity costumes they've made in the past."

More gales of laughter. More leaping dogs.

"The inside of the room is still a bit bleak, as the decorators can't come in for a few weeks," Ziggy said. "Perhaps we could pin up some textiles, or bunting, or do something to make it less... *minimalist*."

"Please, nothing minimalist. All that reminds me of my horrible flat in London!" Beth said with a grimace. "Inexpensive, un-showy but bursting with colour is all I want."

As people began to chat about possibilities, and exchange ideas, Beth went to let the dogs out for a wee, and to have a moment alone. She had not expected this situation, but having been presented with it, something she had been considering for some time seemed destined to become a reality if she was brave enough to suggest it. She had money, enough to last her and Ioan for several years, which meant she could easily pay his small mortgage. Ceri had not asked for maintenance, which everyone *said* was surprisingly noble of her, but everyone *thought* was because Darren could probably afford to buy the whole island if he wanted to. The shop was just about profitable, and she had plans to offer the room she would be vacating in the windmill when she married for overnight guests who could not afford the inflated prices of many rental places on Anglesey. Managing the shop was time-consuming and had never been a long-term goal for her life on the island. She had not known what that was, until now, when she knew without doubt that establishing herself in her new family and becoming a good stepmother to two young children was that goal. This would take all her time and energy if she was to do it as well as she wanted to, so she would need help with the shop, and Lewis and Ziggy might need help with the café too, when things got hectic in August. It was time, finally, to take her brother's advice and delegate. And who better to ask for that help than her calm, organised, patient husband-to-be? Yes, he would probably be less rigorous in his management style than she was, but she saw that as a good thing as things relaxed a little. Her job had been to get things up and running, put a rocket under people and boss them around. And she had. Now it was time for someone who could hold the ship on a steady course in the longer term.

As she went back inside, she felt fired with determination to persuade Ioan to accept her scheme. He was so tired, so ground-down by his job these days that she feared for his health, both physical and mental. It simply was not worth his carrying, almost "running on empty" after every working day, if they could survive without his salary. And they could, easily, at least for a while. If they needed a cash injection later, she would talk to Ziggy about selling the necklace Lucinda had given their mother and had told them was very valuable. All would be well, somehow – she felt it in her bones.

"*Reit 'ta pawb,*/Right then you lot, listen up! I also have a suggestion that it would be more than churlish to refuse, and it's mainly directed at you, Ioan *bach*/dear," she began, which saw Ioan mock-quaking in terror. "I would like to suggest that you leave the hospital, or at least cut your hours right down, and that you take over my role in overseeing the shop and the café. These two likely lads," she pointed at Ziggy and Lewis, who also pretended to cower in fear, "are still going to need a sounding board for their endless wacky ideas, and reining in from making said endless wacky ideas a reality, and I reckon you'd be the perfect person to do both. Whadya say, pardner?"

All faces turned towards Ioan, and nobody spoke, but Beth could feel the eager support for her idea like a warm wave, spreading across the entire room until it reached her on the other side. Ioan looked resolutely down at his knees as if the answer to all life's questions was imprinted on his trousers but said nothing at all. Eventually, Gareth spoke up:

"Dad, think about it now. When you come home from work, you're done in. You've always done your best to help everyone, but you can't go on like this anymore, and you hate it these days."

Envys piped up now. "Yeah, Dad, that job is even making your hair fall out, like Aunty Megan's did."

A ripple of laughter, but nobody felt the need to explain the difference between stress-induced alopecia and baldness just then. It didn't matter. What mattered was getting Ioan to agree to this rescue package, this lifeline to spare him the burnout he was inevitably headed towards.

Beth gently took his hand and made him look up at her. "And one more thing, love. I want you to design and paint the most amazing mural on the biggest wall in the café for our wedding day. I want you to make it bold and beautiful, courageous and kind, vivid and sensitive, just like you."

Ioan's face broke into a smile, and he started to nod, first slowly, and then more vigorously.

"No pressure then," he said, rubbing his hand across his stubbly cheek. "Just another roof of the Sistine Chapel in Aberffraw."

"No pressure at all," Ziggy said.

"None *o gwbwl*/at all," Lewis added, shaking his head.

Another long pause, in which everyone held their breath for so long that Envys started tapping her tap-shoe on the floor as she could not hold hers for much longer.

"OK, I'll do it, for all of us, for 'The Windmill Family'," he said, adding very quietly, "And, perhaps, if I'm honest, for myself."

"Result!" Ziggy said, high-fiving Lewis as they danced around the room, all three dogs scampering around their feet yapping happily.

A little later, Beth found Megan sitting alone outside the mill. The rain had stopped and a weak winter sun was trying to break through the clouds, forming mini-rainbows in the sky. Sitting down beside her, she covered her hand with one of her own.

"Meg, you're worried that Caleb will be at our wedding, aren't you?" she said. "We don't have to invite that side of the family, so we won't, OK?"

Megan turned slowly to look at her friend. Her eyes were calm, and Beth had never seen her look more like the thoughtful, sensitive girl she remembered, and the woman she loved.

"You must invite them, you know you must! I want him to come, and I want to see him," she replied. "It could be the perfect occasion, when everyone's together, and happy... and had a few drinks, let's face it."

Beth hesitated. Perhaps her friend was right, and it could be the best of new beginnings for mother and son. It was her decision.

"Invite them all, please. I won't say a thing unless I feel it's right to do so, I promise, but I will *know* he's my son when I see him," Megan said. "Perhaps that will be enough."

"I need to tell you that one more thing now," Beth said, feeling her heart begin to pound in anticipation. "If I can find the right words, that is."

Megan looked at her directly. "Is it something to do with our sons, Beth?"

The back door burst open, and Ziggy came through it, his mouth open, ready to speak. When his sister mouthed "Not now", he immediately retreated.

"Yes, it is. Very much," Beth began, before taking a deep breath and carrying on. "Meg, Dylan Jones is Lewis's father, not Hugo. I only knew it for sure the other evening, when we saw Dylan again in Beaumaris."

A very long silence greeted these words, but just as Beth was beginning to feel despair seep through her veins, Megan spoke.

"I thought as much, from the state you were in. Those were more than tears for a teenage crush; they were tears of terrible guilt and shame. I'd know those tears anywhere, believe me. I've shed enough of them."

She smiled at her – a tired, but understanding, smile, and one that had been a long time coming.

"But can you ever forgive me?" Beth said, her voice cracking.

"I forgive you, as I forgive myself," Megan said. "Dylan was a beautiful, stupid boy, and to adapt Emily Brontë's perfect words a little–

"We gave him our hearts, and he took and pinched them to death and flung them back at us."

"But we have our beautiful boys because of him, and now we have our hearts back too, don't we?" Beth said.

"Oh yes. We do. Our hearts are ours to give to whomever we choose. But I have to say that I don't think you should tell Hugo or Lewis. What real good would it do? It's a secret best kept with those you can trust to keep it."

"You're right, as always, Meg," Beth whispered.

As they held each other tightly, both knew that all was forgiven.

FORTY

April is a fine month to marry on Anglesey. There can be gloomy, wet days, but there is such a sense of new beginnings that even the soil seems to sing as the first green shoots of new crops peep above the ground. When the sun shines, its warmth fills the soul with hope of the summer to come, and branches on many trees begin to unfurl fresh, new leaves that glow in the spring sunshine like a green-gold veil, covering the blackened twigs of winter. Birds sing for the joy of it as soon as the sun rises as if they, too, have been longing for the darkness, finally, to lift.

As the big day neared, there was an air of excitement in the whole village and the smell of cooking and baking filled the air. A few days beforehand, Ziggy had been lent a vintage jukebox which would provide the music for the disco afterwards, which excited the older people considerably. When it was delivered to the windmill and he scanned the long list of songs on it, he called Beth over straight away. His face was pale, and his eyes full of surprise.

"Beth, look at number 96. It's a song called 'A Song for Tabitha' by a band called Whitefeather," he said. "Do you think, I mean, could it be...?"

"Oh my God. Press the button, Ziggy," Beth said, watching her brother's hands tremble as he did so, and feeling her breath quicken.

As the opening chords emerged from the jukebox and floated across the room, they both knew within seconds that the man playing the guitar was Jed, their father, and that this was a song about the young woman he was falling in love with, Tabitha, their mother.

When the song ended, Ziggy pressed the button again immediately, without saying a word. While it played again, he googled "Whitefeather", and found an old photo of four young men with ponytails and cigarettes in their hands. Beth immediately recognised one of them as a much younger version of the leather-jacketed man who had come to Jed's funeral and left without saying a word to anyone. When she told Ziggy, he remembered him too.

"So, he was in the band with Dad," he said. "How amazing is that?"

They listened more closely the second time the song played. It was lyrical, melody-led, full of the soulful, skilful guitar-playing and gruff singing voice they remembered hearing in *Melin Arian* throughout their childhood, when Jed was on the home-brew. By the end of it, both felt they knew, and understood, their parents a little better than they had ever done.

"That song says it all, really," Beth said.

"It says here it reached the top 40 in the charts," Ziggy said. "But he gave it all up for her. I know they fled after Henry's accident, but they must have loved each other so much to go against her family with all their power and money and come up here, where they had nothing and nobody."

Beth squeezed his arm. "They had us, remember. And love can make you do amazing things."

"I wouldn't know," Ziggy replied sadly. "But hopefully, one day, I will."

"To love and be loved. That's what Mum and Dad would have wanted for you, Zig, and so do I. Most of all, I hope you find someone who deserves you and your heart of pure gold."

The day of Beth and Ioan's wedding was a beautiful one, with a light, cool breeze blowing in off the sea and a blue sky studded with fluffy white cloudlets that did not threaten rain. All the preparations had gone like clockwork in the weeks beforehand, as there were so many willing hands to help. The space in the café was arranged with a small table at one end, to form an informal altar, where the celebrant would marry Ioan and Beth, and all the tables and pews were already lined up and laid, ready for the village to sit and celebrate. Lewis had designed a stunning menu, using almost entirely local produce. Several of his elderly friends agreed to be his sous chefs, the only proviso being that they could sit down whilst they chopped, grated and mixed. As he was so busy, Gareth had taken over the delivery tricycle and the dog walking, and he was soon almost as popular as his predecessor (and had doubled his pocket money within a week).

The shop was closed, the pub was closed, the garage was closed as everyone who knew and loved Ioan and Beth headed to the café. Flora had been invited up from London, and Sabrina came up with her, newly, and happily, divorced. They'd both "had a spot of fizz on the train, to get the party started," reported Cai Hughes, winking furiously, after he'd been to fetch them.

Nesta and Mai had helped Beth alter a beautiful but very delicate second-hand ivory lace wedding dress she had found online, and they were charged with the tricky task of getting her into it without mishap. Once they had, they fastened Tabitha's beautiful necklace around her neck, and it sparkled in the morning sunshine. Finally, Mai slipped a circlet of white wood anemones, pussy willows dusted with yellow pollen and forget-me-nots onto Beth's head, before both twins stepped back, and sighed.

"We never did this, but it feels like you're doing it for us," they chorused.

As Beth prepared to walk from *Melin Arian* to the café to marry Ioan, only one thing niggled at the back of her mind. She had not seen what had been done to make the room a wedding venue, as he had expressly banned her from the café this past week so that she would only see the mural when she walked in to become his wife. He had given in his notice on the emergency ward weeks earlier but agreed to be part of the bank of nurses who could be called upon when needed, which both assuaged his conscience, and safeguarded his pension. Gareth and Envys had been sworn to secrecy about the mural, and when quizzed, merely said that it was *"hollol gwych/*absolutely excellent".

At 11am, the little bridal party set off, Beth's veil fluttering behind her in the wind like the wings of a swan. Envys tapped along in her red shoes behind her, and Megan walked alongside as the maid of honour, both of them proudly holding the hem of The Dress above the ground. Ziggy had agreed to give Beth away and was resplendent in a vintage 1950s suit from Oxfam and blue Dr Martens. Gareth, as the ring-bearer, was already inside, standing nervously next to his dad, Cai Hughes confirmed that everything was "good to go" with Ziggy by text. He was taking his duties as "Chief Wedding Co-ordinator" very seriously indeed.

As she neared the open door, Beth heard all chattering stop, as the first notes of her father's love song to her mother rang out across the village square. It was all she could do not to cry, but she had the most important task of her life to perform and she would complete it well, and punctually, as she always had.

She walked into the room, lit by shafts of sunlight from the new roof windows which made the wooden pews, the tables and pine-boarded floor glow with an incredible warmth. Feeling as if she was floating, Beth glimpsed swags of crocheted flags and home-made patchwork bunting hanging between the old rafters, which had been lovingly restored and sealed with a honey-coloured resin. The air was full of the delicate scent of wildflowers, of late primroses, early bluebells and the first of the cherry blossoms. She breathed it in, and then saw Ioan and Gareth standing seemingly miles ahead of her. How could she possibly walk that far when her knees were already buckling under her? Taking small, steady steps, she felt herself almost glide towards them, turning, as she did so, to register the rows of happy faces looking at her from the left. There was Flora, who appeared to be holding hands with a very flushed Cai Hughes. Next to them was Sabrina, who looked years younger, and next to her stood Alun and his two strapping sons, Llion and Osian. Uncle Alun had wanted to attend, even though he knew Megan would be present too. This trio of strong, farming Welshmen looked so alike, and so *unlike* Caleb, who stood on the very end of their pew.

"I told Caleb about you two having been childhood sweethearts, parted by fate and reunited at last, and he loved it," Alun had told Beth when he accepted the invitation. "I just said that some other family would be there, too, so he's prepared. He's a grown man now, and more than capable of making up his own mind, and of walking away from it all if he wants to."

Despite this reassurance, as Beth saw Caleb, she prayed that Megan would not spot him just yet and be overwhelmed. Right up near the altar, she saw a beaming Lewis, and it struck her that, unbeknownst to him, he was only a few feet from his half-brother. That was a story for another time; today, was her and Ioan's day. Beth looked at her son, now much more man than boy, in his dapper new suit and a spectacular pink bow tie, and she marvelled at how happy he looked just to be *him*, wherever, however and whoever he wanted to be. His beginning was perhaps still a slight source of regret, but the outcome was Lewis, this brilliant young man, the greatest achievement of her life, and she was entirely at peace with that.

When she looked to the people on her right, Beth's eyes were immediately drawn to the wall behind them, and then upwards, towards the roof. Its entire surface was ablaze with colour, movement and light. She knew at once that Ioan had poured his heart and soul into it, and that he had done it for her. It was a huge scene of their home, stretching from floor to ceiling. She saw the beach, the dunes with their mantle of fluttering grasses, the river with its bobbing little boats and prettily painted fisherman's cottages. Then came the green-blue sea, tipped with ripples and waves blown by breezes he could not show in paint. The sky was peppered with birds, wings spread wide, riding freely above the water as if there was nothing more to life than this, because – as Beth saw more clearly than ever today – there wasn't. Finding it almost impossible to hold back her tears, she stumbled.

Ziggy strode towards her and took one of her arms. Megan stepped forward to take her other, and quickly, quietly, first whispered three of Emily Dickinson's words, and then three of her own to her as she steadied herself: "*Come slowly, Eden!*"; "Be happy, Beth."

Her brother and her dearest friend led her towards Ioan and placed one of her hands gently into his. Then, and only then, did Beth feel her whole body relax, as her incipient tears were subsumed by a happiness she had never dared feel, or even imagine. Despite everything she had done, and not done; despite all her apparent successes in life and all her many, many failures, here she was, a woman marrying a man who had loved her for decades and whom she adored with her whole, fallible, newly whole self.

As they knelt to take their vows, the only thing Beth still longed for was that Megan could be granted some of the happiness she had been blessed with.

But did she have the right to ask for that, as well as everything else?

FORTY-ONE

For years, everyone who was present at Ioan and Beth Williams' wedding that glorious April day talked about it. Lots of them wrote how they felt in the book placed near the doorway for people to pass on their good wishes. Some described it as "breathtaking", "like a fairytale", and the kids, as "the best laugh ever". Others remembered the food, the room, the smell of the flowers and many mentioned the amazing mural the groom had painted. Amidst all these comments was a short paragraph laid out like a poem on the page in an elegant, looping italic. This entry described the day as "the distillation of a happiness so tangible, you can almost feel it in the air" and "a coming home of two lost souls, who have found each other again". The entry was signed "Caleb Jones, from the Farm in the Mountains."

While the wedding meal was served and eaten, and speeches made, everyone stayed in their pews, cheering and toasting with great gusto when required. Only after the cake had been cut (an extra-large *bara brith*/currant loaf, courtesy of Nia, who was sadly too unwell that day to come to the wedding) did people begin to mingle. Beth, slightly drowsy as the champagne had kicked in, was proudly surveying her family and friends chatting, drinking and laughing when, out of the corner of her eye, she saw Megan talking with a young man with thick blonde, curly hair: Caleb. Uncle Alun was standing to one side of them but, as she watched, he left them and walked slowly away. A ripple of alarm ran through her and she turned to Ioan, who only had to look at her face to know that something was wrong.

"Look! It's happening! They're talking to each other, Megan and Caleb, over there," she whispered. "What should we do? What if she upsets him, or he upsets her, or is angry with her? I think I should…"

"…let them be, *cariad*/love," Ioan said firmly. "They've waited long enough for this day. Megan will know how things should be done, and Caleb doesn't look capable of hurting a fly. We've played our part in their story. The next chapter is theirs to write as they see fit, and this is their chance to begin it."

But Beth still watched anxiously as Megan very gently touched Caleb's sleeve and then he, in turn, stepped back, his hand over his mouth. Would he reject her, hate her for what he would see as her abandonment of him as a baby? Would Megan be horrified by how much he looked like her betrayer, Dylan Jones, and not be able to see past that to the young man he now was? Holding her breath, she saw Caleb step forward a little, put his hands on Megan's shoulders and enfold her in his arms as she allowed herself to melt into them. It was all going to be all right.

"Right, time to dance, husband, if you'll be my partner," she said, whisking Ioan onto the dance floor and deliberately avoiding looking at the corner where Megan and Caleb still stood together, now talking animatedly. She would not be a *voyeur* any longer; this moment needed to be private.

But as soon as they sat down again ten minutes later,

flushed and giggling, Megan and Caleb came and sat down next to them. Both seemed very calm. As this was the first time she had actually seen him in the flesh, Beth saw so many elements of her friend in this young man's face – his sensitive brow, his deep, soulful eyes. He had his father's hair and jawline, but the gentle *essence* of him was Megan, without a doubt.

After a few moments of slightly awkward silence, Megan spoke first.

"Ioan, Beth, this is Caleb, my son. I think you've met," she said.

Ioan cleared his throat. "We've never *met*, but yes, we know who he is." His steady tone forewarned Beth to keep her emotions in check. As yet, they had no real idea how the reunion had gone, or what might have been said. It was important that they did not react in the wrong way.

"*Neis dy gyfarfod di*/Good to meet you, Caleb," he added, holding his strong hand out to shake his nephew's more delicately boned one.

"And you, Ioan. *Llongyfarchiadau mawr*/Many congratulations. I know you came up to the farm to find me. Dad told me," Caleb said, and Beth smiled to hear that his voice had the same musical lilt as his mother's, as Ioan had heard on the phone.

"You look and sound so like... so like..." Beth, blushing, felt her words dissolve into the air. How could she actually say what she'd intended? How would it make him feel to hear it?

Caleb turned to her, and gently said, "My mam? Oh, I knew who she was the moment I saw her, you know. I knew before she told me. I *felt* it."

Nobody spoke at all for a few seconds, as they all tried to control their feelings.

"Bloody hell, I think we all need more champagne," Megan said, dispelling the tension in an instant. "Shall we fetch a tray of glasses, Caleb?"

And the new husband and wife watched as the new mother

and son drifted off across the room, arm in arm, to forge a future together.

EPILOGUE

A year later

A lot can change in a year, and much did for "The Windmill Family" and all who shared their world on a little island off the top of North Wales. It is perhaps a small world, limited in its distractions and delights, but it is a beautiful one, they all agree.

The café opened at Easter on a blustery day that threatened to whip all the fluttering decorations into the sea but did not. There was a ribbon-cutting ceremony, with Cai Hughes designated as the most appropriate villager to do the deed. A brass band played, and Dai Evans donated a free barrel of beer (mainly to tempt punters to continue the festivities in his pub when it ran out). Nia, Ioan and Megan's mother, came along to watch, her arms looped through her children's, and she declared Lewis's *bara brith*/currant loaf to be "*bendegedig*/marvellous" despite his not having her cherished recipe. Yet.

Within weeks, the café gained a reputation locally, and excellent reviews kept Lewis very busy when the tourist season began and word spread. The cookery masterclasses he started after the summer season were fully booked and he had great plans for expansion. Beth gently advised him to take things one step at a time. In September, Hugo and Hilary called in on their way to a society wedding in Dublin and were "extremely impressed with this bijou little gem" or so they wrote in the book Lewis had placed near the entrance to the café for diners to say what they thought. When Lewis told his father that he was going to frame that page for posterity, Hugo laughed out loud and promised to call in again on their way back to keep him on his toes. Pride in his charming, confident son shone from his every pore and Beth knew, without any doubt, that her decision not to tell them everything was the right one.

Ziggy and Lewis now live together in *Melin Arian* and welcome overnight guests for "the best bed and breakfast in Wales" whenever they can. They have made great improvements, and even managed to repair the wooden sails that had long since lain unloved in a shed and proudly fix them to the windmill once more. Lewis keeps tanks of crickets and locusts after he rescued some that were destined to become reptile-snacks from the local pet shop, which means that evenings in the mill are as noisy as any subtropical rainforest. Ziggy, with Beth's encouragement, has started internet dating, but he is still waiting for someone as wonderful as his sister to appear on his screen and avoid him having to swipe right.

Megan and Caleb meet regularly and share their poetry. There's talk of them publishing a "Mother & Son" anthology in the next few months, to be sold in the shop, and beyond. From what Beth – their trusted creative editor – has read of their work, it could be a big success, as she said that they have managed to capture the essence of their wild, windswept home in words, as Kyffin Williams did in paint. Megan offers occasional poetry readings and calligraphy classes in the café, which all who attend say are inspirational. The phrase she often uses for them to practise their skills is:

"A wounded deer leaps the highest."

Her alopecia has almost vanished, and she looks and feels better than she has in years. Beth hopes that she, too, will find love one day.

Dylan Jones was prosecuted for tax evasion and sentenced to six years in prison, as he could not pay the huge fine he was offered as an alternative. His wife Manon divorced him while he was on remand and now lives in Gran Canaria with their two teenage daughters. They are not in touch.

Almost exactly a year after Ioan and Beth married, their baby girl was born – a miraculous gift for which neither had dared to hope. Gareth and Envys are almost competitive in their zeal to look after her, and now call Beth *"Ail-Mam*/Second Mum" as they decided that the term "step-mother" had too many negative associations. Ioan manages the shop, advises on café decisions and holds weekly "Slap Dash Art Classes for Messy Kids", as well as doing the occasional shift at the hospital, where his compassion, experience and expertise remain unsurpassable. He is now painting regularly and loving it.

They called their new baby Eirlys. From time to time, her father takes her to visit his mam, Nia, who seems to respond to her name every time she hears it. She smiles and holds her granddaughter's tiny fingers with a genuine, gentle tenderness that almost breaks Ioan's heart.

"If she thinks our Eirlys is *her* Eirlys, then that's OK with me," Ioan said, when Beth was troubled that it might upset Nia to think this baby was her lost child. "I hope it brings her peace."

On warm, summer evenings, Beth and Megan still try to meet, once Eirlys is asleep. They swim in the sea in the dying warmth of the sun, and then sit on the headland above Aberffraw, where they always sat as girls, to watch the sun go down beyond the glowing horizon at the end of another day.

They are home, and, for both of them, "home" will always mean each other.

.

A LETTER FROM THE AUTHOR

Thank you for reading *Coming Home to the Windmill by the Sea*. I really hope you enjoyed following Beth and Megan's friendship and getting to know Aberffraw, a village that has always been close to my heart. The island of Anglesey, where my story is set, is the perfect place for reconnecting with what is really important in life, as both friends do in this novel. The power of the natural world to heal us is immeasurable, if we take the time to let it do so.

If you'd like to join readers in hearing all about my new releases and some bonus content too, you can sign up for my newsletter.

www.stormpublishing.co/caroline-young

If you enjoyed this book enough to take the time to leave a review, that would be very helpful to other readers, and much appreciated by me. Even a short review can make all the difference in encouraging a reader to discover my stories for the first time.

Thank you for coming on this journey with me, and do stay in touch. I look forward to sharing more stories with you, and giving you a taste of life on this little Welsh island, the place I am proud to call home.

facebook.com/caroline.young.9250

ACKNOWLEDGEMENTS

The germ of this story was a simple one: the terrible rift between two best friends. I wanted to show how these bonds we share with others are essential to how we live our lives, and should be treasured. Whatever has happened in the past, Beth is lost without Megan, and vice versa. In an age of social media friendships, dating apps and relationships that are often mainly conducted online, I felt that a story about valuing people, and what they offer us, was timely. We need people, and people need us, basically!

I have many people to thank here for enabling this book to be written at all. Firstly, I need to thank my family for supporting me through January, when I became increasingly frustrated that I could not write a single word. I longed for spring as fervently as many of my characters do, but once I saw signs of it, the words came. I wrote the first draft in only three months, which still amazes me! I also need to thank Idris Jones for once again checking my written Welsh, and concealing his astonishment as just how inaccurate it was. Kate Smith, my editor, somehow manages to get the best out of me without my even realising that my plots need tightening up or my characters made clearer for the reader. Thanks, Kate, for everything. I also want to thank Anthony, my brother, who shares my love of the written word and slight obsession with punctuation! And thank you Juliet Greenwood, for guiding me when I risk getting lost.

As friendship is at the centre of this story, so it is at the heart of my life. I am very fortunate to have many, wonderful friends, from all the eras of my life, and I take their kindness and loyalty with me wherever I go, and try to include it in whatever I write. We are nothing without those who love us, and I feel very lucky to be loved by people who forgive my foibles and celebrate my successes without judgement or reservation. *Diolch, ffrindiau*/Thanks, friends.

Printed in Great Britain
by Amazon

48680291R10166